PROJECT ARMA

D1452715

ASHER

NYSSA KATHRYN

UNTITLED

She needs his love. He needs her safe.

When a workplace romance becomes something deeper for Lexie Harper, she's devastated to learn Asher Becket is determined to keep their sensual touches and passionate kisses behind closed doors. But that's not good enough. Lexie won't be anyone's dirty little secret...especially when she's harboring a secret of her own that won't stay hidden for long.

As an ex-special forces soldier with a target on his back, Asher lives each day with just two goals: put an end to Project Arma, the program that changed him forever; and keep his feelings for Lexie locked down tight. His life is a hotbed of danger, and he'll die before letting it touch her.

Then Lexie's secret is discovered by people so evil, Asher's her only hope of staying alive. Instead of pushing her away, he'll have to hold his greatest obsession closer than ever.

ACKNOWLEDGMENTS

Thank you to my editor, Kelli Collins, for your hard work and guidance.

Thank you to my mother, Kathryn, for encouraging me to read when I was growing up and setting up the foundation to my love of romance reading.

Thank you also to my wonderful husband. This wouldn't be possible without your love and support.

CHAPTER 1

"*N*o..." Breathless with disbelief, Lexie shook the stick again.

Maybe it was broken. Maybe they'd sold her a test that had sat on the shelf for too long and was now reading a false positive. Was that a thing? God, she hoped so. Maybe she should google it?

"Please be broken, please be broken, please be broken." Lexie repeated the mantra under her breath like her life depended on it. Which it pretty much did. Life as she knew it.

Pulling a second test from the pharmacy bag, Lexie's fingers shook so badly, she could barely get the packaging open.

She would take another test. And this test would confirm that her life wasn't about to change irrevocably. That she wasn't about to embark on a new journey that she had absolutely no idea how to navigate.

As she sat on the bathroom floor, the cold tiles didn't register. Neither did the churning in her stomach that had been there for the last week.

It will all be okay, Lexie reassured herself.

Quickly taking the test, Lexie returned to the floor and waited to see what the stick would say. Nibbling on her thumbnail, she kept her gaze glued to the window on the test. A shot gun probably wouldn't distract her. Every second that passed seemed more like a minute. Every minute an hour.

When the same symbol that flashed on the first stick came up again, Lexie's breath caught.

Pregnant.

Holy jam on a cracker. Lexie was pregnant.

There was no way two different brands of tests could lie. The odds just didn't seem to be in her favor.

Taking a few deep breaths, Lexie slid down the wall until she lay flat on the tiles.

It was only a week ago that she had been standing at work behind the Marble Protection reception desk with her friends, Evie and Shylah, laughing about nothing, when babies were brought up. That was the moment it had hit Lexie.

She'd missed her period.

Then, wham-bam, it all started happening. The nausea, the exhaustion, the damn light-headedness. She didn't even know if the latter was supposed to be a symptom, but she sure had it.

Placing a hand on her stomach, Lexie felt the threat of tears at the backs of her eyes.

There was a little human baking inside her. A little human that *she* would be the mother of.

She couldn't be a mother. She didn't know the first thing about healthy mothering. Her own was a drunk who hadn't cared for Lexie a day in her life. Now that Lexie was an adult, she only heard from the woman when she needed money.

That was her role model. *That* was her example of how to mother a child.

Good lord, what was she going to do?

Pushing up onto her elbows, Lexie sucked in a long, slow breath.

She had always promised herself that the only possible way

she would bring a baby into this world was if she had her shit together and a ring on her finger.

Well, she sure as hell didn't have her shit together, and not only was she not married, but she was about as far from saying "I do" as possible. Lexie could be president of the unwed ladies' club, she was so single.

Crap, was she turning into her mother? This is exactly how it had been for her. Pregnant to a commitment-phobic douchebag who had left her the moment the stick turned pink. Lexie may as well start filling her cupboards with whiskey now.

To be fair, Asher wasn't a douchebag. He just didn't want Lexie. That made him at least an idiot, right?

Leaning forward, she scrubbed her hands over her face. Christ, she loved that man. Shame he cared for her about as much as he did the stranger down the block.

Asher had made it abundantly clear he didn't want to date. Well, not publicly, anyway. What would he say when she told him she was going to have his baby?

Her breath hitched at the thought. Jeepers, Asher would have a heart attack on the spot. Then probably run as far and fast as possible.

The thought pulled at Lexie's heart.

Pushing up into a standing position, Lexie glanced at her reflection. Her skin was too pale, particularly in contrast to her bright red hair. Hollow bags shadowed her amber eyes, giving her the appearance of being sick.

At least she looked the way she felt. She had barely been able to eat a thing all week.

The thought of telling Asher the news just made her feel even worse. Paralyzing, fall-to-the-floor, never-get-up worse.

Maybe she wouldn't tell him. Not right away, at least.

Pinching her cheeks to add some color back to her face, Lexie felt her body relax at her decision. She would wait to tell him.

When was it that people usually shared the news that they were pregnant? Twelve weeks? She would wait until then.

Pulling her long hair into a ponytail, Lexie did some mental math back to when she'd had her last period. Six weeks, maybe? So, she could be up to six weeks pregnant.

Holy guacamole. *Six weeks pregnant.*

Walking down the hall of her one-bedroom apartment, Lexie entered her bedroom to get changed for work. Her legs felt about as steady as a baby giraffe's.

She prayed she could get through her shift today without throwing up her guts. So far she had avoided being sick at Marble Protection, but there had been some close calls. Just yesterday she'd had to speed walk to the bathroom, thinking she was going to empty the contents of her stomach, only for it to pass a few moments later.

Lexie didn't want to be sick at work. She couldn't. The guys had crazy-good senses. One of their mysterious secrets. One of many. They would know something was going on with her immediately.

Then would come the questions. The investigation.

Lexie had worked at Marble Protection since the place had opened over a year ago. Working for eight former Navy SEALs had felt like winning the lottery at the start. They were all huge and sexy, with muscles for days. They definitely fit the role to run a security and self-defense business.

Unfortunately for Lexie, the last few months had become more torturous than anything else. All because of one man. One man who she hadn't been able to get out of her head. His beautiful brown eyes, his cocky smile. Everything.

It had taken only a month for Asher to get her into his bed. That was her first mistake. She should have made him wait. Sweat it out and work harder. Then maybe he wouldn't be treating her like he could come and go as he pleased. Like she was his dirty little secret.

Just another mistake in the Lexie chronicles.

Rolling her eyes, she pulled out jeans and a sweater. Today was definitely a baggy sweater day.

Stopping in front of the dresser mirror, Lexie let her gaze drift to her midsection. A baby. She was going to have a baby.

Hand reaching for her stomach, she closed her eyes. She was still in disbelief. Probably a bit of shock. But a small shred of excitement began to bubble to the surface, mixed with fear.

If this was real, and she didn't suddenly wake up to find it was all a dream, then she hoped for one thing. That she'd do a better job than her own mother. That she would love and protect the child like no other.

Lexie took a moment to appreciate the gravity of her discovery, goose bumps forming across her skin. She was scared. Heck, she was one step away from a full-blown anxiety attack.

But a small bubble of love had already begun to form.

Swallowing the lump in her throat, Lexie opened her eyes and moved out of the bedroom. Eyeing the kitchen on her way to the door, she considered grabbing something for breakfast, but the thought of putting food in her mouth made her want to gag. She would grab a coffee on the walk to work.

Turning back to the door, she locked up before heading down the stairs.

Pregnant. The word was on repeat in her head. She honestly didn't understand how this had happened. They were always careful. Yes, it was true that sometimes they barely had time to rip each other's clothes off, let alone stop and don a condom. But they did. Every. Single. Time.

Lexie had had so much hope for the two of them at the beginning. She had assumed their nights together would turn into days, and their days would turn into a relationship.

Well, that sure blew up in my face, didn't it?

Asher kept a part of himself locked away from her. The secret phone calls he couldn't discuss, the need to leave at a moment's notice with no explanation.

The man didn't let Lexie in on key parts of his life. He didn't trust her. And if he didn't trust her with his life, then she didn't plan to trust him with her heart any longer.

That's why she'd broken it off. Told him that if he couldn't commit to a relationship, she didn't want to see him anymore. That meant no more kisses behind closed doors, no more late-night visits. Nothing.

Shame he'd already wormed his way into her heart and was slowly tearing it to pieces bit by bit.

Pushing Asher to the back of her mind, Lexie stepped into Mrs. Potter's Bakehouse. Immediately, the smell of freshly baked cakes hit her like a freight train.

Normally, she would be salivating. Buying twice as many as she could eat. Today, her hand flew to her stomach and she prayed the churning would calm.

"Lexie dear, are you okay?" Mrs. Potter's concerned voice sounded from the other side of the counter. "You look a bit pale."

Forcing a smile, Lexie opened her mouth to ask for her usual coffee, only to stop. Were pregnant women allowed to drink coffee? Good lord, she needed to do some research. "I'm okay, Mrs. Potter. I just woke up feeling a bit unwell."

Mrs. Potter's kind eyes turned sympathetic. "I'm sorry to hear that. I know just the thing to help." The older lady turned and ladled a creamy liquid into a takeaway cup before handing it to her. "This is organic chicken broth. Fresh off the stove this morning. Whenever I'm feeling unwell, this is what I turn to."

Lexie didn't know if she could stomach anything at the moment, but she was thankful for Mrs. Potter's effort.

Reaching for her purse, she stopped when Mrs. Potter waved her hands. "No payment needed, dear. I know how dreary it is to feel unwell, so it's the least I can do."

This time, Lexie didn't have to force a smile. It stretched easily across her face. "Thank you."

Not for the first time, Lexie was grateful to live in the small town of Marble Falls. The people here never ceased to amaze her with their kindness.

Taking the cup, she gave Mrs. Potter a small wave before leaving the bakery. Lifting the cup to her lips, she readied her stomach to rebel against the soup. When the warm liquid hit her insides, she stopped walking to close her eyes in appreciation.

Not only was it the first food in a week that hadn't made her stomach turn, it tasted like heaven.

Mrs. Potter was a magician. She wanted to go back and kiss the woman's feet it was that good.

Walking the rest of the short distance to work while trying to quieten the groans of pleasure at the amazing broth in her hand, Lexie came to a stop in front of Marble Protection.

Taking a breath, she told herself she hoped Asher wasn't there. But that was a big fat lie. No matter how much it hurt that the man didn't love her, she craved to be in his presence. Just seeing him gave her butterflies. He was like a drug.

Stepping inside, Lexie waited until she'd slid behind the desk to lift her gaze to the open mat area.

No Asher.

Luca and Bodie both turned to give her a wave, but neither of them were the man she yearned to see. She masked her disappointment as best she could.

Get a grip, woman, and stop being so pathetic, Lexie scolded herself.

Placing the half-empty cup of soup onto the counter, she began sorting the jobs for the day.

Working at the reception desk was a pretty cushy job. Lexie did a lot of organizational work for the guys, which involved ordering equipment, taking phone calls, scheduling classes. She even participated in the occasional class, getting to act out the damsel in distress.

No woman on this planet would complain about getting paid to have former SEALs wrap their arms around them.

Turning to the computer, Lexie powered it up. Lifting her soup, she took another sip and closed her eyes. A moan escaped her lips at the sheer bliss of consuming something that didn't upset her stomach. Even water had been making her feel sick. She needed to order a dozen gallons of this from Mrs. Potter.

"You're sexy when you make that sound."

Jumping out of her skin at the voice in her ear, Lexie instinctively tightened her hand on the cup, squeezing the remaining contents all over her sweater.

The warm liquid soaked into her clothes immediately, the damp material sticking to her chest.

Spinning around, she found her gaze level with Asher's huge chest. It was currently covered in a tight sweater that clung to him, defining his broad shoulders and large muscles. Sexy. That was the only word to describe him.

Did the man not have any loose-fitting clothes?

Lexie lifted her angry gaze to Asher's face, refusing to let his enticing musky scent distract her. She needed to stay angry. Angry was better than attracted. Angry was safe.

CHAPTER 2

*a*sher Becket had seen and done a lot in his thirty-two years. His time as a Navy SEAL had given him the opportunity to jump out of planes, capture terrorists, and scale mountains.

Nothing made his heart pound like Lexie Harper, though. Not a single thing.

Standing in front of her, sweater soaked to her skin, Asher felt his gaze drawn to her ample chest. The thin cotton emphasized her perfect breasts.

That, in combination with the little moan he'd just heard come out of her mouth, was enough to give him the hard-on of a sixteen-year-old kid.

For a moment, Lexie's eyes heated as she looked at him. Unfortunately, the look was fleeting. Her eyes quickly narrowed into slits. "Look what you made me do, Asher."

A lopsided grin stretched across his face. God, she was cute when she was mad. "I'm looking, Lex."

And loving every little thing I'm seeing.

At the deadpan expression Asher received, he assumed his attempt at humor had failed.

Reaching for the bottom of his sweater, he pulled the material over his head and held it out to Lexie.

Her gaze brushed over his bare chest before drawing to the sweater in his hand. "You're giving me your sweater?"

He could tell she was trying to appear unaffected by his naked skin. The pink tinge to her cheeks, along with the slight widening of her eyes, told Asher she was anything but.

"I mean, if you don't want it, I can just turn up the heat and you can remove your wet clothes?"

Yeah, there wasn't a chance Asher would actually let that happen. He would have to kick the ass of every man who dared look at her. With the company he kept—his brothers and business partners—that would not be an easy task.

Asher chuckled at the angry huff from Lexie when she reluctantly took the material from his fingers. As she marched down the hall, Asher couldn't tear his gaze from her perfect behind. "Call out if you need help in there."

"You wish." Lexie muttered the word under her breath, probably intending for no one to hear.

Chuckling again, Asher headed to the office, unable to wipe the smile from his face.

Unfortunately for Lexie, Asher had excellent hearing. Better than excellent; he could hear *everything*—including the way her heart had sped up at the sight of his bare skin a moment earlier.

Not only was his hearing unbelievable, Asher had strength and speed in spades—he was faster than almost any species on Earth—and he healed fast. And that was only a few of his abilities.

Grabbing a spare shirt from a cupboard, Asher threw it over his head.

Lexie knew nothing about Asher's advanced abilities. Not a damn thing. Just like she didn't know about Project Arma, the covert operation that had turned him and his brothers into the genetically altered soldiers they were. The operation that had gone into hiding when the government had discovered their true activity—testing experimental drugs on soldiers. Asher and his brothers had been hunting them ever since.

No. Lexie knew nothing about any of it. And that was how he intended to keep it.

The knowledge was dangerous. Too dangerous for Lexie. Keeping secrets from her wasn't to save *his* ass, it was to save hers.

There was no way in hell Asher was going to expose Lexie to any of it. As far as he could tell, she had a perfect life. Perfectly *normal*.

Asher already worried about the danger Lexie could encounter from working at Marble Protection. He could only hope his enemies didn't use his employees against him, but anything more personal was an exponentially larger risk.

"The group for your next class just arrived, Striker."

Asher glanced up at hearing Mason in the doorway. His teammate, business partner, and brother. Not in blood, but in every other sense of the word. The man was family, just like the rest of the team. The best thing the Navy ever gave Asher was his brothers.

"Be right out."

Mason walked farther into the room. "Who's on to take the class with you?"

"Hunter. And if that asshole tries to pin my head again, he better be ready for a showdown."

Mason chuckled as he headed to the desk. "I don't know that you two are a good pair to run a class together."

They were the best pairing. It didn't get more realistic than what they demonstrated. "I'm the only one who can put up with the big brute. At least Shylah's softened him a bit. Don't need to worry about a broken rib whenever he loses his temper anymore."

Eden, known as Hunter to his teammates, was a different man

than he was a few months ago. Asher remembered too well what he had been like while Shylah had been missing. *Angry* didn't begin to describe it.

Since she'd returned, the team had gotten the old Eden back. The guy still didn't like to be beaten, even if it was only for a self-defense class, but neither did any of them. Asher included.

They had one rule during classes—no one was allowed to show their advanced strength and speed to civilians. Eden liked to bend that rule to save face. Today, Asher might just return the favor.

"Shylah put a stop to that. And the woman is very aware that if she goes anywhere ever again, the whole damn town will drag her ass back," Mason said, only half joking as he dropped into a seat.

"I don't think she's going anywhere." Hell, any fool could see how infatuated Shylah and Eden were with each other. "I'll tell you what, though, I'm damn sick of the people behind Project Arma messing with our women. We need to hurry the fuck up in locating those assholes and putting them behind bars."

Or under the ground.

First Evie, Luca's girlfriend, was attacked by her ex, who happened to be part of Project Arma. Then Shylah, Eden's woman, was set up by the new Marble Falls' doctor, who was also linked to Project Arma.

Both women had almost lost their lives.

"Exactly why we're working overtime to hunt those fuckers down," Mason growled, running his hands through his hair. "Make sure you keep an eye on Lexie, just in case."

Asher's gaze flew to Mason's. Even though he never spoke about his involvement with Lexie, the guys knew something was going on between them. Christ, there wasn't much the team *didn't* know about each other.

"That's exactly why I can't make a commitment to her." Asher left off the part where she'd already decided he was no longer welcome to visit her at all. Not unless he made their involvement public.

About to leave, he stopped when Mason spoke again. "I've been meaning to ask, is she okay?" Asher turned to face his friend. "She's seemed a bit off this last week."

Asher's brows pulled together. "You noticed?"

"That her face has been a shade lighter than the white counter she stands at? Yeah, I noticed."

Running a hand through his hair, Asher felt a knot of unease in his gut. "I asked her about it a few days ago but she brushed me off."

Brushed him off was an understatement. If his memory served him right, which it usually did, Lexie had lit into him in a way she'd never done before, telling him that if he didn't want to share his shit, she wouldn't be sharing hers. She'd then thrown in the whopper—that they were done.

Like hell they were done.

Mason nodded. "We'll all keep an eye on her to make sure she's okay. Just don't do anything stupid."

Stupid like what? Fall for a woman he couldn't have because his life was a hotbed of danger? Too late for that.

Asher left the office to reenter the mat area. Marble Protection had one large open area at the front, which was positioned directly opposite the counter. The same counter where Lexie stood every day. Smaller rooms, used for private lessons and meetings, were off a long corridor.

Asher spared a glance at Lexie, who had returned to the front. She was drowning in his sweater, but the sight of her in his clothes made every territorial instinct in him scream "mine."

Giving himself a mental shake, Asher looked away.

"Ready to get your ass beat?"

Asher narrowed his eyes as he turned to look at Eden. "You even try to cheat and your ass is mine."

Eden chuckled. "You do what you need to do."

Asher intended to do exactly that. Both in the class…and with the rest of his life.

~

LEXIE TRIED NOT to stare at Asher as he flung Eden over his shoulder. The muscles in his back flexed through the tight shirt and his huge biceps rippled.

Good God, he could make a woman orgasm just from watching him.

Lexie dragged her gaze away to face the computer screen. It took much more willpower than it should have, but she'd rather be shot in the foot than have him catch her staring.

It was almost the end of the day, and this was the third class he'd taken. It was damn hard to get over the man when she saw his sexy body all day. He probably stayed out there to torture her. There were other jobs in the company that he could be doing. Office work, private classes in the back rooms, even classes off-site.

"It's not fair. You get to watch Asher all day while Luca doesn't take a single lesson."

Drawing her head up to see Evie exiting the office, Lexie couldn't stop the smile that stretched her lips.

Lexie had known Evie for less than a year but they'd clicked immediately. The other woman had a gentleness about her that Lexie couldn't help but be drawn to.

After moving to Marble Falls, Evie had worked with Lexie at the front desk for a while. Now she spent most of her time working with one of the Marble Protection owners, Wyatt, on their computer system. On the side, Evie was also completing an online IT course. She'd failed to mention when they'd met that she was a genius.

"First of all, you can look at that hunky boyfriend of yours anytime you want. You live with the man." Lexie crossed her arms and leaned her hip against the counter before she continued. "Secondly, that wannabe Hemsworth brother over there can get stuffed. He's been taking group classes all day just to torment me, and I refuse to be affected."

Evie's brow lifted as a slight smile touched her lips. "You're not affected?"

Shaking her head, she lied through her teeth. "Not in the least."

Chuckling, Evie shook her head. "Don't go saying that to any of *them*. They're human lie detectors. They'll see through you quicker than me." Evie cocked her head to the side. "Want to come over for a wine and cake night this Saturday? I've already checked, Shylah's free."

Opening her mouth to say yes—heck yes—Lexie quickly stopped when she remembered her morning discovery.

She was pregnant.

Pregnancy meant no wine. No wine for nine months. Well, seven and a half now.

Holy moly, how would she hide it from Evie? Lexie herself had invented wine night.

Evie's brows pulled together at her hesitation. Placing a hand on Lexie's arm, she lowered her voice. "Hey, are you okay, Lex? You've gone a bit pale."

Of course she was pale. There was the beginnings of a human being growing inside her body.

Glancing down at her friend, Lexie made a decision. She may not want to tell Asher and change his whole world just yet, but surely she could tell Evie. She needed a friend to share her earth-shattering news with.

"Actually, I was wondering if you wanted to grab a coffee with me. There's something I was hoping to get your advice on."

Evie's brows shot up. "Of course. You can talk to me about anything, whenever you need to, Lex. Want to pop over when you finish work?"

And risk Luca walking in on their conversation? No, thank you.

"Could we go to the diner? Maybe tomorrow if you're free?" At the concern on Evie's face, Lexie attempted to downplay it. "It's nothing too serious, I just need a girl's opinion."

Yeah, a girl's opinion on whether to go with disposable or cloth diapers.

"Sure. Tomorrow morning at the diner sounds good."

Releasing a sigh, Lexie tried to hide her relief, but dang did it feel good that someone other than her would know her secret.

At that moment, Luca circled the counter and snaked his arm around Evie's middle. Evie's cheeks colored a rosy-pink shade as Luca nuzzled her neck.

"Ready to go, sweetheart?"

Evie nodded, a gigantic grin on her lips.

Lexie pushed down the piercing jealousy. She was happy for her friend. A gigantic-super-crate worth of happy for her. Evie deserved every bit of joy and love that she had. Especially since she'd been in such a terrible relationship before Luca. Lexie just wished that *her* man loved her that open and fiercely.

Luca and Evie turned to leave, saying their goodbyes on the way out.

Packing up the desk, her eyes lifted to see Asher watching her from across the room. His gaze was heated. Intense. He could almost fool someone into believing he cared about her.

Almost.

Firming her expression, Lexie turned back to the desk, finishing her tidying.

Do not fall for that man's charm, Lexie.

Thinking about the walk home, she cringed. She was tired. Why oh why had she walked to work today rather than driven? Maybe the early pregnancy was affecting her decision-making as well as zapping her energy.

Lifting her bag, Lexie turned—and stepped straight into Asher's big body.

His arm shot out to wrap around Lexie's back, stopping her from landing on the ground. The weak side of her wanted to sink into him. Let his arms of steel wrap around her body and hold her tight.

The strong side, the louder side, knew there was no way she was letting him think he could have her without any sort of commitment. He would take what he wanted, only for Lexie to wake up to cold sheets beside her.

Pushing at his chest, she huffed when Asher remained where he was, like a big old statue.

Lexie's voice hardened as she spoke. "Let go of me, Asher, I'm going home."

A grin stretched his mouth. "I'll take you home."

That was a big fat no. She couldn't trust herself around him for five minutes. "I'll walk, thanks."

Asher lowered his head, his breath brushing against her chilled skin as he spoke. "You look tired. Let me drive you home, Lex."

It was hard to ignore the fact that everyone else in the building had left. It was just her and Asher. Hence his affection.

"So now that everyone's gone home it's okay to touch me?"

She wanted her words to be firm. Angry. But they didn't sound anywhere near that.

"Let me take you home," he repeated, ignoring her words.

At the slight touch of his lips against her neck, a shiver coursed down Lexie's spine. At the same time, his hand ran down her back.

Jeez, she was a goner.

Taking a breath, Lexie gathered her strength before speaking. "Fine, you can take me home under one condition. You remain in the car when we get there. And no touching."

As she said the last word, Asher's lips pressed to Lexie's neck.

Heat spiraled through her core. Holy ham on a cracker, she could light up in flames right then and there.

"Is that what you want?" Asher murmured, lips trailing down her neck.

No. "Yes."

Her voice held less conviction than she would like, but still, Asher lifted his head and stepped back. Her body yearned for his lips to return to her skin. The sudden lack of Asher's warmth caused her skin to chill.

"Let's get going then," Asher said with a hint of a smile.

Dammit, the man knew exactly what he'd done to her.

Stomping past Asher, she didn't acknowledge him until they were in the car on the way to her house.

"Do you have to take every class in the big room at Marble?" Lexie asked, finally breaking the silence.

Humor shone in Asher's eyes as he kept his gaze on the road. "Does it bother you?"

"Yes." What was the point in lying? The man would see right through it, anyway. "Asher, we're not together anymore. For that matter, we never really were. I wanted more, you didn't. Now I need to be given a chance to get over you. I can't do that while you're right in front of me all day, every day. Isn't there some paperwork in the back you can do?"

His gaze darted to Lexie then back to the road, all traces of humor gone. "Why does it have to be one way or the other, Lex? Can't we meet in between?"

"Asher, your version of 'in between' is late-night booty calls and sneaking off before the sun comes up."

"Not true," Asher pushed. "We've had dinner together tons of times."

"Yes, but always at home." Swallowing the lump in her throat, Lexie watched the trees pass by. "I want someone who loves me enough to take me out places. To stay the night and wake up next to me. Someone who'll share their life with me."

Asher shook his head. "I care about you."

Sure didn't feel that way.

The car came to a stop outside Lexie's building. "If you care about me, then either give us a go at being something real or give me some space."

Jeez, she hated the idea of space. It tore her up inside. But so did seeing him every second of every day and knowing he wasn't hers.

"No."

Disbelief coursed through Lexie at his response. "No? No to what?"

"I'm not giving you space to *get over me*, but I can't share my whole life with you."

Anger welled up inside her. He didn't even look like he felt any guilt.

Lexie began unfastening her seat belt but stopped when she saw Asher's hand go to his door handle. "Don't even think about it, Asher," Lexie said firmly, the anger snaking its way into her tone. "You said you wouldn't get out. The least you can do is keep your word."

Asher pulled his hand back.

Climbing out of the car, she ducked her head back in one final time. "And it's not that you can't let me into your life, it's that you *won't*. And that just doesn't work for me."

Slamming the door shut, Lexie walked to her apartment, ignoring the gaping hole in her heart.

CHAPTER 3

*S*tepping into Joan's Diner the next morning, Lexie scanned the tables but couldn't see any signs of Evie.

She needed Evie's support right now. Marble Falls was a small town, and Lexie had dedicated most of her time in the last year to Asher. She hadn't gone out of her way to make new friends.

Lexie needed Evie to tell her everything would be okay. She couldn't do this without a friend.

Moving to a spot in the back, Lexie took a seat away from other diners. She knew no one would be listening—in particular, Asher wasn't here to listen—but the hypersensitive part of her kept picturing him popping out from under a table once the words left her mouth.

Sitting down, she clenched her hands into fists, for no reason other than to stop any nervous fidgeting.

"Coffee?"

Lifting her head, Lexie took one look at the pot of coffee the waitress was holding and reluctantly shook her head. She'd gone home last night and researched it. Apparently, coffee wasn't recommended in the first trimester.

Researching coffee had led her down the rabbit hole of researching everything else pregnant women couldn't eat. The list was miles longer than she'd thought.

Lexie had assumed alcohol was the only no-no during pregnancy. Apparently not.

Lucky, she felt sick to her stomach most of the time and didn't have much of an appetite for food, anyway.

After a few more minutes, Lexie finally saw Evie push through the door of the diner. Only she wasn't alone. Holding the door open was Luca...and trailing behind the couple was the very man she was trying to avoid.

Asher.

What the heck? Were her eyes playing tricks on her or had Evie really brought her boyfriend and the guy Lexie was trying to get over to their meeting?

Asher's gaze landed on Lexie the moment he stepped through the door. Her heart sped up at the sight of the man, and panic began to rise in her chest.

Why would Evie bring him?

On second thought, why would she have brought either of them?

Lexie watched as Evie kissed Luca before weaving her way through the tables to get to her. At the same time, the guys moved to the breakfast bar.

So definitely staying.

Lexie tried to hide the annoyance from her expression, but she was sure it was written all over her face. She didn't know whether to reach over and strangle Evie or walk straight out.

The smell of coffee was already nauseating her, she'd barely slept, and now she was supposed to tell her friend her life-altering news with the baby daddy sitting less than five feet away.

Evie leaned over the table as soon as she was seated. "I'm really sorry, Lex. I just mentioned to Luca that you and I were grabbing breakfast. Asher happened to be over and suggested they both come. I said no, but Asher wouldn't budge."

"I told you I needed to speak to you about something. I may not have said the words, but you should have known it was private."

Squirming in her seat, Evie appeared uncomfortable. "Did I mention I was sorry?" Evie did look apologetic. "They won't be listening. They're all the way over there."

The last words left Evie's mouth with hesitancy. Lexie didn't know if she was more hurt or disappointed by her friend.

"I've worked for the guys for a while now, Evie. I have been witness to their freakishly good hearing many times. One time I was speaking a good twenty feet from Asher and he heard every word I said. You think I don't know that they can hear us?"

A guilty expression washed over Evie's face.

Of course she knew—because Evie knew all the guys' secrets. Luca didn't keep things from her like Asher did from Lexie.

Lexie had never let it bother her that Evie knew more about Asher than *she* did, until this very moment.

"You're supposed to be my friend, Evie."

"I am." Evie's voice was quiet, sadness shading her eyes.

Shaking her head, Lexie swallowed the lump in her throat. "I get that you can't share their secrets with me, it's not your place. But bringing them here, when you knew that I needed to have a private conversation with a friend..."

"I'm sorry," Evie whispered.

So was Lexie.

Lifting her gaze, she saw both Asher and Luca were now watching. No longer trying to hide the fact that they clearly intended to eavesdrop on their entire private conversation.

Standing, Lexie picked up her phone and keys.

"No, Lexie, please. We can go somewhere else." Evie's eyes pleaded with her.

She wasn't sure if it was her hormones, but she felt betrayed.

Too tired to try to make her friend feel better, Lexie spoke in a flat tone. "I'll see you later, Evie."

As she moved toward the exit, Lexie kept her gaze firmly on the door. A part of her wanted to turn back and pour a cup of scalding coffee right over Asher's head. Another part of her, the exhausted and sick part, wanted to fall to the ground and bawl like a baby.

Neither option seemed particularly appealing.

God, she could just strangle Asher. Actually, why the heck was she letting them sit there all high and mighty, thinking that they could invade her privacy?

Spinning around, Lexie stormed over to the nosy assholes.

Placing her hands on her hips, Lexie began with Luca. "To say I expected more from you, Luca, would be one gigantic under-statement. I expect this immature behavior from *him*, but not you. If anyone could have convinced the asshat to do the right thing, it was you. Guess I was the sucker for thinking a man could have integrity." Luca opened his mouth to speak but stopped at Lexie's raised hand. "That wasn't a question and does not require a response."

Turning her head, she looked at Asher with fire in her eyes. "And you—you frustrating, interfering, man-child—it is impos-sible to underestimate the lengths you will go to just to torture me. Do *not* violate my privacy again. Don't even think about it. And while you're at it, don't act like I'm a defenseless, dumb girl who needs protecting. You underestimate me time and again. You are not my boyfriend. I am not *yours*—you made damn sure of that—so I don't have to put up with your boneheadedness. Got it?"

Not waiting for a response, Lexie turned to leave, but was stopped by Asher's hand on her arm. "Lexie—"

"Take your hand off me right now!"

Asher kept his gaze fixed on her for a moment, clearly determining how serious she was. The man must have seen there was no leeway, because his fingers slowly slid from her arm.

"And don't follow me, or so help me God, I'll serve your balls up on a platter."

Spinning back to the door, Lexie walked straight out, ignoring the stares of every single person in the diner.

Lexie had taken only five steps toward her car when she felt a hand on her arm again. Spinning around, she was about to go all kung fu panda on Asher's ass, but paused when she saw it was Evie.

Lexie's face softened slightly at the teary expression on Evie's face. Crossing her arms over her chest, she only just stopped herself from hugging her friend.

"I'm sorry. Like big-bottle-of-wine, huge-tub-of-ice-cream sorry, Lex."

Taking a breath, Lexie closed her eyes for a moment before opening them again. "Today was important, Evie. Really important. I know you have this crazy, out-of-this-world connection with Luca where you can't stand to be apart, but today, I didn't need Luca or any of his super SEAL buddies. I needed you. Just you."

Nodding her head, Evie reached out to touch Lexie's arm. "How can I make this better? We can go to your place and talk? I swear I won't let them follow."

The last thing Lexie felt like doing was sitting on the couch and spilling her guts to Evie right now.

"I think I'm just going to head home. Get some housework done." And by housework, Lexie meant sit on the couch and watch daytime television while contemplating her future.

The sadness in Evie's eyes almost undid Lexie. But Evie had done the wrong thing, dammit, and Lexie couldn't just forget that.

"Please don't hate me, Lex. I'm so sorry."

Shaking her head, Lexie took a step back, Evie's hand dropping from her arm. "I don't hate you, Evie. I just want some space for now."

Evie nodded, the sadness still there in her eyes. Sadness mixed with guilt.

Turning, Lexie headed back to her car. She could not and *would* not feel sorry for Evie, no matter how much she reminded Lexie of Bambi.

Climbing into her car, Lexie put on her seat belt and pushed the key into the ignition. But instead of starting the car, she sat there.

What the heck was she going to do? She needed a friend. Someone to help her, to be in her corner, give her advice.

Evie had shown her today where her priorities lay. Whereas Asher had proven he wasn't at the proper emotional level to deal with such important information.

Who did people normally speak to about stuff like this?

Lexie already knew the answer to that.

People talked to their mothers.

Dropping her head on the wheel, Lexie scrunched her eyes. If she called her mother right now, the woman probably wouldn't even answer on account of being passed out from whatever bottle of alcohol she'd last consumed.

Snapping her head up, Lexie gave herself a little shake. She would not feel sorry for herself. She had managed to take care of herself her whole life, she was not going to lose it now.

She had a baby to think of. Her baby.

Lowering a hand to her stomach, Lexie shut her eyes again, but this time she pictured a tiny hand latching on to her finger. A tiny toothless grin. Beautiful brown eyes staring back at her with trust and love.

Emotion swelled up in Lexie's chest. She would love this baby, and she would love it hard.

If Asher turned out to be just like her father, bailing when she told him, she wouldn't fall apart. She would protect the precious soul and give it an upbringing a hundred times better than what she'd had.

Opening her eyes with renewed hope, Lexie pulled out onto the road. She glanced in her rearview mirror...

Just in time to see Asher, standing outside the diner, watching her car with an intense look on his face.

CHAPTER 4

*A*sher banged on Lexie's door again.

Dammit, where was she? This was the second time this week she'd called in sick to work. He'd been messaging, calling, trying to check in to see if she was okay, but was getting nothing.

The woman had been avoiding him like the plague since he'd screwed up at the diner.

He was done with the bullshit. If something was wrong, if Lexie needed help, Asher would be the one who was there for her.

A moment away from kicking down the whole door, Asher paused when shuffling sounded from the other side. When the door eventually slid open, Asher immediately stiffened.

Lexie looked like hell.

Dark circles shadowed her eyes and her skin was a deathly white shade. Her brows were pinched like she was fighting a headache, and Asher could already hear her labored breathing.

"Jesus, Lex, are you okay?"

He already knew it was a dumb question as the words were coming out of his mouth. Of course she wasn't okay.

Lexie gave a small nod that wouldn't have convinced even a stranger. The woman looked about ready to topple over.

Not waiting for an invitation, Asher moved inside and swept Lexie into his arms, closing the door with his hip. The fact that she didn't even try to push him away was evidence enough that something was seriously wrong.

Carrying her into the bedroom, Asher could see this was where she must have just come from. Rumpled sheets and scattered pillows fanned around the bed. The thing looked like it hadn't been made in days.

Gently depositing her onto the corner chair, Asher went in search of some new sheets. Finding a set in the hall closet, he reentered the room to find Lexie trying to stand.

"Don't even think about it," Asher said with enough authority that Lexie plonked herself back down.

Changing the sheets, Asher made quick work of the job before lifting Lexie again and placing her in the bed.

"I'm going to call the doctor," he said softy, already pulling out his phone.

"No." Lexie's immediate response surprised him. "I'm fine, Asher. I think it's the flu."

Her voice was weak. So damn weak. And her breath had hitched partway through speaking, meaning she'd lied. What the hell was she lying about?

"You're fucking sick, Lex, and you need a doctor." Lifting the phone again, Asher stopped when Lexie began to push out of bed.

"If you came over here to bully me, then you can take your male chauvinistic attitude with you and shut the door on your way out."

Placing the phone back in his pocket, Asher sat on the edge of the bed and gently pushed Lexie into a lying position. "Lex, why can't I call the doctor?"

Her eyes darted away before slowly drawing back to him.

"Because I'm okay, and he won't tell me anything I don't already know."

Asher studied her face, frowning when he realized she'd just spoken the truth. "Fine, but I'm not leaving until I know you're okay." Studying the rest of her, he noticed she'd lost weight. The problem was the woman didn't have any weight to lose. "When was the last time you ate?"

Closing her eyes, Lexie's brows furrowed. "I'm not sure."

A deep growl emanated from his chest. "I'm going to make you a sandwich. Maybe a BLT—"

Before Asher could finish what he was saying, a pained groan escaped Lexie's lips. "Please, God, no bacon. Or tomato. Or bread."

Reaching out, Asher moved a piece of hair from her face. "But you love all those things."

Lexie didn't respond, simply shook her head.

"You need to eat, Lex." There was no way he was letting her go days on end with no food. Christ, she would perish away into nothing. "Tell me what I can get you, because you can bet your ass you're going to eat something."

There was a beat of silence before her eyes slid open. "Could you pop down to Mrs. Potter's Bakehouse and see if she has any chicken broth left?"

"Chicken broth?" The woman hadn't eaten in who knew how long, and she wanted chicken broth?

"I was going to head out for some before but didn't feel up to it."

Concern for Lexie was at the forefront of his mind. Maybe she really did have the flu.

"Like I said, I'm not leaving your side until you're better, but I'll send one of the guys out."

Lexie grunted some type of acknowledgment before she rolled to her side. It only took a moment for her breaths to begin evening out.

Reaching out his hand, Asher smoothed some of the worry lines around her eyes. She looked exhausted.

Why hadn't he come the first day she'd called in sick? Asher could kick his own ass. He knew it was unusual for her not to come in to work, but his stubborn pride had gotten in the way.

Standing, he hit dial on his phone.

"Mrs. Potter's Bakehouse."

Asher was relieved when Mrs. Potter herself answered on the first ring. "Mrs. Potter, it's Asher."

"Asher, so nice to hear from you, dear. What can I help you with?"

"Lexie's not feeling too well. I was wondering if you had any chicken broth."

A small gasp sounded through the line. "Oh, the poor dear is still unwell, is she? How dreadful that must be. Of course, I've got a stash that I froze. I'll take it out for her."

"That would be great. I'll send one of the guys to pick it up. Thanks, Mrs. Potter."

"Not a problem, dear. Send Lexie my best."

After hanging up, Asher sent a quick message to Luca. Then, moving across the room, he sat in the chair and watched Lexie sleep.

Damn, she was beautiful. Even sick and pale, she was still the most beautiful woman he'd ever laid eyes on.

The memory of the first time he'd seen her was still fresh in his mind. It had been like a sucker punch to his gut. Then she'd spoken, and he'd been lost. She always had a witty comeback for his remarks.

Lexie was everything Asher wanted plus more. That was why he knew he couldn't keep her. If something happened to her because of him—if someone from Project Arma got to her—it would destroy him.

Not ten minutes later, Asher heard footsteps in the hallway.

Silently moving toward the door, he opened it to Luca holding a bag.

"Thanks, Rocket. I appreciate it." Asher used his friends nickname as he took the bag.

His friend had a concerned looked on his face. "How is she?"

"Weak and sick. Not herself at all. Might be the flu." At least Asher hoped it was nothing worse.

An expression passed over Luca's face. Like he was having the same thoughts as Asher. It wouldn't surprise him. Luca was perceptive. The whole team was. Lexie hadn't been herself lately. And calling in sick two days in a row was definitely out of character.

"Look after her," Luca said before retreating down the hall.

Stepping back inside, he noticed Mrs. Potter had sent more than one serving. A lot more.

That was good. If broth was going to make his woman feel better, broth was what she would have.

Asher stopped for a moment when he realized he'd referred to her as *his* woman.

Well, she wasn't anyone else's. The very thought of any other man touching her sent him into a blind rage. But, Christ, if he didn't claim the woman, eventually someone else would.

Asher scrubbed a hand over his face as he headed to the kitchen. He needed to sort his shit out and fast.

Heating up a bowl of broth, Asher placed the rest in the fridge before returning to the bedroom.

Lexie still lay in a ball under the covers, looking small and fragile.

He hated to wake her. But Asher knew from his years as a sleep-deprived SEAL that rest with food in your stomach was essential to the body's recovery.

Sitting on the edge of the bed, Asher gently roused Lexie.

When her sleep-glazed eyes opened, he smiled. "I got you some broth, sweetness."

Her eyes slid closed again and a frown marred her brows. "What have I told you about calling me that, Asher?"

"That you love the endearment and would love to hear it more?"

The slightest smile spread across her lips. Some of the tightness in Asher's chest eased at the sight of it.

"Not even close," she mumbled.

After Lexie pushed herself into a sitting position, Asher fed her the soup, surprised that she let him. Once the bowl was empty, she resumed her ball position under the covers, but some of the color had returned to her skin.

When her eyes drifted shut, Asher placed the empty bowl on the side table.

For the first time, he noticed a light thumping in the room. It was quick but quiet. It almost sounded like a clock ticking, but faster.

He was about to look for the culprit when a soft moan sounded from the bed. Without thinking twice, Asher moved around the bed to slide in behind her.

Lexie's body was warm and soft as he pulled her into him. So damn irresistible.

Resting his eyes, knowing he couldn't be with her forever, Asher memorized the moment, determined to remember the feel of Lexie in his arms.

～

LEXIE TOOK A DEEP BREATH. For the first time in days, she didn't wake wanting to be sick.

Squinting one eye open, she noticed that it wasn't actually morning. The room wasn't bright enough. Too many shadows spread across the room.

Then the warm body behind her registered, and the memory of that morning came back to her. Asher had come over. Was *still* over. In bed with her. He had fed Lexie broth.

Scrunching her eyes shut, Lexie wanted to groan from embarrassment. But that would alert Asher to her consciousness.

She'd felt like death every morning this week, and her stomach had been empty most of that time. But not now. It must have been the broth. Mrs. Potter's magical broth.

She had to remember to eat. She'd researched that eating regular small meals while pregnant kept the nausea at bay. Not to mention her baby needed nutrients.

Crap, Lexie needed to do better.

A good night's sleep was also essential for both mom and baby during pregnancy. But worry had kept her awake. Asher's warm body probably went a long way in soothing her tired body into a calm sleep.

At the thought of Asher's body, it moved behind her, his hardness rubbing against Lexie's butt. As if it had a mind of its own, her butt wiggled against him, though she knew it would do nothing to calm him.

"Lexie," Asher growled.

Jeez, the man even had a sexy afternoon voice.

Rolling onto her back, she looked at Asher's huge body as he leaned over her.

His brows pulled into a frown. "How do you look so much better?"

Lexie scrambled for a response. "I probably just ate something that made me temporarily ill. I'm feeling a lot better."

Asher's perceptive eyes inspected her face. Crap, the man could sense a lie a mile off. "A few hours ago, you looked a step away from needing a trip to the emergency department."

Giving a little shrug, Lexie struggled to think of a plausible excuse. "I don't know what to say, Asher, Mrs. Potter's soup has magical healing powers."

Which was the truth.

As his gaze continued to inspect her far too closely, she

lowered her own to his muscular chest. His naked, muscular chest.

The man was a piece of art. And she wanted him.

The exhaustion and fear of the last week suddenly felt too much for Lexie. Keeping the secret of her pregnancy was both challenging and lonely. The knowledge that her world was about to change scared the absolute heck out of her.

And in this moment, being with Asher, felt like an escape. An escape she needed so very badly. She almost felt a desperate need to be touched by him. Held.

Even though she had told him she was done. Told *herself* she was done. She wanted him with a ferocity she had rarely felt in her life.

Giving in to the desperate yearning inside her, Lexie reached out to touch his powerful chest. Her fingertips slid across warm skin. At the same time, she lifted her left leg until her foot hooked around his muscular thigh.

"Lexie..." Asher's voice was deep, guttural.

Pulling his hips down with her leg, she knew Asher could easily have remained where he was, but instead, he lowered his hips, his hardness pressing against Lexie's core, making her heat up.

Lifting her head, Lexie placed her lips against Asher's neck, suckling the skin. "Asher, I'm okay." Her words came out in a whisper. Rocking her hips against his, she felt his muscles bunch from obvious self-restraint. "I need you."

She needed him with an intensity so strong, she was scared of what might happen if he rolled away.

"You kill me, Lexie."

The deep words were the only warning she got before his lips crashed onto hers. All thoughts of going slow were wiped away by the explosive kiss.

His hand pushed up her shirt, engulfing her breast.

A groan escaped Lexie, swallowed by Asher's lips. Grabbing

his hair, she pressed against him harder, the barrier of clothing frustrating her.

As if reading her mind, Asher lifted her shirt over her head in one swift move, then pushed her pajama shorts down her body.

Lexie lay bare beneath him, loving the heat in his eyes as he scanned her from head to toe. The man looked at her like she'd been made just for him.

And it sure as hell felt that way to Lexie.

Pushing down his pants, Asher came back to her, mouth going straight to Lexie's.

There was no slow or gentle in their lovemaking. It was hard and fast, like every other time. As though neither of them could wait to be connected.

Asher nipped her neck at the same time his hand lowered between her thighs, immediately pressing a finger inside her. Lexie jolted at the glorious invasion.

Arching her back, she groaned as she reached down and wrapped her fingers around him. He was rock solid.

She needed him, and she needed him now. It had always been like that between them. Too much need, never enough patience.

Asher's chest rumbled as she firmed her grip. "Fuck, what do you do to me, Lex?"

Lexie knew exactly what she did to him. It was the same thing he did to her.

"I want you inside me." Lexie's words were almost incomprehensible. Drawn from her chest in a gasp.

Lifting her right leg, Asher pushed it to the side to widen her thighs farther. His fingers slid back to her core, this time rubbing her sensitive clit.

Whimpering in desperation, Lexie wanted to scream.

Asher's fingers rubbed and circled as she thrashed her head side to side. Just when she thought she couldn't take the torture any longer, he lifted his body away from hers.

A desperate need came over her to pull him back. But then

heard the crackle from the end of the bed. Asher was putting on a condom.

Lexie went still, momentarily pulled out of her lust-filled craze. But then Asher was back, positioning himself at her entrance, and all coherent thought was lost.

Lowering his hips, Asher pushed inside Lexie, filling her. She gasped quick breaths in and out as he began to thrust. Each time he lowered, a new round of pleasure rocked her body.

This. This is what she'd needed. Craved. Him. All of him. To take her away from everything and throw her into bliss.

Increasing his pace, Asher drove into Lexie, pushing her closer to her release. Each sensation was so intense, she was afraid she might just explode from pleasure right there and then. But she wanted to hold off. Make it last as long as possible.

Lowering his head, Asher sealed his lips to Lexie's, tongue immediately invading her mouth and massaging. Lexie pulled at his hair. Back arching off the bed, she grazed her sensitive nipples against his chest, creating a new wave of sensations.

As an orgasm rippled through her body, fast and hard, Lexie cried out and latched on to his shoulders as her walls tightened around him.

Asher kept thrusting. Relentless. Prolonging her feelings of ecstasy. Then, his powerful body shuddered above her.

Letting out a deep growl, he hung his head. His chest rose and fell as he held himself above her before he rolled to the side.

The room was silent for a moment, barring their deep breaths.

"Every time I convince myself I can live without you, you do something like that," Lexie said quietly.

Although, it wasn't just the sex. It was his coming to check on her when she'd called in sick for work. The making sure she was fed. Caring about her health and wellbeing

Maybe she should just tell him about the pregnancy now. There was no way what she felt for him could be one-sided.

Every time she was with him, there was an undeniable connection.

Turning her head, Lexie opened her mouth to speak—but Asher jumped in first.

"We're amazing together, Lex. What we've had has always been amazing."

She paused, turning his words over in her mind. "What we've always had?"

Asher rolled to his side, resting his head on his hand. "Yeah. Us keeping things private. Just you and me."

And by private, Asher meant free of commitment. Labels.

Asher began to stroke the crevice between Lexie's breasts. Normally, that would send her right back into his arms. This time, she wanted to rip his arm right from its socket and feed it to the wolves.

Instead of yelling and screaming at the brainless man, Lexie gave him a sweet smile. "You're right. Complete absence of romantic date nights, the odd fuck here and there—oh, and let's not forget the lack of commitments and no one sharing any secrets. What's not to love?"

The smile dropped from Asher's face at the same time that Lexie shoved at his gigantic chest. Her effort was futile, because the man didn't move an inch, but it sure made her feel better.

Rising from the bed, Lexie grabbed her oversized shirt and threw it over her head.

"Lexie—"

"I appreciate you coming over and checking on me, but I'd like you to leave now."

Before I break down in tears in front of you.

Walking to the front door, Lexie opened it then waited. It took a few moments for Asher to join her. When he did he was fully dressed.

Lexie wanted to slap herself for falling into the same routine time and again. It was her fault. Entirely her fault. For wanting the man. For willingly giving him her body again even when she'd sworn to herself that she wouldn't.

Lexie felt weak. And she hated that.

Asher's hair was tousled as he stood in front of her, the shirt pulled tightly against his broad chest and shoulders. He looked exactly like the no-commitment bachelor that he was. Probably what he would always be.

"Lexie, you don't need to push me away."

"I do, Asher. Because I care about you a lot. Too much. So much that your wanting to keep this *casual*," Lexie said the word with air quotes, "is like you reaching into my chest and tearing out my heart. I want a partner who wants *me* just as much. It has to be all or nothing."

Asher took a step closer, but she placed a hand to his chest.

This time when she spoke, her voice cracked slightly. "Please, Asher, if you care about me at all, you'll commit to me, be my boyfriend and share your life with me...or leave me alone."

It was difficult to say those last four words, but she couldn't see any alternative.

War raged in Asher's eyes. A small amount of hope built inside her that he would choose her over whatever block that was stopping him from letting her in.

Until he nodded and left.

Lexie released a pained breath and slowly shut the door.

Yep, that was the feeling of her heart shattering.

CHAPTER 5

*L*exie dragged her feet as she walked to work.

She was ten weeks pregnant. Ten weeks and two days, to be exact.

A month had passed since taking the tests, and two weeks since she'd dragged herself to a doctor. She'd driven over an hour out of town to see one.

The drive had been worth it. Marble Falls was small. Too small. Even walking into a doctor's clinic would make people talk. Raise questions that she wasn't ready to answer yet.

The doctor had said nausea and fatigue were normal during pregnancy, but the prenatal vitamins prescribed should help.

Well, two weeks later and those vitamins had done nothing. She never felt a hundred percent well. Feeling sick and tired had become her new normal.

Mornings were the hardest. Lexie had quickly realized that the only way to not end up bedridden half the day was to force herself to eat something as soon as her eyes opened. If her stomach was empty, functioning was impossible.

She had resorted to keeping ginger cookies and dry crackers next to her bed.

Dragging herself out into the fresh air helped, too. That was why she was making herself walk to work even though each step was the world's greatest effort.

In two more weeks, she planned to tell Asher. The thought edged her close to mild panic attacks. They'd barely spoken since she'd kicked him out of her apartment. No late-night texts, no sneaking up on her at work when no one was around.

What would happen once he knew she was carrying his baby? Her own father had picked up and left.

Lexie didn't think Asher would go that far, but she also doubted he'd be throwing her in the air and doing a happy dance.

As Lexie neared Marble Protection, the ringing of her phone jolted her from her thoughts. Fishing it out of her bag, Lexie groaned out loud when she saw who it was.

Gwen. Her mother.

The woman only ever called for one thing. Money.

"Hi, Mom."

Her mother's husky voice sounded through the phone. The woman was getting older, and Lexie could hear it. She was sure the alcohol abuse did nothing to slow the aging process. "Lexie, baby, how are you?" Raising a brow, Lexie didn't have the energy for her mother's problems today. "I'm fine, Mom, how are *you*?"

"I—I'm good." The hesitation in Gwen's voice was telling. Lexie already knew what was coming next. "I was wondering if I'd be able to borrow some money."

Lexie wanted to laugh out loud at the word *borrow*. Borrow inferred any money given would be paid back. Her mother called multiple times a year, always asking for money, and not once had Gwen paid back a single cent.

Not that Lexie expected her to. She knew exactly how quickly that money would be spent and what it would be used for. You couldn't get a refund for alcohol once the bottle was empty.

She had considered saying no in the past. But she worried

about the lengths to which her mother would go to feed her addiction.

"How much do you need, Mom?"

Lexie didn't have a lot of spare money, though the guys at Marble Protection paid her well. Very well for a receptionist. She made sure to put a little bit of each paycheck away, ready for the next call from Gwen.

"Just a few hundred dollars. And I'll get it back to you this time, baby, I promise."

She rolled her eyes even though her mother wouldn't be able to see. "I'll transfer it today."

Lexie stopped walking once she was standing outside Marble. She subconsciously tapped her foot, eager to get off the phone.

"Thank you, baby girl."

"Bye, Mom." Lexie hung up.

She hadn't been her mother's baby girl in a long time. Possibly ever. She had pretty much raised herself, all while ensuring her mother didn't kill herself along the way.

Massaging her forehead, Lexie felt the beginnings of a headache coming on. *Dammit.* Add that to the grocery list of ailments Lexie was experiencing.

Pushing through the door, Lexie went straight behind the counter and set up for the day. God, she hated being a grump. She needed to cheer the heck up, and fast. There was the chance that she would be feeling unwell for the next six and a half months. No way did she want to be gloomy that whole time.

Then another thought hit Lexie. Did being stressed affect the baby?

Hand subconsciously going to her stomach, she rubbed her slightly protruding belly. Not that anyone would notice the tiny bump. Particularly in her baggy sweater.

"Hey."

Whipping around at the sound of Shylah's voice, Lexie

quickly dropped her hand to her side. "Hey, Shy, what are you doing here?"

Even though Shylah was in a relationship with Eden, she rarely made it down to Marble. Partly due to her shiftwork at the hospital, and partly because she and Eden lived a bit farther out from the main town area.

"The guys are just looking at my car around the back. It's been making some strange noises. Then Eden and I are going to Joan's Diner for breakfast. I'm on my lunch break at the hospital, well, breakfast for me, so figured we could fit in a sneaky date."

"Early as in…"

"Five a.m. start."

Lexie's eyes widened. Jeez Louise, even when she felt in tip-top shape, there was no way she was out of bed that early, let alone at work already.

"You've definitely earned yourself some breakfast."

Shylah shrugged, causing her brown ponytail to swish. "Could be worse. I could be given night shift."

That *was* worse. The only thing worse than rising before the sun was never making it to bed to begin with. "You're right, that is worse, and a definite nonoption if anyone ever asked me. This lady needs her beauty sleep."

Not that she was getting it at the moment. Apparently, baby didn't want her mama to sleep.

Shylah glanced around the room before taking a small step closer to Lexie and lowering her voice. "I've been meaning to check in with you. I wanted to make sure that everything was okay? You've seemed a bit off the last month or so. Not the normal high-energy Lexie. Even today you look a bit tense."

Lexie wanted to slap her forehead for not hiding it better. If Shylah could tell she wasn't herself, then she could bet her preg-nant ass the nosy SEAL boys knew something was up.

"I'm okay. I've just got a headache today." Shylah opened her mouth to say something else but Lexie quickly cut in before she could. "I'm just going to pop into the back room and grab some supplies."

Moving down the hall, Lexie didn't look back, too scared her friend would see the word *pregnant* stamped across her forehead.

The storage room was at the back of the building, beside a door leading out to the parking lot. Once she'd stepped inside, Lexie frowned. She didn't actually need anything but if she returned to the front with nothing, Shylah would see her leaving for the avoidance tactic that it was.

Lexie scanned the room. A cupboard at the back stored cleaning supplies while boxes were stacked on open shelving to the right. Lifting her gaze to an upper shelf, Lexie spotted a box that she'd refilled only last week. It contained highlighters and sticky notes. Heck, she never had enough of either at the desk.

Grabbing the ladder from across the room, Lexie moved it below the shelf, then climbed up. Once she was eye level with the box, she began to shuffle it backward when the window to the side caught her gaze. The small window was near the roof, so anyone standing on the ground wouldn't be able to see through it.

Noticing Asher immediately, Lexie's heart stuttered. He was wearing another one of his skintight shirts that was two sizes too small. He had what looked like a grease stains across his biceps.

Holy moly, the guy was sex on a stick.

Eden and Luca stood with him, and they all surrounded Shylah's car. Lexie was pretty sure a licensed mechanic would have been the better choice if something was in fact wrong with the engine, but it was Shylah's car, so her choice.

As Lexie's eyes remained trained on Asher, she frowned when he crouched, reaching for the bottom of the car's front bumper.

What the heck is he planning to do?

In the next moment, Asher did something that had Lexie grabbing at the shelf so she didn't topple to the ground in shock.

Asher lifted the car.

Holy shit.

That car had to weigh at least a ton, and Asher was lifting one end like it was a sack of potatoes. The guy didn't even look like it was straining his muscles.

Breaths coming out shorter, Lexie shut her eyes for a moment. Maybe her tired pregnant brain was playing tricks on her. Were hallucinations a symptom of pregnancy?

Lexie opened her eyes again, and her breath hitched. Nope. No hallucination. Asher still held the car in his hands, laughing, but now Luca and Eden stood under the hood, inspecting the engine.

Luca said something that made Asher laugh again, but Eden appeared angry. In the next moment, Eden tried to shove Luca, only to have him move away.

Only he didn't move at the pace of a normal person. Luca moved so fast that he was a blur.

Taking a quick step down the ladder, Lexie grabbed at her head as the room whirled around her. Leaning against the ladder, she took a couple of deep breaths.

Okay, so Asher is strong. She knew he was strong, just not lift-a-car, hulk-type strong.

And Luca was *fast.* She knew they called him Rocket, so she should expect him to be fast. But not like that.

Opening her eyes, the room was still moving around her.

"Lexie?"

Lexie squinted at the doorway. There were two Shylahs standing there.

Oh no, she was going to pass out.

Not able to keep her hold on the ladder any longer, Lexie slipped, falling to the ground with a thud. The sound of Shylah's quick steps moving toward her echoed through the room.

"Lexie? Can you hear me? Are you okay?"

Scrunching her eyes shut, Lexie quickly reopened them to

glance up at Shylah. Blinking a couple of times, she made herself focus.

Shylah had Lexie's wrist in her hand and seemed to be counting the beats.

Pulling away from her friend, Lexie began to push herself into a sitting position. "I'm fine, Shylah."

"What the hell?"

Ah, crap. That was Asher.

Both Lexie's and Shylah's eyes shot up to see him standing in the doorway, with Eden and Luca close behind.

At least she was only seeing one of everybody now.

Rushing forward, Asher kneeled beside her. "What happened?"

Shylah opened her mouth to speak, but Lexie quickly cut in. "I was halfway up the ladder when my foot caught. I fell."

Lexie could feel Shylah's eyes boring into her but was grateful when the other woman didn't say anything.

Asher frowned. Damn, she'd forgotten he was a human lie detector.

Wait—was that connected to how strong he was? How fast Luca was?

"Lexie..." Asher began, warning in his tone.

"I'm okay." Standing up, Lexie ignored the fuzzy haze that still clouded her vision. Asher moved to one side to support her as Shylah went to the other. "I'm going to go back out to the desk."

"Lexie." Asher's voice firmed as he held her biceps, preventing her from moving. He could probably prevent an elephant from moving with the strength he had.

Lexie looked at his hand for a moment before trailing her gaze up to his face. She had so many questions. But she also felt like some of the weight on her chest had finally lifted—because she knew one of his secrets.

"Asher, please remove your hand."

Asher and Lexie shared a moment where their gazes held. It

was almost a competition of wills. But eventually Asher removed his hand.

Walking out of the room, she didn't spare anyone a glance. She had a secret of her own to hide, and too many thoughts racing through her head on what she'd just seen.

Moving behind the counter, Lexie felt Asher hot on her tail.

"You also passed out on me a couple months ago."

Crap, Lexie had all but forgotten about that incident out in the parking lot. It happened a week before she found out she was pregnant. "That was a long time ago, Asher, and I told you it was because I hadn't eaten anything. And I didn't pass out just now, I lost my footing."

"I know that you're lying."

Turning to face him, Lexie tipped her head back to look at him. "And how exactly do you know that, Asher?"

Asher's face hardened and he remained silent.

Of course the man didn't say anything. He could lift a damn car, was a human lie detector, and he could hear things a mile away, but why was any of that important information for Lexie?

"I need to get back to work." She was already turning toward the desk as the words left her mouth.

"I'm not leaving your side, Lex. Next time, you'll hit your head on something and do some real damage."

She opened up a folder on the computer, all but dismissing him. "There won't be a next time."

"Why are you so stubborn, woman?"

"Why are you?" This time, Lexie *did* look at Asher. Their gazes locked. "Tell me your secrets, Asher. Tell me the parts of your life that you keep locked away from me."

She prayed the man would say something. Anything. Anything real about his life.

A moment passed...and he didn't utter a thing. Not a single word. The silence was broken by the sound of his phone ringing.

He released a growl before pulling the phone to his ear. "I'm busy—"

Asher went still as he listened to whoever was on the phone. His eyes darted to the front door.

Here he goes again, Lexie thought, trying to fight her disappointment, already knowing what was about to happen.

"Leaving now." Hanging up the phone, Asher turned back to her. "Lex—"

"Secret duties call."

He remained where he was for a moment longer. Lexie thought he was going to turn away, when his hand suddenly lifted to cup her cheek.

"Don't go climbing any ladders while I'm gone. You're too damn important for me to lose."

Then he was out the door.

His simple touch, that was so rare in public, heated Lexie. Then Asher's words sank in and warmed her further.

Quickly, Lexie shook her head. No. If they didn't have trust, they didn't have anything.

Now that she knew one of his secrets, it brought up a hundred more questions for her. Questions that she would get answers to—regardless of whether Asher wanted her to have them or not.

CHAPTER 6

*G*oddammit.

Asher swallowed his frustration as he raced to his car. The timing couldn't be worse for the team to have a lead on Project Arma.

Asher needed time with Lexie. Time to figure out what was going on. Because he sure as hell knew there was something.

But not going after this lead wasn't an option. Not going after any lead on Project Arma was never an option.

Oliver and Kye had been on assignment since dawn, researching a suspicious license plate from out of town. It was suspicious because the driver had only arrived yesterday, yet he'd already been spotted lurking around Marble Protection multiple times.

The team had discovered that the car was a hire car. And whoever the driver was had used a fake license so there was no way to identify them.

Asher knew it didn't necessarily mean the guy was connected to Project Arma. But it was suspicious. And they were going to make damn sure they confirmed one way or the other. No stone unturned.

Oliver and Kye had tracked him across town. When the perp had caught on to the fact he was being followed, he'd taken off, speeding around town, driving through red lights.

Kye and Oliver had reported that the driver was good. So good that they'd lost him. That was why they'd called Asher, Luca, and Bodie. Each man had a different part of Marble Falls they were responsible for searching.

Jumping into his sports car, he wasted no time pressing his foot on the accelerator. Black Toyota Prius. That was the car he needed to find.

He drove around for exactly three minutes before he spotted the asshole.

Gotcha.

The car turned onto Lacy Drive. Overtaking a vehicle, he knew he was exceeding the speed limit. Way exceeding it. But there was no way he was going to let this lead slip. Not a chance.

Taking the corner sharply, Asher drew closer to the other driver.

Asher stomped his foot harder on the accelerator, and his tires squealed as he sped closer to the car. He knew the exact moment the driver noticed him. The Toyota immediately sped up, taking a sharp turn that almost flipped the car on the spot.

Asher took the turn easily, keeping the black car in his sights. The guy was headed for the highway, no doubt trying to hightail it as far from town as possible.

Not gonna happen, buddy.

Asher's car was easily faster than the Toyota. Designed for speed, his Nissan made the sharp corners with much more ease than the Toyota.

The other driver had good skills, but not as good as Asher's. And certainly not good enough to get away.

Hitting the highway, Asher took the long stretch of road as his opportunity to speed up. Swerving into the other lane, Asher kept pace next to the car, getting a good look at the driver. Dark hair and a clean-shaven jaw.

It wasn't much, but Asher stored the details in his memory on the off chance the asshole got away. Not that Asher would let that happen.

When the driver turned his head, his eyes widened. Fear. Cold, stark fear. That was all Asher could see.

Good. So he knew exactly who he was dealing with and how this would all pan out.

Accelerating, Asher waited until he was a nose in front of the other car. Then he swerved toward it before pulling back. His intention was to give the illusion that his vehicle was going to hit the other.

Yeah right, like Asher would risk his sweet ride for this jerk.

The other car swerved immediately, just as Asher had anticipated. Losing control, his car hit the dirt on the shoulder and spun—and kept spinning before colliding with a tree.

Slowing the Nissan, Asher pulled over in front of the crashed vehicle. Smoke leaked from the hood of the other car, telling him that the driver wasn't going anywhere.

Pulling out his phone, Asher sent Kye a quick text to tell him he had the driver and included his location.

Jumping out, he went straight for the crushed driver's door. Making sure the road beside him was empty, Asher pulled the entire door off the car, throwing it to the side. Bending down, he took a close look at the driver.

Blood dripped from his head as he sat hunched over the wheel. Most would wonder if he was alive, but Asher could hear his heart beating in his chest. Alive. For now.

Reaching over, Asher snapped off his seat belt before he began to pull the body out of the car.

As he was partway out, the other man's eyes popped open— and he lifted a spray can.

Before Asher could react, a chemical was sprayed into his eyes.

Pain immediately bombarded his face as he fell back onto the ground.

"Motherfucker," Asher cursed, eyes scrunching shut.

What the hell was that? He'd been sprayed with pepper spray before, but this felt worse.

The jerk was going to pay for that one.

It took Asher a moment to recover, but when he did, rage pounded through his body. Jumping to his feet, he took off in the direction of the trees, where the guy had gone.

The man was no soldier. His movements were too slow and clumsy. The asshole either wasn't trying to be quiet or didn't know how. Asher suspected the latter.

Sprinting in the direction of the heavy footsteps, it took Asher less than thirty seconds to have the man in his sights. The man's injuries from the crash were probably contributing to his sluggish movements, making his job easy.

Speeding up, Asher jumped onto the man's back and they both crashed to the ground. Flipping him over immediately, Asher was about to deliver a punch when the man whimpered and covered his face.

What kind of a villain is this?

"Please don't hurt me! I'm—I'm sorry I sprayed that shit into your eyes." His voice trembled along with his body as he spoke.

Asher immediately smelled the stench of urine.

"Who the fuck are you and why did you run?"

The man opened and closed his mouth multiple times before any words came out. "My name's John. John Roberts. They made me do it. They told me you'd notice I was from out of town, and that you'd follow me. I was just told to make you follow!"

"Who's they?"

"I don't know."

Asher's eyes turned to slits and he firmed his grip on the man. John wailed beneath him.

"Please, I really don't know! I owed the wrong people money and they turned me over to this group of doctors and scientists. They threatened to kill me if I didn't do this."

"Why? Why did they want us to follow you?"

"I was a distraction."

A distraction?

Asher opened his mouth to ask his next question but before he could speak, a bullet hit the man between the eyes.

John's body fell still.

Rolling away from the dead man, Asher dropped behind the nearest tree.

Fuck. How had a shooter snuck up on him? Asher wanted to kick his own ass.

The bullet had come from higher up. Peeking his head out, he just caught sight of a retreating figure. They were moving quick. Real quick.

Leaving the shelter of the tree, Asher chased after the shooter. It was another man. Maybe six-two or -three, two hundred fifty pounds.

Asher sped through the trees, ignoring the sting of branches whipping against his skin and the howling of the wind. His focus remained on the figure in front of him.

Just then, the man swung his arm back and shot at him.

Swearing under his breath, Asher dove behind a tree. Leaves and dirt flew up from where the bullet hit the earth.

Dammit, he needed a gun. Any form of weapon.

When he jumped back out from behind the tree, the shooter was gone. Silence echoed through the woods.

Breathing through his nose, he let the fury inside him settle. Not only had he allowed a man who had answers about Project Arma to be shot right in front of him, he had also lost sight of the shooter. All leads were gone.

Clenching his jaw, Asher pushed down the cold, raw anger in his chest.

He had been so close. So fucking close to getting some answers. He had so many questions. Where were the people from Project Arma hiding? What was the end goal of the program? It was taking too damn long.

Turning around, Asher headed back to the body, not surprised when he saw Kye and Oliver were already waiting.

"When we said we wanted you to catch the guy, we meant alive, Striker," Kye said, crossing his arms over his chest.

Asher bent down and began to search the dead guy. "Someone snuck up on me and shot him."

"You let someone sneak up on you?" Oliver asked.

"*Let* is not quite the way I would describe it."

Asher found what he was looking for inside the man's jacket pocket. He tossed the phone to Kye. "That should have a tracking device on it. Pretty certain that's how the shooter knew our location. Not that it will be much use. Probably a tracker phone with no leads."

"I'll take it to Jobs to get checked." Kye pocketed the phone. "It doesn't appear that you caught the shooter. I assume that means—"

"Someone with altered DNA? Yes. That's how he snuck up on me and that's how he was able to get away. That, and the damn gun that he had. I need to remember to carry mine."

Asher knew exactly why he wasn't armed. Her name was Lexie.

When he began seeing her more frequently, he started leaving his weapon at home. The possibility of her finding it would raise questions. Questions he didn't want to answer. After all, why would a retired SEAL, in the small town of Marble Falls, need to carry a loaded gun all day?

"We'll get Jobs or Evie to run a facial-recognition check on him," Oliver said, studying the dead man. "We'll see if we can work out who he is. Did you get anything from him before he was shot?"

"He said his name was John Roberts. Sounded like the truth. He also said he was a distraction."

Both Kye and Oliver went still.

"A distraction for what?" Oliver questioned, muscles in his arms visibly tensing.

Shrugging his shoulders, Asher looked into the trees in the direction the shooter ran. "No idea. He was shot before he could tell me. The shooter was probably watching and listening. Waiting for the guy to say something he shouldn't so he could shoot."

"He didn't shoot you, though," Oliver commented, also glancing out at the trees.

No, he hadn't. Asher hadn't been his target. He knew well that a good soldier always followed orders.

Kye pulled out his phone. "After your text we called Rocket and Red off the search. We need to let everyone know what's happened here. We all need to be on watch. If something is going on in Marble Falls, we need to figure out what, and fast."

As Kye walked toward the trees, Oliver pulled a bottle out of his pocket. "This was by the car on the side of the road. Know what it is?"

Asher's anger deepened at the sight of the spray bottle. "The asshole sprayed it in my eyes. That's how he got away. Felt like my eyes were on fire for few minutes. It was almost like pepper spray but stronger. A lot stronger."

Oliver turned the bottle around and inspected it. "We can send it off to have the contents tested."

CHAPTER 7

𝓛 exie pulled up in front of Eden and Shylah's home.

This evening was the hospital fundraiser. Lexie, Shylah, and Evie had agreed to get ready and go together a couple months ago.

Before Lexie had found out she was pregnant, and before she'd had the argument with Evie.

Well, less of an argument, more Lexie getting emotional.

Sitting in her car, Lexie took a moment to massage her forehead. The headaches were getting worse. Worse than worse, they were brutal. Not to mention the constant nausea and fatigue. It felt like her body was shutting down. Never in her life had Lexie felt so run-down and unwell.

She had gone in to see the doctor only a week earlier. The same doctor that was located an hour's drive from Marble Falls. But the older man hadn't seemed concerned and didn't seem to think any tests were required. Instead, he'd prescribed her some iron pills. Lexie had been taking the medicine yet feeling no better.

What's more, today was the dreaded twelve-week mark. Not

dreaded because she'd reached the milestone, dreaded because that meant time was up. She needed to tell Asher.

Lexie was usually a brave person, but the idea of sharing this news with Asher made her want to run for the hills. And she knew exactly why. Fear of him running as far and fast from Lexie as humanly possible. Or inhumanly, if Luca's speed was anything to go by.

Breathing in a shaky breath, Lexie pushed out of her car and headed for the door.

Evie and Luca had gone on a holiday together for three weeks to stay in a cabin in Canyon Lake. That meant Lexie hadn't had a chance to talk with her friend much since the diner incident.

If tonight would be good for anything, it was giving Evie a hug and moving on. Lexie missed her friend. Needed her friend's support.

The stress of everything was becoming too much lately. Hiding the secret, feeling unwell, missing Evie, anticipating Asher's reaction. It was like a tsunami of stress.

Raising her hand, Lexie went to knock but the door was pulled open before she had a chance.

Evie stood on the other side, a small, tentative smile on her face. "Hey. I saw you walking up."

Just seeing her friend made it that bit easier for Lexie to breathe. "Hey."

"I wanted to say sorry," Evie rushed before Lexie could step inside. "And that I miss you and that I really, really, really want us to be friends again. I wanted to skip the trip altogether to spend time with you, but the accommodation was nonrefundable. And did I mention I'm sorry and nothing like that will ever happen again?"

Not hesitating, Lexie pulled her friend into a warm embrace. "I know. And I'm sorry I got so mad. I'm just a bit hormonal at the moment."

Evie wrapped her arms around Lexie. "No, I was dumb. So

dumb. I should have stood up for you and your privacy. Next time, I promise to be a better friend and put you first."

Pulling back, Lexie kept her hands on her friend's shoulders. "Let's never fight again."

Evie nodded her head vigorously as she took Lexie's hand and walked inside.

Thank the lord, one less stress on her plate. As they headed upstairs to the main bedroom, Lexie felt like a small weight had been lifted off her chest. She just needed to concentrate on that— and not the next hard conversation she needed to have.

As Lexie stepped into the bedroom, Shylah's head popped up. "Are we all friends again?"

A smile stretched across Lexie's face as she glanced down at Evie, nodding.

Shylah let out a squeal before jumping to her feet and wrapping her arms around both women. The three of them stood embracing each other for a moment.

Lexie soaked in the feeling, forever grateful for the women in her life.

"It feels good to be back to normal," Lexie murmured.

Finally separating, she glanced at her friends to find the two women sharing a strange look between them, followed by small smiles.

"What?"

Shylah stuck her head out the bedroom door, looking around, then closed it. "I think he's outside. Should we tell her now?"

Seeming nervous, Evie nodded.

Jeez. Were her friends about to tell her about a dead body? Ask her to help them bury it? Hide it some place far away?

In all fairness, she probably would.

"Okay, spill, what are you two up to?"

"You tell her," Shylah said quietly.

Focusing on Evie, Lexie waited for the other woman to speak.

"Shylah and I were talking...and we agree that you should know Asher's secret."

Lexie immediately tensed at the mention of Asher.

"It's not just Asher's secret, it involves all the guys. Shy and I are also involved, in a way." Pausing, Evie wet her lips before she continued, "Not tonight, because Eden's too close. We were thinking breakfast tomorrow at your place."

"Even though Luca and Eden will murder us when they find out, but the secret is driving a wedge between us," Shylah added, placing a hand on Lexie's arm.

Evie's eyes softened. "It's really Asher's place to tell you, but we're not sure if he will anymore. And you deserve to know."

"A hundred percent you deserve to know." Shylah nodded.

Nibbling her lip, Lexie didn't know what to say. It hurt that her friends knew and she didn't, but she understood why they hadn't told her.

The fact that Evie and Shylah were willing to share the information now, even though they would get in trouble with the men they loved, told Lexie a lot about their relationship.

"Thanks, guys." Biting her bottom lip again, Lexie hesitated a moment before deciding to tell them what she knew. "Can I tell you something, and you promise not to tell Luca or Eden?"

Evie and Shylah nodded, but that wasn't enough for her.

"No, you have to swear not to say a word."

"We swear, Lex," Evie said, frowning.

"Yeah, come on, spill," Shylah urged.

"I think I kind of discovered part of the secret by accident." Taking a breath, Lexie turned her gaze to Shylah. "You know the other day when you found me on the ground in the storage room?"

Shylah nodded quickly.

"Before I fell, I saw something out the window. I saw Asher. Lifting your car. By himself."

Evie and Shylah shared a glance between them, neither appearing surprised.

"Then I saw Luca move at an impossible speed." At the continued silence, Lexie knew she'd hit the nail on the head. "I know I should have been shocked by what I saw, but I wasn't. Or at least, not very shocked. I've picked up on things over the time I've been working at Marble Protection. The guys have crazy-good hearing—like, they can hear things two rooms over through double brick walls. Asher rarely gets sick, even if he's standing in a freezer without a shirt on. He can even see in the dark."

Shylah shook her head, a small smile on her face. "The guys are so dumb. Do they think you're stupid? Of course you've cottoned on to things. You work at the place every single day."

"It's all true," Evie said quietly. "Tomorrow we'll spill everything. We promise."

Lexie breathed out a long breath. She wasn't crazy. Witnessing Asher lift the car hadn't been some hormonally fueled episode. Her mind wasn't playing tricks on her. Asher was like some kind of superhuman.

In the days since she had seen him lift a car, she'd tried to convince herself that it had been some kind of hallucination. Apparently not.

Smiling at her friends, Lexie nodded as she took it all in. "I appreciate it. I appreciate both of you. Now, are we going to make ourselves look hot for these men or what?"

Both women laughed as they turned to start getting dressed for the fundraiser. Lexie bent down to grab her bag—and immediately grimaced at the shooting pain in her head. Her vision fuzzed and a round of nausea hit.

Grabbing on to the chest of drawers beside her, Lexie closed her eyes for a moment and waited for the dizziness to pass.

"Lex, are you okay?" Evie's voice came from right beside her.

Slowly straightening, Lexie blinked a few times to clear her vision. "I'm okay. I've just got a headache today."

Like a gigantic, splitting-my-head-open headache.

Shylah quickly appeared on her other side. "Do you need some water? An aspirin?"

"Have you eaten? It might be low blood sugar. I brought some of Mrs. Potter's cinnamon rolls home with me?" Evie added.

Oh Christ, the mention of any form of sugary baked good made Lexie's stomach recoil.

"No, I'm okay." When neither woman appeared convinced, she picked up her bag, this time not almost passing out in the process. "Come on, girls, let's get ready. Evie, I want to hear every last detail about your romantic getaway with Luca."

Evie still appeared concerned, but she soon began talking about her trip. Lexie was grateful to have the attention off her as she dropped the bag on the bed and began pulling out her outfit.

She made a mental note to call the doctor the next day. This time, she would be putting her foot down on wanting tests done. It was time to figure out if these headaches and dizzy spells were normal or not.

CHAPTER 8

*A*sher lifted the beer to his lips as his eyes followed Lexie around the ballroom.

She stood with Evie and Shylah. The red dress she wore pulled tightly across her chest, making her breasts appear more plump than usual. The rest of the thin material flowed loosely down her body, stopping midthigh. Asher could barely drag his gaze from her silky, shapely long legs.

Lexie was both slender and strong. Soft and powerful. And Asher couldn't forget sexy. The woman always looked damn sexy.

Man, he was in trouble. Being away from her this last month, not being able to touch her creamy skin, was causing him physical pain.

He should be thinking about Project Arma. About locating the assholes. Bringing them down.

As it was, they'd found nothing of importance about John Roberts. But the test results for the spray had come back.

The bottle contained a mixture of chemicals with similar properties to both pepper spray and tear gas. To a normal person, being sprayed close range in the face with the stuff would be lethal. To Asher, it simply slowed him down.

Someone was experimenting with chemicals. Creating weapons designed to maim but not kill Asher and his team.

That should be his focus. That should be consuming his every thought. Not the beautiful redhead who refused to give him the time of day.

"I don't know what the fuck you're doing over here, Striker."

Asher turned his head as Mason came to stand beside him. "She's avoiding me."

And it was pissing him off. He never made public displays of affection, but he was a moment away from dragging the woman into his arms and planting his lips on hers.

Mason shrugged. "When has that ever stopped you?"

Since she'd made him feel like he was tearing her heart out of her chest by not giving her the committed relationship she wanted. "I can't give her what she wants."

Asher could feel Mason's disapproving eyes on him even before he turned to look at his friend. "You can. You choose not to."

"It's not that easy, Eagle. Look at her. She's perfect. And happy. If I date her, I have to pull her into our world."

"First of all, no one's life is perfect. That girl might look like she's had an easy ride, but she's tough. You only get that way from experiencing some tough shit. Secondly, she's already in our world. The woman's around us every single day at work. And she's fallen for you. Who's to say you're not doing more damage by staying away?"

Looking back over at Lexie, he saw her eyes flicker to him before quickly pulling away. "If something happened to her because of me—"

"What if something happened to her because you stayed away?" Mason interrupted. "Because you weren't there to protect her?"

Fuck. That would destroy him.

Mason clapped a hand to Asher's shoulder. "Nothing in life is guaranteed. Least of all our survival. If I had a woman to love, there wouldn't be a damn thing that could keep me away from her."

Asher stood there for another moment before turning to his friend. "When did you become so wise?"

"I've always been the smartest man on the team, you fools were just too blind to see it."

Asher chuckled and clapped his hand on Mason's back. The guy wasn't a fool, that was for damn sure.

Downing the last of his beer, Asher left it on the nearest table before he walked straight over to Lexie.

He knew the exact moment she was aware he was headed her way. Her back went ramrod straight and her hand clenched her glass of water so tightly, her knuckles whitened.

"Evening, ladies." Even though Asher spoke the words to all three women, he only had eyes for one.

"Shylah and I might go find our men," Evie said lightly as she took Shylah's hand.

Lexie's gaze immediately narrowed on her friends. If looks could kill, Evie and Shylah would have been in trouble. Lucky for Asher, he wasn't deterred easily.

Taking ahold of Lexie's hand, Asher pulled her toward the dance floor.

"What are you doing?" Lexie asked, voice not nearly as angry as he was sure she was hoping for.

"Dancing with you."

"Aren't there a few too many watching eyes at the moment?"

Stopping when they reached the center of the dance floor, Asher pulled Lexie into his arms, pressing her body against his.

"Maybe just for tonight I want to bend the rules a little."

"But maybe I don't want to dance with you." Lexie's breathy voice set his blood racing.

Lowering his mouth to her neck, Asher pressed his lips just below her ear. He felt a shiver course down her spine as he lifted his lips to her ear. "Liar."

Lexie took a moment to respond. "No, that was the truth."

Asher almost laughed. That lie was even less convincing than the first one.

Arms tightening around her waist, he smiled. "Your breathing hitched. Your pupils just dilated. I know when you're being honest with me, and I know when you're not. You're too honest for your own good, Lex."

He left out the part about hearing her heart thumping away in her chest.

"And that's all, is it?"

Asher paused for a moment before he answered. "Should there be something else?"

"I think that's a question only you can answer, Asher."

He pulled Lexie an inch closer. Trying to distract her from getting too close to the truth seemed the safest option at that moment.

The entire front of her body was now pressed to his. Desire swirled in his gut.

"You look beautiful."

Lexie remained silent, still rigid in his arms.

"No alcohol tonight?"

Lexie scoffed. "How do you know it wasn't alcohol in my glass?"

"I heard you ask for water," Asher murmured as he swayed to the music. "I think the last time I saw you drink water was after you ran to work because you were running late. Your car had a dead battery."

This time her heart didn't just race, it galloped.

Asher's brows pulled together. Why would that comment make her anxious?

"Maybe I'm not as predictable as you think, Asher."

She tried to push away but Asher kept his arms around her waist, unyielding. "Maybe. Or maybe it's not that you're predictable, but that I know you."

Fiery amber eyes lifted up to stare him down. "There's more to me than you could possibly know."

His heated palm glided up her back, pressing her closer so that her hard nipples brushed his chest. He suddenly wished they were alone, and that there was no clothing between them.

Asher lowered his mouth to her ear again. "Tell me, Lex."

When he glanced into her eyes, she seemed conflicted. Then she quickly masked all emotions and looked away.

Was it possible there was something going on in her life that she was hiding from him? Something painful? Or hard?

"You want me to tell you my deep dark secrets, but you won't tell me yours?"

That was a question, but Asher had a feeling it didn't require a response. There was pain behind her words.

He cringed. "I don't want to lose you, Lex." Pressing his lips to her hair, Asher could have sworn she leaned into him. "Losing you feels too painful. I've felt enough pain. I want to feel good."

"You can't lose what you never had."

Asher kept quiet. He had her. He knew he did. Just not in the way she wanted.

"You don't talk about that—having a painful past," she said quietly.

"Because you're my safe place, Lexie. The place where there's no lies or betrayal, it's just you and me." And maybe if he never let her get close enough, then his shit would never touch her.

Lexie pulled back so she could look Asher in the eye. "I want a relationship. Something real and genuine. That means we share the good *and* the bad."

He knew that. He knew exactly what she wanted, and what that would require.

Deep down, he had always known that eventually he'd have to

choose. Did he let her in and possibly risk her future, or did he watch her walk away, safe but alone?

The thought of Lexie walking away from him, from them, was like a dagger being dug deep into his chest.

He was a selfish bastard for what he was about to do, wasn't he?

Asher opened his mouth to tell her he was ready. She was his, and he wanted to let her in.

Before he could utter the first word, Lexie's breathing suddenly changed. Her fingers tightened on his biceps and her face paled.

Going still, Asher pulled away slightly so he could see her while keeping a firm hold on her.

"Whoa, you okay, Lex?"

TAKING A FEW DEEP BREATHS, Lexie blinked a couple of times before looking up at Asher.

It happened again. The wave of light-headedness, almost passing out. The headache now resembled what she imagined someone taking a sledgehammer to her skull would feel like.

The slight blurring of her vision was doing nothing to alleviate the pain. She'd never had a migraine before, but she imagined that this was what one felt like.

Lexie forced a small smile before she spoke. "I'm okay, I've just had a headache today."

Clenching his jaw, Asher looked angry. "This is more than a headache, Lex. It's been going on for weeks. Months even. You need to tell me what's going on, and you need to tell me now."

Lexie knew she did. It was time. Past time. She'd put it off for long enough.

But here at a hospital fundraiser was not the place to do it. She could just picture it, Asher turning white as a ghost and having a heart attack right in the middle of the dance floor. That would put a definite damper on things.

"I will."

Asher reeled back at her response, obviously having expected Lexie to refuse.

"Tomorrow. I'll tell you everything."

Eyes narrowing, Asher looked suspicious. Jeez, the man always saw more than she wanted. "What's wrong with now?"

Squirming under the scrutiny, Lexie placed a hand to her forehead to try to dull the ache. "Asher, we're at a fundraiser. I want to tell you when it's just you and me." Blowing out a breath, she shut her eyes for a moment before opening them again. "I'm really not feeling that well. It might be a migraine. I'm going to head home."

Hands tightening on Lexie's arms, Asher went unnaturally still. "Are you sick? Is that the secret you've been keeping? Fuck, Lexie, if something is seriously wrong—"

Reaching her hand up, she placed it over Asher's lips. At that point, she didn't know how else to get him to stop speaking. "Asher, stop. I'm okay. I'm not going to die. There's just something I need to share with you." Taking a moment to breathe through the nausea, Lexie swallowed before continuing. "I'm going to use the bathroom then go home for an early night."

"I'm taking you home."

"Asher—"

"I'm taking you home, Lex." Asher's voice was firm.

Not having the energy to fight him, she just nodded, regretting it immediately when it made the pounding in her head intensify. "I'll meet you at the door," Lexie said quietly.

"I'm coming with you."

That was where Lexie drew the line. "Asher, I'm going to the bathroom. You are not going to chaperone me to the bathroom."

Asher attempted to stare her down, but she held her ground. Eventually, he loosened his grip and stepped away.

"I'll be back," she murmured.

Moving through the crowd, Lexie didn't feel steady on her feet. Crap, maybe she should have allowed Asher to go with her. What would he have done, though? Gone into the cubicle with her? That was a hard no.

Stepping around a group of people, Lexie hit the shoulder of a tall man, almost falling backward. His hand shot out to steady her.

As she looked up, a pair of black eyes caught hers. The man didn't say anything, but his hand lingered a moment longer than was polite. Then slowly, he untangled his fingers and disappearing into the crowd.

Standing there a moment longer, Lexie frowned. Something about his eyes gave her an uncomfortable feeling. They were almost emotionless. Empty.

Pushing the thought aside, she went to the bathroom.

As she came out of the stall, Lexie caught sight of her reflection in the mirror. Jeepers, she looked like death.

Fingers immediately rising to the dark circles under her eyes, Lexie traced the skin.

Even though she had coated on the concealer and foundation, it was impossible to miss the black shadows. They made her skin look pale in comparison, her eyes too big for her face.

Hanging her head for a moment, Lexie shut her eyes. She needed the pounding in her head to stop and the nausea to fade. She just needed a break, a small reprieve from the never-ending unwell feeling.

The thought that she could feel this way for the next six months made her want to cry.

Glancing back up, she straightened her shoulders. What she needed was a good night's sleep. Thoughts of telling Asher about the pregnancy, worrying about her alcoholic mother, and not speaking with Evie had kept her up for consecutive nights.

Maybe she should try meditation to decrease the stress?

Lexie silently scoffed as she walked out of the bathroom. Like she could sit in silence for an extended amount of time and think about nothing. Was that what mediation was?

She had no idea.

All Lexie knew was that it was supposed to alleviate stress, but the chances of her actually being able to meditate were slim to none.

About to head to the front door, she suddenly remembered her coat. Lexie had handed it to a coat checker on her way in, and he'd taken it upstairs. The fundraiser was being held in a grand historical house. Her jacket must have been placed in one of the bedrooms.

Looking around, there was no sight of any coat checkers, or any staff. Breathing out a deep breath, Lexie turned and headed toward the stairs. She got about halfway up when the dizziness hit again.

Oh jeez, maybe she should forget the jacket.

Turning her head to look out a window, she saw the trees moving in a strong breeze.

Nibbling her lip, she looked down at her thin dress. It was likely too cold to go without.

Holding on to the handrail, Lexie moved up the steps slowly, one at a time. When she reached the top, she wanted to wave her hands in the air and celebrate. The only problem was that she felt like she'd exerted all her energy.

She checked a couple of rooms, and it was the third one where she found the stash of jackets. Five minutes into looking, Lexie found hers.

About to turn toward the door, her vision blurred to the point she had to hold on to the wall and pause a moment.

Okay, this was definitely not normal pregnancy sickness. Maybe she should get Asher to take her to the hospital. There had to be something the doctor had missed the previous week.

Forcing herself to straighten, Lexie slowly made her way back to the staircase. Glancing down, she swallowed. Had there been that many steps on the way up? It looked ten times higher.

Taking a firm hold of the balustrade, Lexie moved down the steps slowly.

One at a time. That was all she kept telling herself.

Lexie blinked a few times, the stairs starting to blur, her legs becoming shaky.

On her next step, Lexie's foot hit the edge of the stair and her legs crumbled.

Reaching for something to break her fall, she felt nothing but air. As her body began to pitch forward, she just made out Asher's voice before she hit the stairs with a thud.

Too weak to stop herself, Lexie began to tumble down the staircase until, halfway down, strong arms lifted her.

Lexie's eyes felt too heavy to open, but she didn't need to see to know that it was Asher carrying her.

As darkness started to descend, she could faintly hear Asher speaking to her but couldn't make out what he was saying.

Opening her mouth, Lexie whispered the words she needed him to hear. He was the only one who could help her and their baby in that moment.

"I'm pregnant." Then she lost consciousness.

CHAPTER 9

"What do you mean, her results are unusual?"

Asher shouted the words at the doctor. He was out of patience. Lexie lay unconscious in the hospital bed and this man, who should have the answers, couldn't even tell him what was wrong with her.

"Like I said, the results of her bloodwork are unusual for the stage of pregnancy that she's at. That's all I can discuss with you. Everything else needs to go through Miss Harper or her family."

Asher took a threatening step closer to the elderly doctor.

"Striker." Bodie pressed a firm hand to his shoulder before looking down at the doctor. "Doctor, could you give us a minute?"

The older man regarded Asher for a moment longer before nodding and leaving the room.

Once it was just Asher and Bodie, Asher ran his hands through his hair. "Fuck."

"I think we need to see if we can get Dr. Porter down here," Bodie said.

Darting his gaze to his friend, Asher nodded. Dr. Sage Porter had checked over the team after Project Arma was shut down.

Due to experimental drugs being injected into their system for months, both the team and the government had deemed it safest to have full medical checks.

The doctor had gone on to study their altered DNA and as such, she both knew about the project and was familiar with their bloodwork. If Lexie needed special care because she was pregnant with Asher's baby, Sage was their best chance of getting it.

"If something happens to her because of me—because I got her pregnant—I don't know what I'll do, Red."

Bodie took a step closer to Asher and grabbed on to his shoulders. "Nothing is going to happen to Lexie."

Bodie didn't know that. There were no certainties. The reality was, Lexie was still unconscious, the doctors were struggling to understand what was wrong with her, and there wasn't a damn thing Asher could do. Never had he felt so helpless in his life.

"I'll go make the call. But before I do, I need to ask, are you okay?"

Was he okay? Apart from the fact that Lexie had tumbled down stairs while pregnant with his child, then proceeded to fall unconscious, he was fan-fucking-tastic.

"She's pregnant, Red. Why didn't she tell me?"

"It was probably a lot for her to process. I'm sure she was planning to tell you."

She had said she was going to tell him something tomorrow. Was it this?

"I don't understand how this happened. We always used protection. I was so damn careful with her. We don't know enough about our own DNA. What if this pregnancy hurts her?" Christ, it already was. Each time he looked at her, guilt almost suffocated him.

"No, we don't know everything about our altered DNA, but we are going to figure this out. This may be between you and her, but we're all here for you. Both of you."

Asher had gone through many emotions since seeing Lexie fall down the stairs. Fear. Frustration. Anger. Bodie had just added another to the list.

Gratefulness. He was grateful for his brothers and lucky to have them in his corner.

Asher gave his friend a nod before Bodie took his phone out of his pocket and left the room.

The rest of the team were in the hall except for Luca and Eden, who were taking their women home. Both Evie and Shylah had wanted to come, but it was now the middle of the night, so Luca and Eden had insisted they go home and rest. There was no doubt in Asher's mind that, come daylight, both women would be in this room.

Grabbing a chair, Asher pulled it next to Lexie's bed. Her face was pale. Unnaturally so. He would do anything to see her smile light her face. Anything to listen to her infectious laugh.

Damn, why hadn't he just let her in? Trusted her? Maybe she would have trusted him with the fact that she was pregnant. He could have gotten her the help she needed before it got to this stage.

Taking her hand in his, Asher rested his head on Lexie's hip, willing her to open her eyes.

One thing was certain—he wasn't leaving her side. Not a chance.

A COUPLE of hours passed before the door to Lexie's room opened. Dr. Sage Porter walked in, followed by the rest of Asher's team.

Sage looked exactly as Asher remembered her. She was a short blonde lady who wore square-framed red glasses while working. Looking at her, you would never think she was old enough to be a doctor, but the team had been told about her brilliant mind when they'd first met her.

"Asher, it's good to see you again." Stopping at the end of the bed, Sage glanced down at Lexie.

"Thanks for coming, Dr. Porter." Considering she lived a few hours away and it was the early hours of the morning, he was grateful she'd made it so quickly.

"Of course, and remember, please call me Sage." Looking at the file in her hands, Sage studied it a moment before glancing up again. "I've looked over her notes and seen the bloodwork results. I'm going to order an iron infusion. I believe that will help her gain the energy to wake up. After that, I'll chat with her on what the rest of her results mean."

Mason stepped forward. "We need to know whatever *you* know—now, Sage."

Sage turned her gaze to him, her voice firming. "Mason, Lexie Harper is my patient. All information on her health is confidential. I will not be sharing her private details with her employers while she lies unconscious in a hospital bed."

Mason's body visibly tensed. He was clearly unhappy with her response.

"I'm the father of the baby." Christ, saying he was a father, out loud, was as surreal as it got.

Sage's eyes softened as she turned to Asher. "I know. And I'm sorry you're going through this. It must be very difficult to see the mother of your unborn child sick. Unfortunately, you're not married, and therefore not family, so it needs to be Lexie's decision whether you're privy to her medical information. I'm certain that once she receives the iron, she'll wake." Sage hesitated for a moment before she continued, "Does Lexie know about Project Arma? About your DNA?"

Taking a breath, Asher shook his head. "No."

Disapproval was written all over the doctor's face, although she tried her darndest to hide it. "My advice would be for you to speak to her soon. Tell her everything. She may not have had anything to do with Project Arma before, but she does now. This pregnancy will be affected."

~

LEXIE TURNED her head to the side. Readying herself for the pain of a pounding skull, she scrunched her eyes in anticipation. But the pain never came.

"Lexie?"

Eyes popping open at the sound of Asher's voice, she had to blink a few times at the brightness of the room.

Was she in a hospital bed?

Brows pulling together, she turned her head to see Asher's worried gaze. The beeping of machines and the smell of antiseptic bombarded her.

Yep, definitely a hospital bed.

"Do you remember what happened, Lex?" Asher spoke to her gently, his usual banter absent.

Her brows pulled together. Then, bit by bit, memories from the fundraiser came back to her. "I fell down the stairs."

Nodding his head solemnly, Asher leaned forward. "I couldn't get to you until you were about halfway down."

Anger tinged his voice.

Shooting her hand to her stomach, panic hit her full force. "The baby—"

"Is fine," Asher jumped in quickly.

Relief spiraled through Lexie as she closed her eyes. "Thank God."

Once the relief settled, it hit her.

Asher knew.

She vaguely remembered telling him before she'd passed out. Just now, his voice hadn't faltered, and he hadn't winced at the mention of a baby.

Popping her eyes back open, she studied him. "You heard me?"

Asher nodded. And to Lexie's bewilderment, he didn't appear on the verge of bolting. Instead, she saw hurt on his face. "You should have told me, Lex."

Guilt assailed her. "I know. I'm sorry. I was scared about how you'd react. You didn't want a relationship, so I couldn't imagine how you would react to a baby." Although Lexie had tried to think of how the man would react and it had never ended well. "It was always my intention to tell you. I was waiting for the twelve-week mark."

"I'm glad to hear that. It's a lot to process, but right now, I just want to focus on making sure you're okay."

At least he isn't halfway to Canada by now, Lexie thought optimistically.

"The doctor will be here soon but before she arrives, I need to tell you something." Asher's jaw clenched and the muscles in his arms flexed.

Oh God, something's wrong with the baby. Her breaths began coming out shorter, her hand gripping her stomach tighter.

"The baby is fine. Relax." Asher reached for her hand and snaked his fingers through hers. "And I know that you freaked out just then because...I can hear your heart beating in your chest."

Asher paused, studying her reaction, but Lexie didn't react in the slightest. After seeing him lift a car, she doubted she would be surprised if the guy said he could fly to the moon.

"There are other things I'm capable of, too, like—"

"Lifting a car?" Lexie interrupted. "Breaking records with how fast you can move?"

Asher remained still at her comments. The only evidence that she'd shocked him was the slight tightening of his hand on hers. "How do you know that?"

She kept her voice even as she spoke. "That day I fell from the ladder, I saw you lift Shylah's car. I also saw Luca move so fast, he would probably beat a speeding vehicle. I mean, it wasn't a huge shock. We've known each other for a while now, I did pick up on things. Your excellent hearing. Your ability to see when it's pitch black. What else can you guys do? See through walls? Throw fire with your eyes?"

A slight smile touched Asher's lips. "No, but that would be pretty awesome." His thumb began a gentle stroke of Lexie's wrist. "You're right, I have twenty-twenty vision no matter how dark it is. I can see in almost any condition, and I heal quick. I don't need as much sleep as most, and I don't feel the cold much."

Raising her brows, Lexie was proud of herself for not jumping out of bed in hysterics. "You must have been one heck of a SEAL."

It sounded like he had all the traits to make the ultimate warrior.

Anger filtered into Asher's eyes as he pressed his lips together. "We only developed these...abilities less than two years ago."

Asher paused while Lexie waited for him to continue.

"I was part of a program. It was called Project Arma. It was designed to help SEALs, as well as other members of the military, train more efficiently. Recover quicker. Our commander signed us up. You have to understand that Navy SEALs are taught to push themselves to the absolute limit, and then keep going. It takes a toll on even the most conditioned soldier."

Asher dropped his head for a moment but didn't stop the gentle strokes on her wrist.

"We were part of the project for almost a year. Shylah was a nurse at the facility. We'd only just started realizing that our bodies were changing when Shylah discovered something. She found out that the drugs we were receiving were actually experimental. Drugs designed to alter our DNA—which they did. Me and the guys are now genetically altered. Faster. Stronger. They turned us into weapons."

Asher's looked angry when his gaze lifted. Angrier than she'd ever seen him. "They found out about the raid and went into hiding. We've been hunting the people who did this to us ever since. Trying to locate them. Shut them down for good."

Holy shit. That was a lot for Lexie to take in.

Swallowing, she raised a hand to Asher's cheek. "I'm sorry that was done to you without your permission. It was a violation of your trust. It must have been painful when you discovered the truth."

Painful was an understatement. Lexie couldn't imagine what it felt like to place your trust in people, in your government, only to have it broken so completely.

"It was. We each deal with the deception in our own way. It's a mental battle."

There was something that was still bugging Lexie. "How do you know the people involved in Arma are still working on the project?"

Asher removed a hand from her to scrub it over his face. "When Evie was attacked by her ex, we later found out that her ex was a SEAL who was part of the project. He wasn't a good guy, though. None of his team were."

Lexie knew he wasn't a good guy. She'd seen Evie after the guy had attacked her. Beaten and bloody. It had killed Lexie to see her friend like that.

"We killed him," Asher continued. "But other members of his team paid her a visit in hospital while she was recovering. They told us that the project was alive and running. That it was too valuable to discard. Basically, they told us to leave them alone, or they'd come after us."

"Oh my gosh. And he was still chasing them?"

Fear coursed through Lexie at the thought of Asher being hunted by these people.

"Yes. They're dangerous and they need to be stopped. I think eventually they'll come after us, anyway, whether we hunt them down or not. We're valuable to them. But they haven't directly come after any of our team yet. They need a way to control us first. It doesn't matter who finds who first, because one way or another, we're going to end them once and for all."

The secret was so much more than Lexie had thought. But it wasn't more than she could handle. "Why didn't you tell me this before, Asher? You know I don't scare easily."

A war raged in his eyes. The normally laid-back joker nowhere to be seen. "I didn't want this to touch you. I don't want to be the reason your life is in danger. I would die to protect you, Lexie. But if someone hurt you to get to me..."

Turning her hand over in Asher's, Lexie ran her fingers over the hard ridges. "No one can protect anyone else from everything. And you can't live your life not letting anyone get close to you for fear you may lose them."

The look on Asher's face told Lexie he thought otherwise.

The door to the room suddenly opened and a short, curvy female in a white coat walked in. She was beautiful, with intelligent blue eyes.

"Hi, Lexie, I'm Dr. Porter, but I would love for you to call me Sage. I'll be looking after you today."

Lexie returned the smile. "It's nice to meet you, Sage."

"How are you feeling?"

Compared to the last few weeks, Lexie felt like she could run a marathon. "I feel great, actually."

Sage's smile grew. "I'm so glad to hear that. Now, would you like Asher to be present while we chat, or would you like it to be just between you and me?"

Shifting her gaze to Asher, she noticed his features were stubbornly set. Lexie had a feeling it would be difficult to remove him even if that was what she wanted.

"I'm not leaving," Asher said, confirming her thoughts.

Good. Because she didn't want him anywhere else. "He can stay."

Nodding her head, Sage moved her glasses down to her nose

as she read from the file in her hands. "They did bloodwork when you first arrived. The first thing they noticed was how low your iron levels were. Low iron can be normal in pregnancy, but yours were exceptionally low, particularly for someone still in their first trimester."

"So she needs more iron? Like meat?" Asher asked.

"Unfortunately, I don't think it will be that easy." Sage looked at Asher, then she shifted her gaze back to Lexie. "We're in uncharted territory here. For a normal pregnancy, a woman needs more than three times the iron that a nonpregnant woman needs."

"Normal pregnancy?" Lexie frowned. "Are you saying this isn't a normal pregnancy?"

Placing the file on top of the sheets, Sage walked around the bed and sat on the edge. "Did Asher tell you that I was the doctor who checked them over after the truth about Project Arma was revealed?"

Shaking her head, Lexie remained silent. There was so much information to take in.

"The guys called me down here tonight because I'm familiar with their DNA. Their *altered* DNA. That means your pregnancy might be slightly different from most. We already know you have significantly higher iron requirements. Your bloodwork also shows an abnormally low white blood cell count. That means you have a lowered immune system and you'll be more susceptible to sickness."

"More susceptible to sickness?" Asher jumped in, reminding Lexie that he was there.

"All these things can be supported with nutrition, lifestyle choices, supplementation, and modern medicine, where required." Placing her hand on Lexie's arm, the doctor leaned closer. "What I suspect is that this baby has greater needs than most. Currently, bubs is taking what it needs and depleting your stores. It's our job to ensure you have enough for both of you."

Okay, Lexie now understood why she'd been feeling like death the last few months—she was growing superbaby in her belly.

"How do we do that?" Lexie questioned.

"We've given you an iron infusion. Now we'll give you supplements as well as nutritional recommendations. In terms of lifestyle, rest and avoid stress. I'd like to see you for weekly checkups, too, if that's okay with you."

"Are you local?" Lexie hadn't seen the doctor around town.

"No, I work a couple of hours away, but I have special permission to be here with you as my patient in this hospital. So, I will be remaining in Marble Falls for the duration of your pregnancy. That way, I can be close by and we can work together to adjust your requirements weekly."

The doctor was just going to leave her life to work with Lexie, someone she didn't know from a bar of soap? "I really appreciate you supporting me, and I'll do whatever I need to do to keep this baby safe and healthy, but I don't want to uproot you from your life?"

"I'm taking a leave of absence for you, Lexie. Now, before you question it"—Sage held up her hands—"I need you to understand that I can't let any other doctor treat you. I have studied the DNA of these men. I am the best person to take care of you. I take my responsibilities very seriously, and Lexie, you are now my responsibility. You and this baby."

Lexie didn't know whether to smile or cry. Finally, she felt like she had support. A team. People around her to make sure that her baby had the best start to life.

"Thank you." Although the words felt inadequate, she said them anyway. "Both of you."

CHAPTER 10

"*S*top being so stubborn and stay in bed, woman."

Asher blocked the exit to his bedroom as Lexie's hands went to her hips.

He lived in a warehouse apartment in the center of town, above several small businesses. It had taken a good hour at the hospital to convince Lexie that here was a better option than her apartment at the moment. He had better security and more space.

They'd been home less than an hour, and Asher had already carried Lexie back to bed more times than he could count.

"Get out of my way, you big bully, I feel fine," Lexie huffed, moving to shove past Asher.

Hell no. That was not happening.

Lifting Lexie into his arms, Asher carried her back to the bed, ignoring her fists pummeling his chest.

"Cut it out, Lexie. You're going to hurt yourself. Sage said you need rest," Asher ground out as he placed Lexie back on the bed.

"She also said no stress. Guess what, Einstein, you're stressing me out."

She pushed up onto her elbows, only to have Asher hover

over her. "I've restrained the meanest sons of bitches you can think of. You think I would hesitate to restrain *you*?"

A moment of silence passed, but she looked about ready to kill him. Or at least cause some bodily harm.

Give it your best shot, Asher thought, sticking to the fact that Lexie needed to rest.

She opened her mouth, but the knock on the door cut off whatever blistering insult he was sure she was about to spew.

"Stay. Here," Asher commanded, his patience thoroughly drained.

Crossing her arms, Lexie leaned back against the headboard. The likelihood of her still being there when he returned was slim.

Breathing out his frustration, Asher moved to the door, already knowing who it was.

Pulling it open, he found Luca with a bemused look on his face. The bastard had obviously heard the exchange between him and Lexie. Evie and Shylah stood beside him, concerned expressions on their faces.

"Hey. She's—" Asher turned his head at the sound of footsteps. Lexie stood in the bedroom doorway. "Not in bed," he finished, not surprised at all that Lexie couldn't do what he asked for a single second.

Both Shylah and Evie brushed past Asher and rushed over to hug Lexie.

Shutting the front door, Asher ground his teeth as the women disappeared into the bedroom, closing the door behind them.

"Now she willingly goes in there," Asher muttered to himself. He was about ready to throw a damn lock on the door.

Chuckling, Luca dropped down to the couch. "I can see the pregnancy has done wonders to keep the peace between you two."

"Yeah, it's celebration central in here." Asher went to the fridge to grab a couple of beers. "The woman was just released from the hospital. She was told to rest, and she wants to be up and doing shit."

Asher knew a lot of his frustration grew from worry. Worry for Lexie. For the baby. It was taking a toll on his relaxed nature.

Dropping into the seat beside Luca, he let exhaustion wash over him as he passed a beer over.

"Lexie is a high-energy person. Asking her to rest in bed all day would be near impossible. Christ, imagine if someone told *you* to do that."

Rolling his eyes, Asher lifted the beer to his lips. "I don't have a baby growing in my stomach, zapping all my energy."

Luca leaned forward, all humor leaving his face. "How are you doing with that? The news that you're going to be a father?"

"Honestly, man, I haven't had a moment to sit down and process it." He scrubbed a hand over his face, and anxiety hit him hard. "The whole reason I didn't want to publicly date Lexie was because I wanted to keep her safe. Protected. Separate from my shit. Now she's pregnant. If that information gets back to the people behind Project Arma…"

"It won't," Luca reassured, his hand going to Asher's shoulder.

"We don't know that. We don't know nearly enough about them."

Hell, the team didn't even know where they were located. Project Arma could have people scattered everywhere, even Marble Falls.

"But we will, Striker."

It would be nice if Asher had his friend's confidence. "It's not just people from the project that I'm worried about. I know you guys were outside Lexie's room listening to what Sage said. We're in uncharted fucking territory. Who knows what this pregnancy could do to her health?"

"That's why we keep an eye on her. Watch for any threats externally, and make sure she maintains her health." Luca paused, firming his grip on Asher's shoulder. "You and Lexie aren't alone.

We're your brothers, and now Lexie and your child are family, too. We'll do everything in our power to keep her and that baby safe. You're *not* alone, Striker."

Some of the tightness in Asher's chest loosened at hearing those words.

He never took his brothers for granted. Not for a second. He knew exactly how lucky he was to have the seven men in his life.

"Thank you, brother."

❧

"LEX, ARE YOU OKAY?"

Lexie was unsure how to answer Evie's question. She *was* okay. Better than okay. Health-wise, she felt better than she had in months. Plus, there were no longer any secrets between her and Asher. It was like a gigantic rock had been lifted off her chest.

But at the same time Lexie felt grouchy and hormonal.

Shylah leaned forward. "We saw you fall down the stairs before Asher got to you but the guys didn't want us at the hospital."

Plonking herself on the bed, Lexie shook her head. "Probably because they're controlling chumps who like to tell women what to do."

Shoot, there was that hormonal crabbiness again.

Shylah and Evie shared a look between them before turning back to Lexie.

"Is Asher not taking good care of you?" Evie asked, concerned.

"I can get Eden onto him if you want?" Shylah added. It sounded like it should have been a joke but the look on her face told Lexie she was dead serious.

Lexie let out a laugh at the thought. Boy, it was good to laugh again. "Thanks, Shy, but I'll pass. Asher's been amazing, just a bit overbearing since the hospital, that's all. He thinks I should be strapped to the bed and resting for the next six months. Can you imagine?"

Evie cocked her head to the side. "Why? What happens in six months?"

At Evie's confused expression, Lexie's eyes widened. *She doesn't know?*

Lexie turned her attention to Shylah to find the same confused expression on her face.

Uh, jeez. The guys hadn't told them. That meant Lexie had to do the honors.

She shot Shylah a nervous glance. Shylah couldn't get pregnant. She had shared that personal information with Evie and Lexie only a couple of months ago. When Shylah had spoken the words, Lexie had seen the pain in her friend's eyes. The yearning.

Crap, she dreaded the thought of telling her she was pregnant. Would Shylah resent her?

Lexie must have looked at the woman a moment too long, because Shylah's eyes suddenly widened.

"You're not?"

Biting her lip, Lexie nodded.

"Not what? What am I missing?" Evie's eyes darted between her friends.

"Oh my God. That day I saw you in the hospital hallway and you were acting so strange. Were you...?"

"I was going to see a doctor to get tested," Lexie finished for her. The moment Lexie had spotted Shylah, though, she had freaked out and run right back home. A week later, she'd taken the tests. "We were talking about babies that morning, and it suddenly dawned on me that I was late."

"Late?" Evie asked before her mouth opened in an O shape. "You're not...I mean, you can't be...?"

Shrugging, a small smile curved Lexie's lips.

"You're pregnant?" Evie shouted the words. It was the loudest she'd ever heard her soft-spoken friend.

Lexie nodded. "I'm pregnant."

The scream that left Evie's lips was probably heard by neighbors two streets over. She jumped at Lexie, wrapping her arms around her.

It was lucky Evie was so light, or she could have done some damage with that movement. Lexie fell back onto the pillows, embraced in her friend's arms.

In the next moment, a second pair of arms wrapped around them.

Cocooned by her friends, Lexie closed her eyes. She hadn't had this kind of support before meeting these women. Not once.

They had become family to her, and Lexie was forever grateful to have them.

When they eventually separated, Lexie looked to Shylah to see her friend smiling. Not a huge, overexcited, let's-have-a-party smile. But a smile all the same.

Reaching out, she placed her hand on Lexie's. "Congratulations, Lexie. I'm happy for you."

Shylah's words rang with sincerity. Lexie breathed out a sigh of relief. She hadn't realized how much anxiety she'd held over telling her friend until that moment.

Immediately, the knot in her stomach released. Lexie squeezed Shylah's hand.

"You said you have six months to go. Does that mean you're three months pregnant?" Excitement kept Evie's eyes wide.

"Yep, twelve weeks."

"Why the heck are we only just hearing about it now, woman?"

Shylah tightened her fingers on Lexie. "I hope it's not because of me. I think it's amazing that you're having a baby with Asher, and I can't wait to go through everything with you."

Lexie smiled at her friend. "Thank you. I was just waiting until I hit the twelve-week mark to tell anyone. I hadn't even told Asher."

Both Evie and Shylah reeled back in shock.

"He's only just found out that you're twelve weeks pregnant with his baby?" Shylah asked, shock all over her face.

Lexie nodded. It even sounded crazy to her ears.

"What did he say when he found out?" Evie asked gently.

Lexie chuckled. "Well, I told him after I fell down a staircase just before I blacked out. So I didn't quite catch his reaction. When I woke up, he told me about Project Arma. After that, the doctor came in and started telling me about my abnormally low iron and white blood cell count. So, we haven't really had a chance to discuss cribs and car seats yet."

The silence that followed pretty much summed up how Lexie felt about it all, too.

Concern came over Shylah's face. "That's a lot for you to process, especially after what happened at the fundraiser."

Evie nodded, hand extending to Lexie's knee. "Let's start with the Project Arma stuff. So, now you know. No more secrets. That's great. Amazing. How do you feel about it?"

If Lexie was honest with herself, she didn't feel much about it because she'd always suspected something massive was being kept from her. A huge chunk of Asher's life had been locked away, and now she finally had a key.

"Relieved to know the truth. Grateful that he finally told me. I guess I'll always wonder if he would have told me on his own, without the baby bombshell." Taking a breath, Lexie shrugged. "In regard to them being all superhuman, it wasn't much of a surprise. Even before I saw Asher lift the car, I had suspicions that his secret was huge. I mean, I knew he was different. All the guys are."

"I'm so relieved you know," Evie said.

"Now, tell us about what the doctor said. How are you and the baby?" Shylah asked.

"We're both alive and healthy. Apparently, this baby is a bit high-need, because he or she keeps sucking all my nutrients. I was super low on almost everything, especially iron. I had an iron infusion and I'm on high doses of supplements. I might have to go back for more iron infusions during the pregnancy. I also need weekly checkups and low stress. Not that Asher cares about the stress part, he keeps forcing me back into the bedroom because I need 'rest' but doesn't seem to get that him doing that is stressing me out."

Lexie appreciated his concern but wasn't made of glass.

Evie leaned forward. "I'm sure he just wants to help."

Shylah nodded. "The guy is crazy for you and I bet he doesn't know how to handle the situation. All the guys are so used to jumping in and saving the day. He probably wants to do something. Help in some way."

That was true. Heck, Lexie knew that Asher was being amazing. So much more amazing than she had anticipated. He was desperate for her to rest and be healthy and he hadn't left her side at the hospital. Not once. "Other than not letting me leave this bed, he has been pretty good to me."

Good. Amazing. The best thing since sliced bread. All of it.

Shylah raised her brows in a suggestive way. "Not letting you leave your bed might have its perks."

Lexie couldn't hold back the laugh. "So he can get it on with his baby mama? Yeah, right. I wouldn't be surprised if our sexy time is put on hold. At least for another six to twelve months."

Evie laughed out loud. "I don't think so. The man can't keep his eyes off you all day at Marble Protection. I doubt he's going to be able to go over six months without having sex with you."

The real question was, could Lexie go six months without having sex with him. Doubtful.

"If the man doesn't play his cards right, that's exactly what's going to happen," Lexie said, lying through her teeth.

All the women laughed at that one. They each knew what it was like to date one of the former SEALs. Living in the same house and not having sex with the guy would be impossible.

CHAPTER 11

*T*he sound of a ringing phone pulled Lexie from her sleep.

It took her tired brain a moment to recognize it was *her* phone ringing. Asher's arm tightened around her waist as she went to sit up.

"Who would be calling you at such an early hour?" The man sounded wide awake.

She had her suspicions about who it was, but there was no way she would share them until she knew for sure.

Grabbing her phone, she noticed it was three in the morning. And the name on the phone confirmed her suspicions on who it was.

Crap. Not now.

Pushing up to get out of bed, Lexie intended to take the call in another room but the arm around her waist kept her rooted to the spot. She threw an elbow into Asher's chest, but he didn't so much as grunt, let alone loosen his titanium hold.

Well, it wasn't like moving to another room would stop the guy from hearing. Lexie answered the call where she was. "Hello."

"Darling, it's Mom. Have I caught you at a bad time?"

Only if a person requires sleep. "Mom, it's three in the morning. Of course it's a bad time." Lexie let out a yawn as if confirming her words.

"Oh, I'm sorry, sweetheart, time got away from me."

Her words slurred through the line, telling Lexie exactly where that time had gone.

"What do you need?" Because that was the only time she ever heard from the woman who'd birthed her.

"Actually, I'm in a bit of a tricky situation. My friend Jo needs some money, and I'm, ah, a bit low right now."

Swallowing her resentment, Lexie ignored the hovering two hundred and fifty pounds of muscle next to her who was eaves-dropping on every word. "I'll transfer you some in the morning."

"No, dear, I need it *now*." Gwen's response was instant. Desperate, even. "In cash."

Groaning out loud, Lexie didn't try to hide her frustration. "It's the middle of the night."

"I know, I'm sorry, baby girl. Are you...are you able to drive over here now?"

Falling back onto the pillow, she scrunched her eyes shut. "How much this time?"

Gwen paused before she spoke. "Five hundred."

Christ, Lexie would be short for the rest of the month. If she didn't give her mother the money, though, who knew what lengths the woman would go to get it.

"I'll be there in an hour."

Hanging up the phone, Lexie didn't wait to hear whatever her mother said next.

Grabbing the pillow, Lexie shoved it over her face. This was the first decent night's sleep she'd had in weeks, and it was cut short by her one dysfunctional family member.

"That was your mother?"

Lexie went still at Asher's question. Damn, she'd almost forgotten he was there.

"Why does she need money at three in the morning?"

Time to break the news to Asher that her life was not all puppies and rainbows, like he'd thought.

Removing the pillow from her face, Lexie pushed out of bed, relieved that Asher let her go this time. Her mother lived in Austin so if Lexie wanted to be there in an hour, she didn't have time to spare.

"Possibly to feed her alcoholism. Although by how urgent she sounds, she might be using again."

Lexie avoided Asher's gaze as she began to dress. She didn't want the guy to feel sorry for her. She hated pity. She'd experienced it enough growing up. Everyone pitied her, but no one would do a damn thing to help her.

That was fine. That's how she'd learned to look after herself. You don't get strong from having an easy life.

"You're not leaving."

Scoffing at Asher's words, Lexie pulled a shirt over her head. Damn, her clothes were getting tight. She'd need new ones soon. Maternity clothes.

"I am, Asher." Although she wished she wasn't. "My mother might be a dud in the parenting department, but I still love her. If I don't give her the money, she'll just find other ways to get it."

Suddenly, Asher appeared in front of her. He'd moved so quickly, Lexie hadn't heard a sound from him.

"Lex, you're pregnant, you just got out of the hospital. and it's 3:00 a.m." Asher's voice was firm. "I'll send one of the guys."

So that they could all learn about her pathetic upbringing? No, thanks.

"Asher, I appreciate your concern, but I'm going. Besides giving her the money, I need to talk to my mother. Check for myself that she's okay."

"Lexie—" Asher took hold of her wrist as she tried to brush past him.

"Asher, don't. I know you can physically stop me from leaving your home, but I'm asking you not to."

His eyes narrowed and his jaw clenched. They stood there, daring each other to back down for what felt like an eternity, both as stubborn as the other, before Asher eventually broke the silence.

"Fine, but I'm going with you."

"Asher—"

"Either I go with you, or you don't go, Lex. Take your pick."

At the sight of Asher's set features, Lexie knew there was no changing his mind. "Fine."

That probably worked better, anyway. Lexie may be able to fit in a car nap. If she was lucky.

With a quick nod, Asher pulled on a pair of jeans and a shirt, drawing Lexie's gaze to his muscular body. The man even looked sexy in the middle of the night.

Going to his drawer, Asher pulled something out that Lexie didn't see before he ushered her to the door.

Once in the car, Lexie let out another yawn.

Growling, Asher took off. "You should be sleeping. You and the baby need rest."

"I'm fine." But she knew he was right. She would have to break it to her mom that she couldn't do this again. The further she got into this pregnancy, the more important sleep would be. "Can you stop at the ATM, then I'll give you directions to my mom's place."

"I've got the money you need, and I know where your mom lives."

Shocked, Lexie swung her gaze toward him. "First, I'm not taking your money. Second, how the heck do you know where my mother lives?"

Asher didn't take his eyes from the road. "You're an employee at our business, we did a background check on you."

"And that background check included my mother's address?"

"Yes."

Yes? That was his only response?

Huffing out an angry breath, Lexie crossed her arms. "I'm still not taking your money."

"You're taking the damn money, Lex."

"No, I'm not." She could feel a battle of wills coming on, and usually she would argue to the end, but at that current point in time, her body felt exhausted.

"I'm not stopping the car, so tell me, how do you expect to get it?"

Christ, the man drove her insane. "Fine, but I'm paying you back."

Shrugging, Asher didn't seem bothered. "You'll just receive it back again as a work bonus."

The man was infuriating. Sweet, but infuriating.

"Tell me about your mother."

Gosh, that was the last thing Lexie felt like doing. "I thought you did a background check?"

"There was nothing about your mother being an alcoholic."

That was because the woman was good at pretending she had her shit together when it counted.

Shrugging, Lexie glanced out the side window into the dark night. "My dad left my mom when she was pregnant with me. She loved him, so when he left, it destroyed her. Add in being a single parent and it was all a bit too much. She turned to alcohol."

That was the very short and condensed version of the story.

"That must have been hard for you growing up."

Hard. Lonely. Scary. It had been all those things. But no way in hell would Lexie let it affect who she was today. She was strong because of what she'd been through.

And Lexie would never subject her baby to an upbringing like that.

Lexie's hand went to her stomach. "This baby is going to have a different childhood. I'm going to make sure of it."

Asher's hand immediately left the wheel, intertwining with Lexie's fingers over her stomach. *"We're* going to make sure of it."

Swallowing the lump in her throat, she looked down at Asher's much larger hand encompassing her hand and stomach. She hoped that was true. For her baby's sake and for her own.

Lexie knew she couldn't control his actions. All she could do was wait and see whether he kept his word. Trust didn't come easily to her, but slowly, he was gaining hers.

Resting her head back, Lexie closed her eyes.

What felt like a moment later, Asher's hand on her arm caused Lexie to jolt forward. Looking around, she noticed they were outside her mother's house.

Jeez, she had fallen asleep quickly.

Unbuckling her seat belt, Lexie was about to push out of the car when she caught Asher doing the same.

"You're not coming in."

Asher laughed. "Yes, I am, darlin'."

"I need to speak to my mother. Alone. I won't be long."

"Lexie, this isn't a good area and it's pitch black out there."

Raising a brow, Lexie cocked her head to the side. "Aren't you supposed to be a supersoldier? If some thug sneaks up on me between here and the door, won't you get to me in time?"

Asher's eyes narrowed but he sat back. Taking her hand, he placed a wad of notes in it. "You have five minutes or I'm coming in there."

Lexie was about to climb out of the car but stopped at the last moment. Turning, she leaned over and planted a kiss to Asher's lips. "Thank you. I know I'm a lot…but thank you."

Shutting the door after her, Lexie had a smile on her face as she walked up to the house. Even though she should be in bed, and even though she was at her mother's house, it didn't feel completely awful. Because she wasn't alone.

Before she knocked, Lexie took a moment to gather herself. Talking to her mother was not her favorite activity. Especially in person. It always brought her back to her childhood. Of craving the mother everyone seemed to have, bar her.

After a moment, she straightened her spine and raised her hand to the door. Once she'd knocked, there were some muffled noises on the other side before the door opened. Only it wasn't her mother standing in front of her.

One hand on the door and one on the frame, a middle-aged man stood there. He was tall, with a large protruding stomach hanging out from his undershirt. The man reeked of alcohol.

His eyes immediately scanned Lexie's body, lingering too long on her chest. She had the urge to cover herself, even though she didn't have much skin exposed.

Standing taller, Lexie refused to be intimidated by the stranger. "Is Gwen here?"

Finally, the man's gaze rose to Lexie's face.

About damn time.

"So, you're little Lexie, huh? Gwen didn't mention how hot you were." Smiling, the man exposed his brown crooked teeth, making Lexie want to gag.

"Is she here or not?"

The stranger took a step forward, no doubt attempting to intimidate her. "What's with the attitude, girlie? Think you're too good for me?"

"Damn straight she is."

Lexie swung her head around to see Asher taking a step in front of her, dwarfing the man in the doorway.

Christ, that was the second time tonight she hadn't even heard him coming. She hadn't so much as heard the car door shut, let alone him walking right up next to them. The man moved like a cat.

"Who the fuck are you?" the older man sneered, losing some of his confidence from a moment ago.

Asher's fists clenched. "That's none of your business. The lady asked you a question. Is Gwen here or not?"

It was clear the man didn't want to back down but his gaze kept darting to Asher's muscular arms. "I'm here to get the money—"

"I didn't ask what you were fucking here for. Get Gwen out here, now, or I'll search the house myself. And you can bet if I have to search the place, and I find things I don't like, the police will be pretty fucking interested."

The man's face began turning red from anger, his fingers tightening on the door. Opening his mouth, he shouted down the hall, "Gwen, get your ass out here!"

There were some shuffling noises before Gwen came into view behind the man.

Lexie breathed in a pained breath. It had been a year since she'd seen her mother in person, but Gwen looked like she'd aged ten. Her once pretty eyes were now red-rimmed and new wrinkles feathered her lips and eyes.

"Lexie, darling, you're here!" Moving next to the man, Gwen put her hand on his arm. "Albert, I'm going to sit on the steps and talk to my daughter."

Albert crossed his arms. "I'll stay."

Asher took another threatening step toward the man. They were so close that they almost touched. "The woman wants to talk to her daughter alone, so if you like your bones unbroken, you're going to go back inside, close the door, and stay the hell in there until we leave."

If Lexie was Albert she would be turning and running. Evidently, the man wasn't so smart.

His gaze flickered from Asher to Gwen, seemingly weighing his options. If he decided to stay, he was even more stupid than Lexie had already suspected. And she hadn't thought much of him to begin with.

Eventually, Albert turned to Gwen. "Don't take long, and don't come back inside without the money."

Giving Asher a final withering stare, the man disappeared inside.

Gwen stepped out of the house, gently shutting the door. At the same time, Asher turned to Lexie.

"I'll wait in the car." His voice was angry. As if he were just waiting for a threat to jump out.

Nodding, Lexie watched him walk to his car before turning back to her mother.

"Boyfriend?" Gwen asked.

"Mom..." Lexie didn't want to talk about her personal life. Not while the stench of alcohol was on her mother's breath.

Gwen followed suit and sat next to her. "You don't have to tell me. Thanks for coming, honey."

Swallowing the lump in her throat, Lexie crossed her arms. "This can't continue, Mom."

"What do you mean?"

What an absurd question. Shaking her head, Lexie wrapped her arms around her legs. "I'm pregnant. I'm going to be a mother, and I am determined to give this child a better upbringing than I had. So, what I *mean*, is that next time you call me at three in the morning, I will not be answering the phone. My child is my priority now."

There was a beat of silence. Then Lexie saw tears begin to form in Gwen's eyes. "You're pregnant. Wow. You're...you're going to make a wonderful mother. You always took care of me."

Lexie nodded. "I did. I tried to get you help numerous times, but it never went anywhere because you were never open to change."

Tears fell down Gwen's cheeks. "That's true. I was never—" She took a breath, her gaze darting around before she continued. "I was never as strong as you."

Lexie wanted to yell at the woman. Either that or cry with her. "My strength was a choice. To take my struggles and over-come them."

Gwen would understand what Lexie was saying. That she'd crumbled when she should have been stronger. Both for herself and her daughter.

Extending her hand, Lexie held out the money. "I want you to be safe, Mom. But me constantly bailing you out isn't helping. If you want help to turn your life around, real help, come to me and I'll do whatever I can. If not…I need you to refrain from contacting me again."

Gwen's face crumbled slightly but to her credit, she didn't fall apart. Lexie wished her mother would say that she was ready to change. Follow her to the car. But she knew the woman wasn't ready for that. She might never be ready.

"Bye, Mom."

Standing, Lexie had taken one step before she stopped at her mother's voice.

"I love you, Lex. I know it doesn't always seem like it, but I do."

Lexie's heart clenched at her mother's words. A huge part of her felt that if that were true, she would have tried harder.

"I love you, Mom." Even when the woman didn't deserve it, Lexie couldn't help but love her.

CHAPTER 12

"*I* swear to God, Asher, if you don't let me exit this car myself, I'm gonna nunchuck your butt to Timbuktu."

Asher raised a brow as he took a step away from the passenger door. "Nunchuck?"

The woman was damn cute when she was mad. Her brows furrowed, making her resemble an angry rabbit.

Lexie climbed out of the car with a huff. "Just because you have this superstrength thing going on, don't make the mistake of thinking I won't beat your SEAL ass if I have to."

Asher laughed out loud. Lexie might be tall for a woman at five foot nine, but her slender body was made for anything but fighting.

Shutting the door after her, Asher took her elbow as they headed into Marino's Pizzeria. "Let's keep your pregnant butt out of any fights with my SEAL one, okay?"

Lexie was pursing her lips, but Asher could see she was trying to hide a smile. Trying and failing.

It had been a week since Asher had found out Lexie was pregnant. He could understand her frustration; Asher *had* been hovering. But dammit, he needed to ensure both Lexie and their baby were safe. Healthy.

"Asher! Lexie! So good to see you," Bill Marino, the restaurant owner, called as he stepped out from behind the counter.

Giving both Lexie and Asher a kiss on the cheek, Bill led them to a corner booth.

"What can I get you to start? Some wine? Garlic bread?"

"Apple juice would be lovely, thanks, Bill," Lexie said without looking at the menu.

Bill's brows pulled together. "No Heath Sparkling?"

"No thanks, just juice."

Bill turned a questioning look to Asher. The man's confusion didn't surprise him. He had probably never seen Lexie in his restaurant without a glass. It was her favorite.

"We're not drinking tonight. I'll have a Coke." Asher smiled, noticing Lexie's raised brow. "And some garlic bread."

Bill still appeared somewhat confused but simply nodded before heading back to the kitchen.

Asher turned his attention to Lexie. God, she was stunning. He felt like he needed a moment to take her in. She had always been the most beautiful woman Asher had ever laid eyes on. Her radiant red hair and bright amber eyes made her stand out from a visual perspective.

It was her fiery personality, though, that really drew Asher in. She always kept him on his toes with her quick wit and was never afraid to voice her opinion, even if she knew it wouldn't be received well.

"How's the nausea? Feeling okay?" Asher asked as he lifted the menu.

"This past week, I've been feeling better than I have in months. Whatever's in that concoction of supplements that Sage is having me take, it's a game changer."

Raising his brows, Asher studied the menu without really taking it in. "Is it the pills making you feel better, or the overbearing man you're going to nunchuck to Timbuktu?" Hearing her chuckle, Asher let a small smile creep across his face. Every time he heard that lyrical sound from her, his blood pumped that bit faster.

"Hmm, doctor-prescribed iron, magnesium, and iodine...or a man who threatens to throw me over his shoulder and carry me everywhere regardless of my own desires? That's a tough one."

Finally looking up, Asher shook is head. "I don't think it's tough at all, Lex. Clearly the sexy man opposite you is stronger than any pill. Also, I would not throw a pregnant woman over my shoulder. I would cradle her delectable body in my arms."

God, he loved the sight of Lexie's cheeks when they turned that rosy pink shade. Bill returned with their drinks and garlic bread.

"What will it be tonight, folks? The seafood marinara pizza?"

A choking sound came from Lexie's direction, causing both Asher and Bill to look over to her. Her face had gone a shade paler.

It looked like seafood was off the menu for the foreseeable future.

"Chicken pizza?" Asher asked, smiling at Lexie's vigorous nod.

"And a margherita," Lexie added eagerly.

Bill's eyes slanted as he looked at Lexie suspiciously. "First no alcohol, now no seafood—your favorite. Anyone would think you were..." Bill's eyes grew large as he stopped midsentence.

Ah, shit.

"Santo mio. You're pregnant?"

Lexie opened and shut her mouth before eventually giving a small nod. "I am."

"Che grande!" Bill cried as he threw his arms into the air. Leaning down, he kissed Lexie on both cheeks before slapping Asher on the back. "Tonight, I make your dinner extra special."

Then Bill turned and hurried back to the kitchen.

Lexie's laughter pulled Asher's attention and he studied the beautiful woman in front of him. "You don't mind that Bill knows? You know the whole town will probably find out about this by morning?"

Lexie shrugged as she turned her attention back to Asher. The joy on her face made his breath catch. Perfection.

"I'm already showing. Soon enough, I'll be the size of a house. People will sure know then."

The humor in her eyes made her whole face light up. "Fuck, you're gorgeous, Lex."

He said it because he couldn't keep the words in any longer. He needed her to hear. He needed the whole world to hear.

Lexie's smile softened. "Like I said. Soon I'll be the size of a house. Will you still find me gorgeous then?"

"You could be pregnant with triplets and my thoughts about you wouldn't change," Asher promised, all humor gone. "Any shape or size, you'll still be the most beautiful woman in the room."

~

LEXIE COULDN'T TEAR her eyes from Asher.

Since they sat down only twenty minutes ago, he'd been looking at her like she was the only woman in the room. The only woman in the world.

And man oh man had he been saying things that turned her to mush and made her heart sing.

Just then, Bill returned with their pizzas and they smelled divine.

Once the food was set down in front of her, Lexie's hand had a mind of its own, swiping the first piece even before Bill had a chance to leave.

"Oh my God, carbs are my soul food at the moment." Biting into the slice of margherita, Lexie shut her eyes and let out a groan. "It's like a slice of heaven." She took a moment to appreciate the cheesy goodness.

Please, God almighty, don't ever let me get full.

Or at least not for a while. Lexie wanted to feel just like this while eating another ten slices.

Slowly opening her eyes, she saw Asher smiling while Bill looked proud. Probably knowing his pizza was good. Damn good.

Let them stare, Lexie thought. She didn't care. The pizza was like all her dreams come true.

Bill clapped his hand on Asher's shoulder. "I think your woman will be returning in the next few months."

"Don't close on me, man," Asher laughed.

"Wouldn't dream of it." Bill shook his head as he went back to the kitchen.

Picking up a slice of his own, Asher bit into it and frowned exaggeratedly. "Not quite a slice of heaven, but not terrible."

Lexie was already halfway through her piece, already eyeing a second. "Leave it for me then. I know how to treat it with proper appreciation."

Asher's chuckle rippled through his big chest. "I don't think so. You may be pregnant with our child, but no way am I letting you have it all."

Lexie laughed as Asher shoved half the piece in his mouth. Damn, she needed to eat faster or the man would finish the whole chicken pizza before Lexie had a chance to try it.

She piled another three slices onto her plate, all the while ignoring Asher's raised brow.

"Let the race begin," Lexie eventually said.

After half an hour, Asher and Lexie had effectively eaten everything in front of them. Sitting back, she placed her hands on her stomach. "Baby may not be letting me have a glass of Shiraz, but I'm sure glad it likes pizza!"

Bill popped by their table. "Ahh, you finished. More?"

That was a no from Lexie. Her stomach was popping out, and it wasn't all baby.

"I think we're done," Asher said with a smirk.

Lexie pushed out of the booth. "I'm just going to visit the restroom before we go."

As she headed down the hall, Asher's behavior over the last week was at the forefront of her mind. Even though the man had been ridiculously overbearing, Lexie would never admit it out loud, but his attention was kind of sweet. He made her feel protected. Cared for.

A flutter of hope built up inside her. Hope for a future that involved Asher and her together and her baby with two full-time parents.

Lexie's hand went to her stomach, thumb rubbing up and down.

Since she'd been feeling better—*better* meaning not almost passing out every second of every day—she'd been able to appreciate her pregnancy more. Every day, she'd let the excitement increase. Lexie had even gone as far as to research car seats and cribs.

Her next appointment with Sage was tomorrow. So far, all her bloodwork had come back great. And based on how she was feeling, Lexie wasn't worried about tomorrow.

Coming out of the bathroom into the hallway, she had taken only a step when a man walking toward her blocked her exit. She waited a moment for him to politely move to the side. When he didn't she glanced up to see familiar black eyes looking at her. It took Lexie a moment to place them.

He was the stranger she had bumped shoulders with at the hospital fundraiser.

A nervous moment passed when Lexie wondered why the man didn't step to the side. As she was about to open her mouth and ask him to move, he turned his body to let her pass just before she did.

Lexie took a step around him and kept walking.

What a creep.

Noticing Bill at the counter, Lexie walked up to him before returning to the table.

Leaning over, she spoke quietly. "Bill, do you know who that man is?"

Bill glanced in the direction Lexie indicated with her head before turning back to her. "Dominic," Bill said, nodding. "He's renting the room upstairs. I wouldn't worry about him. He's quiet and pays his rent on time. Why, did he do something?"

Bill was quickly on alert as his body straightened.

"No, no," Lexie reassured him quickly. "I saw him at the fundraiser last week is all."

Lexie looked over her shoulder in the direction the man had walked but he was gone. That was twice now. Twice she'd bumped into him and twice he'd creeped her out.

Heading back to the table, Lexie shook her head. He hadn't done anything. Absolutely nothing. She had to be overthinking things.

When she returned to the table, Asher was waiting and holding her jacket.

"We should stop by your apartment and get some more of your things," Asher said as he helped her into her jacket.

Lexie was definitely keen on that. She'd been borrowing too many of Asher's things. She needed her own stuff.

"I really need my charger. Sharing with you is a pain in the butt."

Stepping outside, Asher laughed. "Woman, if your phone isn't in your hand, it lives on the charger. You would struggle to share with anyone."

The drive to her place was short. Both Asher and Lexie lived in the center of town. That was probably why they had such a problem staying away from each other.

Lexie almost laughed out loud at the thought. That definitely was not the main reason they struggled to stay away from each other. More like, Lexie couldn't keep her hands off the ten-pack.

When they stopped outside her apartment building, Asher stilled behind the wheel for a moment. Lexie started to grab her door handle but was stopped by Asher's hand on her arm.

Eyes shooting back to him, Lexie frowned. "What is it?"

Silent, Asher kept his eyes on the rearview mirror a moment longer before he glanced toward her. There was no humor in his expression. "Someone was following us."

Twisting her head around, Lexie didn't see anything. "What do you mean, someone was following us? Maybe they were just going in the same direction."

Climbing out of the car, Asher was at Lexie's door before she could blink. "No. They were trying to stay hidden, but I saw the tail."

Swallowing, Lexie kept glancing down the street as she walked next to Asher. The idea of someone following them creeped her out to no end.

On the way up to her apartment, Asher pulled out his phone. "Jobs. I'm at Lexie's apartment. There was a Mazda on our tail. They followed us from the restaurant."

There was a moment of silence before Asher continued. "Didn't catch the plate number or the color of the car. Can you contact the guys to do a drive-around?"

When they were only a few feet from her apartment door, Asher's arm extended across Lexie's body, halting her steps.

"What?" Lexie asked quietly. Nervous tension entered her limbs. There was nothing that she could see that appeared out of place or warranted his stillness. She looked up to see Asher's gaze narrowed on her door.

"Someone's been at Lexie's apartment, Jobs. Call the guys."

Dropping the phone back into his pocket, Asher edged closer to the door, keeping Lexie behind him. When they got close enough, she finally saw what Asher saw.

Her door sat ajar, the handle hanging. Almost like someone had broken it off.

Holy shit. Someone had broken in to Lexie's apartment.

A chill swept its way down her body at the thought that she could have been home alone when that happened. Hand instinctively going to her stomach, she crept a bit closer to Asher.

Tension was coming off him in waves. His body was ready for action.

After a moment, Lexie realized he was listening.

"There's no one inside." Asher spoke the words quietly as he took a step forward.

Lexie hesitated. "Are you sure?"

She thought she was a brave person but now that it was crunch time, she wanted to hide behind her big protector and ask him to carry her out of there.

"Trust me."

Looking up into his brown eyes, Lexie knew that she would trust the man with her life.

Giving Asher a nod, she followed him inside, his hand firmly clasping hers.

Immediately glancing around her living room, Lexie couldn't see anything out of place. Her books sat perfectly on her coffee table, dishes all intact in the kitchen.

Asher pulled Lexie down the hall to the bedroom. When they stepped inside, they saw the same thing. Nothing looked touched. Even her jewelry remained.

"They didn't take anything."

At Asher's continued silence, she glanced at him to see his eyes black with rage. "That means they weren't after your belongings."

Lexie's breath caught. If they weren't after her belongings, they were after something else. Her.

CHAPTER 13

*L*exie gasped for air as she bolted into a sitting position. Hands shooting to her stomach, she closed her eyes, trying to force the nightmare away.

The vision of her crying baby being taken from her arms was on replay in her mind. The image of those little fists reaching for her made her want to cry and scream even now, just like she had in her dream.

Sweat beaded on Lexie's forehead and her heart raced.

It was just a dream. My baby is safe.

Lexie repeated the mantra in her head, praying her mind would accept it.

"Lexie?"

Asher sat up next to her in bed, eyes wide. The man looked ready to kick someone's ass. Unfortunately, he couldn't fight off what existed in her mind.

Throat clogged, Lexie took a deep, calming breath. "I just had a nightmare."

Only it hadn't felt like a nightmare. It had felt as real as the sheets beneath her fingers.

Asher growled in his throat. The anger on his face in complete contrast to the gentle touch of his fingers grazing Lexie's cheek. "This is the third time in a week you've woken from a nightmare. Nothing is going to happen to you, Lex."

God, she wished she could believe his words. There was something inside her, though, urging Lexie to run. Hide. She knew how absurd that sounded but she couldn't shake the feeling.

"I just can't get rid of this feeling inside me that something's going to happen."

It was like a dark cloud hanging over her. The pregnancy had made her dreams vivid. Real. Now, since the break-in, they'd become nightmares on repeat. Torturing her. Stealing her sleep and her sanity.

"Tell me about them," Asher encouraged gently.

Hesitating, Lexie didn't particularly want to relive it any more times than she had to. Asher's hand began to rub gentle circles across her back, giving her the strength she needed.

"I'm standing in my apartment. Pregnant. Really pregnant. There's a knock on my door. When I open it, these people wearing white lab coats, holding briefcases, are standing there. I immediately know why they're there, so I turn and walk into my bedroom. When I walk out, I'm no longer pregnant. I'm holding my baby in my arms." Lexie's breath caught as she pictured the perfect little face staring up at her. Trusting her. Counting on her love and protection. Only she didn't protect them. Not in her dream, anyway. "The people are still there waiting, and when they open one of the briefcases, they take out this paper bag."

And she'd known what was in it. Alcohol.

Lexie closed her eyes as the next part returned to her.

"It's okay, Lex."

Turning her head, she looked at Asher, tears filling her eyes. "I just hand my perfect baby to these strangers." Scrunching her eyes again, she tried to get the baby's cries out of her head. "It's like my arms had a mind of their own. As soon as they take the baby, I want it back, but it's too late."

Even thinking about the soft cries made her heart wrench in pain.

"It was just a dream," Asher whispered, his mouth close to her ear.

Shaking her head, Lexie felt a physical pain in her chest. "What if it's trying to tell me something? Like I'm going to be a terrible mother to my baby? I'm going to fail like my mother failed me. Run away, like my father. Asher, I don't know the first thing about being a parent."

It was a nightmare that took all her fears and rolled them up into a neat scenario that seemed too real to forget.

Asher pulled her onto his lap, lifting her in one swift action. Placing two fingers under her chin, he tilted her face up until their eyes met. "Lexie, I don't need to see you holding your baby in your arms to know that you are going to protect that child with your life. You will be an amazing mother and will love and protect your child with an unbreakable strength. I know that with absolute clarity."

Shaking her head, Lexie didn't have that same blind faith in herself. "I've never experienced good parenting. How will I know what to do?"

Asher brushed some of her red hair behind her ear, his fingers touching her temple. That simple touch soothed some of her frayed nerves. "Something tells me you did a lot of parenting when you were only a child." Pausing, he looked Lexie in the eye. "And even if you hadn't, you're the strongest, fiercest woman I know, Lex. You are loyal and you love hard. If that doesn't describe a good mother, I don't know what does."

Swallowing, Lexie couldn't draw her gaze from Asher's. He was right about one thing. She did love hard. She would adore this baby with a fierce kind of love.

Just like she loved Asher. She loved him harder than she'd

ever loved another soul. If she loved her baby with even a fraction of the amount that she loved Asher, there was no doubt her child would be greatly cared for.

Eyes dipping from Asher's eyes to his mouth, Lexie slowly lifted her head and pressed her lips to his. He didn't pull back, but rather, met her halfway. His lips were soft but firm, immediately moving over hers.

Groaning, Asher used the moment to push his tongue past her lips. Invading her mouth and igniting a fire inside Lexie's body.

Hands going to Asher's wide shoulders, she grabbed on and anchored herself. Pushing herself up, she wrapped her legs around his waist.

Pure, raw lust shot through her body.

Asher's hardness pushed into the V between her thighs. As if having a mind of their own, Lexie's hips pressed down, grinding against him.

In that moment, everything else faded. The nightmare. The fear. It disappeared. All that existed was her and Asher. Peace and chaos rolled into one.

Asher reached for the bottom of Lexie's sleep shirt, his hand brushing against her small protruding stomach, then reaching up to cup Lexie's breast.

Passion sawed through her. Tossing her head back, she moaned at the ecstasy of his touch. Taking immediate advantage of her exposed neck, Asher latched on and suckled her sensitive skin.

Desperation hung in the air, like it always did between them. There was no slow. It wasn't possible.

The only barrier between her core and him was Lexie's thin panties. She had never been so glad that the man slept bare of any clothes.

Lowering her hand, Lexie wrapped her fingers around his hard length, loving the growl that vibrated through his chest.

Firming her grip, she began to move her hand in slow, sure movements.

Hunger exploded inside her as his hand immediately lowered, tore off her underwear, then plastered to her core. His hand covered her completely.

Asher's lips caught hers again, his tongue plundering her mouth as his fingers began to play with her clit.

Her throbbing increased, all moans muffled by his mouth, prevented from being more than a whimper.

She needed Asher inside her now. Never had she needed something more in her life.

Lexie pushed herself up and placed him at her entrance, positioning him where she wanted. Asher's hands stilled, then went to her hips. His tip slid inside her a mere quarter of an inch.

"Lex…" His groan was raw. Pained.

"I want you. Inside me."

Shimmying her hips, she slid down another inch. Asher's breaths were short. Lexie felt like she would combust from frustration.

He reached for the bottom of Lexie's shirt and tore it off, leaving them both bare. Her breasts bounced at his actions, Asher's heated gaze watching their movement through the moonlight.

Latching his hands back on to her hips, he slid her down until he was seated inside her completely.

Lord almighty, it was pure heaven. A feeling unrivaled by anything on this Earth.

Digging her nails into his shoulders, Lexie pulled herself close so there wasn't an inch of space separating them. Her softness against his hard ridges.

Then, Asher thrust his own hips. The movement caused a ripple of pleasure within Lexie. As he repeated the movement, she used her legs to lift and drop down to meet each thrust.

Pleasure cut through her body. Her heart raced.

Each thrust was harder than the last. Bringing them together in the most primal way.

Lowering his head, Asher engulfed Lexie's nipple, suckling her breast. Her skin burned for the man inside her. Throbbing with need, she moved faster, urging Asher, deeper, harder.

Suddenly, he flipped them so that she lay beneath him. His body huge as it hovered above hers.

Lifting her left leg, Asher pressed it into the mattress before he began to thrust again, this time at a new angle. Hitting a new spot inside her.

"I can't last much longer." Lexie gasped the words, the pleasure so great it was bordering on pain.

Even a minute longer sounded like a lifetime. Her body threatened to explode.

"Let go."

As he whispered the words, he plunged harder, deeper. Every thrust pushing her closer to the edge, until it became too much.

Lexie screamed Asher's name as she exploded. Her entire body tipped over the edge and her core pulsated against him.

As he kept thrusting, the spasms kept going, hitting her hard. Asher's mouth dropped to hers before his body tightened. Then a coarse growl vibrated against her lips as he came. Heat filled Lexie and he throbbed inside her.

Taking a moment to catch her breath, Lexie wrapped her arms around the man on top of her.

She loved him. With every fiber of her being, she loved him. She wanted to say it out loud. Scream it to make sure he heard. But she hesitated. Fear rendering her silent.

Asher lifted his head, a small smile curving his lips. "You are amazing, woman."

Leaning down, he pressed a long kiss to her lips before rolling to the side. He pulled her body against his, and she leaned into his warm, damp skin.

Falling back to sleep in the arms of the man she loved, Lexie prayed that he could also be the man she needed him to be.

CHAPTER 14

"How many weeks is she now, Striker?"

Asher didn't have to think about his response to Bodie's question. "Fifteen."

They weren't even halfway there but already they had a never-ending list of things to do and buy. Asher was loving every minute of it.

Taking a seat at the long table in the office of Marble Protection, Asher had a look around at his team. They tried to meet a few times a week but someone was invariable missing. Usually more than one person.

At today's meeting, Asher, Luca, Bodie, Wyatt, and Mason were present. Eden couldn't make it because he was picking up Shylah from work, while Oliver and Kye were taking a class out front.

"She's been looking much better these last couple weeks," Mason said from across the table.

Bodie nodded. "A few weeks ago, I thought the woman was going to topple over on me every time I saw her."

Asher was damn glad she was better, but his concern wasn't

gone. "She was great right after her infusion, but her levels have all been going down again. She's tired. Low on energy."

Grouchy. Asher left that one off the list.

Luca raised his brows. "She told you that?"

Asher scoffed. "Christ no. It would be a dark day in hell before Lexie admitted she wasn't a hundred percent. Her stubbornness is a pain in my ass."

But most days, a welcome pain in his ass.

Bodie had a smirk on his face as he leaned back in his chair. "That's why you're so infatuated with her. The first woman to put you in your place and not fall all over herself for you."

Asher chuckled. She sure was good at the former. "I've spoken to Sage and she's going to adjust Lexie's supplements. If her levels don't go back up, she'll go in for another iron infusion."

The woman needed to take better care of herself, not push herself so much. And learn to ask for help when she needed it.

"I could see if Evie would talk to her?" Luca suggested.

At this current moment, Evie sat with Lexie at the front desk. Lexie was working while Evie studied. Although, Asher had no doubt they were probably talking more than anything else. The women were stuck at the hip.

"I'll let you know." Needing to focus his attention on something else, Asher drew back to the matters at hand. "Any news on the 'distraction' John Roberts referred to?"

The man had died for almost sharing the information. It had to be important.

"Nothing." Frustration coated Wyatt's voice. "Cage did spot a man in town the other day who looked suspicious. He followed the guy but lost track of him."

"How did he lose him?"

Wyatt's gaze hardened. "I'd like to know that, too."

"What about the background information on John?" Luca asked.

Wyatt crossed his arms over his chest. "He was exactly who he said he was. A businessman from Austin. All evidence points to him being a low-level drug user. Likely owed the wrong people money."

Bodie frowned. "But how did Project Arma get him? John said he was handed over to them."

"Is Project Arma buying people now?" Mason growled.

"Wouldn't be surprised," Luca spat under his breath.

At this rate, not much would surprise any of them about the lengths those behind Arma would go to.

"So, nothing on John and nothing on what he was supposedly distracting us from?" Bodie asked, tone somewhat defeated.

The whole team felt it. Every time they found a lead, it led to a dead end.

Wyatt glanced around the table as he spoke. "We can't find anything unusual that happened on that day."

"Damn," Bodie muttered.

Asher's frustration built. "Is there a chance it's connected to Lexie? To the break-in?"

"I can't see how that's possible," Luca said, frowning. "The only reason I can think of why someone might want her is because she's pregnant with your baby. You didn't even know about it when you caught John."

Bodie tapped the table before speaking. "If the person who broke in knows she's pregnant, how did they find out?"

That was a damn good question. One that Asher had been asking himself for days.

Wyatt turned to Asher. "Is it possible someone heard at the fundraiser?"

Shaking his head, he already knew it wasn't. "I only just heard her, and I was right there next to her."

"Would it be possible"—Mason paused, seeming to consider his next words—"that Sage leaked information."

A moment of silence followed. The five men looked around at each other.

"If our own commander could be a part of such an evil project, I don't see why Sage couldn't," Asher eventually answered.

The thought of Sage passing on medical information about Lexie to the wrong people made Asher see red. She was Lexie's doctor and care provider. She was supposed to help her. Protect her. Not sell her to the highest bidder.

"We did a background check on her before she checked us out after Arma, didn't we?" Luca directed his question to Wyatt.

Asher knew they did. Once the project shut, trust was lost. They didn't let a person get close unless a thorough background check had been performed.

"She was clear," Wyatt confirmed. "Grew up in Florida. Two parents who are still alive and a twin brother who studied at MIT."

"Doesn't mean she couldn't have been bought after coming here," Bodie responded.

Unfortunately, Asher knew some people were more easily "persuaded" than others. He just hoped that Sage wasn't one of them.

~

"Crap."

Evie's curse drew Lexie's attention. Her friend was standing at the end of the counter, frowning at the screen as though everything was written in a foreign language. Whenever Lexie looked at the screen, it sure appeared that way.

"Everything okay over there, Brainiac?"

Evie huffed before she glanced up. "My professor thought I needed a challenge and has given me this ridiculous code to crack. It's killing me."

Popping her hip against the counter, Lexie raised a brow. "Want me to get Wyatt out here to give you a hand?" Holding back a laugh, she saw Evie's frown deepen. Lexie knew exactly how much that comment would aggravate her friend, which is precisely why she'd said it. Evie was too damn serious, especially when it came to anything related to computers.

"I don't need help," Evie grumbled. "I've got it." She leaned closer to the screen, so that she was only an inch away. If the woman got any closer, her face would be plastered to the thing.

At the sound of the company phone ringing, Lexie drew her eyes away and lifted it.

"Marble Protection, Lexie speaking."

"Lexie, it's Bill. I have the pizzas Mason ordered. I told him I could deliver them, but we just got a huge order and I'm pushed for time."

At the sound of the word *pizza*, Lexie's stomach grumbled. The carb cravings were still coming in hard and strong. "Not a problem, Bill. I'll pop over and grab them."

And maybe eat them, too.

Lexie wondered if Mason's superhearing included that of pizza being eaten.

"You're a lifesaver. I'll place them on the counter. Mason's already paid."

Even better. "Perfect, I'll leave now."

Hanging up, Lexie turned to Evie, who was still staring at the screen like it held the world's answers to everything.

"Hey, Einstein, I'm just going to head across the road and pick up pizza from Bill."

Finally, Evie gave Lexie her full attention. "Aren't you supposed to have one of the guys go with you?"

Turning her head to look at Oliver and Kye and noting that they were busy running a class, Lexie shot her gaze across the road. "Everyone's busy, and we can literally see Marino's Pizzeria from here. I'll be fine."

Lexie walked around the desk while Evie nibbled her lip.

"Maybe I'll go, Lex. I need to run out to my car and grab some folders, anyway."

"And take away time that you could be working your IT magic? No. I'll be back before you can blink."

Stepping outside, Lexie wrapped her arms tighter around her waist as she was hit by a sudden chill.

Jeepers, when did those gray clouds roll in?

Crossing the road, Lexie stepped into the pizzeria. Breathing in a whiff of melted cheese and pizza dough, Lexie considered not returning to work. Surely no one would notice if she spent her afternoon here, eating every pizza in sight. Even if they did notice, that was acceptable behavior for a pregnant lady, wasn't it?

Plonking a pile of pizzas on the counter in front of her, Bill put his hands on his hips.

"I should have told you to bring a friend. You gonna be okay with all of them, Lexie?"

Assessing the stack, Lexie nodded. "I should be fine. If not, I'll eat them on the way." She cracked a smile. It was wasted on Bill, though, because he'd already turned back to the wood oven.

"Thanks. Say hi to the guys for me," Bill called over his shoulder.

Wrapping her arms around the boxes, Lexie turned to go. They weren't as heavy as they looked, and the heat warmed her already chilly fingers.

Using her shoulder to push outside, Lexie stepped out onto the path. She had only taken a few steps when rough hands grabbed on to her arms from behind.

Dropping the boxes, Lexie let out a yelp as the punishing grip began to drag her toward the side alley.

It took Lexie's shocked brain a moment to process what was happening. Once she did, she began to kick out her legs, hoping to land hit anything that might cause the person pain.

When her foot landed a few times on the attacker's legs—and did nothing—panic began to rise in Lexie's chest.

Holy crap, she was being kidnapped right across the road from Marble Protection.

Just before they rounded the corner, Lexie caught sight of Evie's shocked face. The other woman stood by her car on the street. Then Lexie lost sight of her as she was dragged into the alley.

Struggling as much as she could, she began to flail, fingers stretching to grab on to anything within reach.

Too soon, she caught sight of a van—and her heart jumped into her throat.

Shit. Shit, shit, shit.

Lexie had seen crime shows. She knew that if they got her into a vehicle, her chance of survival dramatically decreased.

Thrashing harder, Lexie opened her mouth to scream. Before she could utter a sound, a hand came over her mouth. Then, her body was lifted and roughly thrown into the back of the van.

Her head hit the metal interior, pain exploding through her skull. In the next moment, she heard doors slamming and the engine roaring to life. Then the van began to move, forcing her to hold on.

Dizziness rocked her vision. As the van took a hard corner, Lexie rolled to the side and grabbed on to whatever she could.

Once her body was somewhat steady, she took a moment to gather herself. It was like one big fat nightmare. One minute she was walking down the street holding pizza, the next, she was in the back of a van protecting her bump from all the knocks.

Nausea began to roll through her; whether it was from hitting her head or being thrown from side to side in the back of a van, Lexie wasn't sure.

Eyes darting around, she searched for something, anything that might help her situation. There was nothing. No weapons and no windows.

Holding on to the side of the van, she slowly slid her body to the back door. She said a silent prayer before testing the handle, sure it would be locked.

To her surprise, the handle moved easily.

What sort of kidnapper leaves the door unlocked? It was as if they thought she wouldn't try to escape.

Opening it slightly, Lexie immediately noticed that the van moved at an alarming speed. Buildings and trees passed in a blur. Crap, there was no way she could jump out without injuring herself or her baby.

For a moment, Lexie wondered if it might be possible to sneak out when the van stopped. Surely it would need to at a red light or for a pedestrian?

That idea was quickly dashed when she acknowledged again how fast they were moving. If the assholes didn't drive within the speed limit, she doubted a red light would stop them.

Pushing herself into the corner of the van, Lexie placed her hand on her stomach.

"Don't worry, bubba. I'll get us out of this," she whispered while forcing her body to remain calm. Panicking wouldn't help her.

A few minutes passed before an idea hit. A stupid idea, but seeing as she was all out of good ones, Lexie had no choice but to go with it.

Grabbing the handle of the back door, Lexie opened it again, allowing it to swing wide. At the same time, she latched on to the side wall grab handles, grateful they were there. She held on as tightly as her fingers allowed.

She was betting on either someone coming up behind them who would see her, or the driver stopping when he noticed the door was open.

Looking out, Lexie swallowed her disappointment as she saw nothing but road. Not a soul in sight to help.

Before the disappointment consumed her, she felt the van begin to slow. Her gaze darted to the forest next to the road.

She had been hoping they were still in town. The forest wouldn't give her nearly enough protection, and she didn't need to know whether or not they had enhanced abilities to know they were likely faster than her regardless.

What choice did she have but to run, though?

Taking a calming breath, Lexie waited until the van was almost stopped before jumping out the back.

Knees caving, Lexie rolled across the ground, protecting her stomach as much as possible. Quickly pushing up, she began to sprint through the trees.

Lexie's heart beat through her chest. She wasn't moving nearly fast enough. In the next moment, rain began to fall, causing her feet to slide.

Shuffling sounds behind her made her breath catch. They were close. So damn close that there was no way she would make it much farther before they caught her.

Lexie had taken only a couple more steps when a hand grabbed a fistful of her hair. Crying out, she was flung backward. Her head hitting the dirt before the rest of her.

A large body loomed over her, head covered in a black hood.

"You got a fucking death wish, woman?" Lexie pushed her body back into the dirt, trying to put space between herself and the pair of dark eyes that stared down at her. "Because if you want me to kill you *and* the baby, I won't fucking hesitate."

At the mention of her baby, Lexie's body went still. Was he after her baby? Because of Asher and what he could do?

"Yeah, you get me now, don't you."

Before Lexie could blink, his fist flew hard and fast, punching her in the temple.

Lexie cried out as the pain spiked through her skull.

"That was for making me stop," the man sneered. "Don't cause me anymore fucking trouble."

His long, unrelenting fingers wrapped around Lexie's wrist before he began to drag her across the ground, back in the direction on the van.

Using her free hand, Lexie tried to pull herself up to protect her body from the unforgiving hardness of the rocks and tree. The farther he dragged her, though, the more futile her attempt. Giving up, Lexie closed her eyes as she felt pain ricochet through her body.

"Fuck, man, you can't carry the bitch? We weren't supposed to hurt her."

Eyes snapping open at the second voice, Lexie tried to turn her head, but the slight movement made a new round of pain hit her skull.

"Fuck them. We're the ones getting the job done," a third man's voice sounded.

Three. She had three kidnappers.

Exiting the trees moments later, the man dropped her next to the van.

"Who the fuck did this?"

Forcing her head up, Lexie caught sight of what they were looking at. All four tires were flat.

CHAPTER 15

*A*sher watched from across the room as Luca fished his ringing phone out of his pocket. The team was almost done with their meeting and Asher was ready to see his woman again.

The huge smile that stretched across Luca's face before answering gave away who it was immediately.

"Missing me already, darlin'?"

"Luca, someone took Lexie."

Asher's body stilled as he heard what Evie said through the phone line. Every man in the room stopped moving and listened.

Luca sat forward, no longer smiling. "Where are you, Evie?"

The sound of a car engine rumbled through the line. "I was by my car when they took her. Now I'm following the van they threw her in. It's going really fast, though. I'm struggling to keep up."

Asher pushed to his feet, unable to remain seated. He needed to go to her but he had to find out where she was first.

"I can't see them anymore. I'm on the highway, I just passed Walmart but I can't..."

A tense moment of silence across the line had Asher's skin turn to ice.

"What is it, Evie?" Luca stood as he spoke.

"I can see the van ahead. It's stopped." Evie's breathing was heavy through the line. "Three men in black hoods jumped out and they're running toward the forest. Oh God, the back of the van is open. She must have made a run for it."

Asher was already moving. He could hear the guys following closely behind. Luca was still on the line with Evie.

"Evie, keep driving," Luca ordered.

More silence followed before Evie eventually spoke. "I've got a knife. I'm going to pop their tires so when they come back, they can't take her anywhere."

Asher jumped into his Nissan, Luca taking the passenger side while Mason jumped in the back. Wyatt and Bodie took a second car.

"*No*, Evie. It's too dangerous." Fear laced his voice.

"I'm doing it, Luca."

The line went dead.

"Fuck!" Luca shouted as Asher pressed the accelerator to the floor.

Racing through town, Asher didn't pay attention to speed limits or red lights. He'd always thought his car was fast but, dammit, in this moment, it wasn't fast enough.

"When we get there, you guys hunt them and bring back Lexie. I'm going to find Evie," Luca said through gritted teeth.

Asher nodded but kept quiet, his mind focused on getting to his woman as quickly as possible. She'd better be unharmed. If not, someone was going to pay.

When Asher got her back—because he *would* get her back—she was going to be so heavily protected, Project Arma wouldn't be able to so much as catch a glimpse of her without also seeing Asher, let alone take her.

After what felt like far too long, he spotted a vehicle on the side of the road. Slowing down, he wasted no time jumping out of the car and running toward the van.

Empty. And not a soul in sight.

Mason hunched over a clear track. "They dragged her back up here."

Bodie walked over to another track. "They must have seen the flat tires then headed back into the woods."

Asher breathed through his rage, ready to tear people apart with his bare hands. Everyone who was part of this would pay with their lives.

"I'm going after her," he growled, already taking off at a run along the trail leading back into the woods.

Aware that Wyatt and Bodie were following, Asher kept his eyes ahead. The farther he went, the more his fury grew. The assholes had dragged her far into the woods. What kind of a man dragged a pregnant woman?

Asher already knew the answer to that. One with no moral compass. No morality.

When the trail suddenly changed, Asher bent down to study it. One of the sets of prints had become deeper, indicating the man was suddenly heavier. "This is where they stopped dragging her and began carrying her."

Wyatt stepped forward, touching the next imprint ahead. "It won't be as easy to follow them from here. They were smart. Mostly treading on tree roots. Avoiding most of the softer ground."

Rising to his feet, Asher looked forward. "We'll catch them. They won't be far."

And when he did catch them, he would make sure they regretted touching her.

~

LEXIE HURT ALL OVER.

The intensity of the pain to her head and back almost caused her to lose consciousness multiple times. But she held on, needing to protect her baby from any impact.

She had been able to convince the asshole to start carrying her, rather than continue dragging her. She knew it would be harder for anyone to follow their trail, but the pain of being pulled across the uneven ground had become unbearable.

Unfortunately, rather than any relief, Lexie experienced a new pain when she'd then been thrown over a hard shoulder. The jerks clearly had no intention of trying to keep her or her baby unharmed.

Lexie had been using all her strength to push herself up the entire walk. She needed to relieve as much pressure to her stomach as possible. Her arms now trembled from the strain. Every minute, it became harder.

She'd come to realize that the tall man with the black eyes was in charge. He had an air of authority about him, whereas the other two reminded Lexie of low-level criminals.

She'd also picked up that the man carrying her was called Packer, and the other man Thomas. The leader had yet to be named.

A ringing sounded from the pocket of the man with the black eyes. Stopping, he pulled out his phone. The call lasted less than thirty seconds and only involved a couple yeses before he hung up.

"They need me. I'm going to move ahead." His voice was flat.

The jerk carrying her groaned. "Fuck, I need a break."

Before Lexie could comprehend what was happening, she was unceremoniously dropped to the ground like a sack of potatoes.

Grunting in pain as her hip took the brunt of the impact, she remained still and took a few deep breaths. She was grateful she no longer had to leverage her body on his shoulder, but dammit, couldn't they make a tiny bit of effort to not injure her?

The black-eyed man was suddenly in Packer's face, grabbing

him by the throat. "You are under strict instructions not to harm the baby."

Packer coughed and choked as he spluttered out a response. "You already punched her."

His words seemed to anger the man further as his fingers visibly tightened. "Is her face connected to her stomach?"

Lexie watched wide-eyed as Packer was thrown against a tree so hard that the entire thing rocked.

She swallowed her fear and pushed her body backward. The big guy was scary *before* he was angry. Now he was absolutely terrifying.

"First you break into her apartment by busting the door handle. You fucking alerted those assholes to our presence," the man said quietly as he kneeled in front of Packer. "Then you leave the back fucking door of the van unlocked!"

The last words were yelled.

Packer's chest was rising and falling quickly, giving away his fear.

"You and Thomas are going to get her to base and the baby will remain unharmed. If you don't, I'm going to break every bone in your body, one by one."

Stark fear showed in Packer's eyes as he nodded.

The black-eyed man stood and left. And Lexie noticed one thing—he was fast. Unbelievably so. Possibly as fast as Luca.

Or maybe faster.

Silence descended over the three of them. When Lexie looked toward Packer, it was to see red-hot anger replace the fear in the man's eyes.

"I fucking hate that guy."

Thomas shrugged. "You should do what you're told."

Packer's eyes narrowed. "He's not the fucking boss of me. Fuck him."

Thomas turned to look at the path. "Whatever, let's go."

"I told you assholes I'm tired. I'm having a break."

Frustration came over Thomas's face. "We'll be late."

"Whatever. We'll blame it on *her*. I'm tired."

Thomas grunted. "Can't even carry the bitch? No wonder you're so desperate to get more of that ability-enhancing shit."

Christ, Lexie was getting sick of being called a bitch.

"You fucking carry her then."

"Here's an idea, how about no one carries me and I walk?" Lexie ground out the words, her voice raspy.

"Shut your face, bitch." Packer spat the words at her as he stood, then dropped onto a nearby log. "I'm taking a break."

Thomas didn't look happy. But he conceded. "Five minutes, Packer. Then we move again."

Packer pulled his mask off as Thomas shook his head.

So, the asshole was either confident that she wouldn't escape or just too lazy to care. Probably both.

Lexie took a moment to inspect Packer. He was tall, with light brown hair and eyes. There wasn't anything that stood out to her.

All she could tell about asshole number two, who was still wearing a mask, was that he had lighter eyes. Maybe hazel.

Lexie wrapped her sore arms around her legs. Her arms were shaking from earlier strain. Her body was exhausted.

Resting her head on her knees, she tried to push the pain she was feeling in every limb from her mind.

"She's pretty hot, you know. For a pregnant bitch."

Lexie's eyes shot up at Packer's words. "I'm right here, asshole."

Packer laughed at her retort before turning to his friend. "Yeah, she's fucking here, Thomas. Should we have some fun with her before we take her to the doc?"

Eyes widening, Lexie felt her skin crawl at the thought of the man putting his hands on her. Shrinking back, she could only pray that the other man, Thomas, didn't let it happen.

"Get yourself under control. Remember that comment about

every bone in your body being broken? He wasn't fucking joking. If we rape her, we're dead men walking."

Packer's slimy gaze slid back to Lexie, trailing down her body. "Don't see how they would find out."

Rolling his eyes, Thomas glanced back in the direction they'd come from. "I'm gonna go make sure we didn't leave tracks. The rain's starting to get heavier, which will help. You stay here—and if you touch her, I'll kill you myself."

Lexie watched Thomas go as she fought a rising panic.

He's just going to leave me here with the rapist?

When Lexie's gaze shot back to Packer, she noticed he was still watching her. Assessing.

Wrapping her arms tighter around her legs, Lexie narrowed her eyes. "He's gonna kill you, you know."

Scoffing, Packer didn't look the least bit concerned. "Thomas? Sorry to break it to you, but he ain't hurtin' no one but you."

Shaking her head, Lexie glared at the slimeball. "Not him, dumbass. Asher. The father of this baby. He's going to tear you limb from limb."

There was a brief moment of fear on Packer's face before it cleared, a scowl taking its place. "Tell me, doesn't he have to know where I am to be able to tear me limb from limb?"

Yes. But he would find them. Lexie had to believe that. Or else the desolation would destroy her.

"You like fucking superhumans?"

Lexie drew back at Packer's sneered words. She tried to appear surprised. Not wanting to give away that she knew about Asher's altered DNA.

"I don't know what you're talking about."

"Of course you do, you lying bitch." She could already smell the disgusting acid on his breath and there was over a foot separating them. "I've had some of that shit. I may not be as advanced as lover boy, but hell, I can hold my own."

Standing, Packer began to unbuckle his belt.

Lexie's breath caught and every muscle in her body tensed. "Thomas said you weren't allowed to touch me." Suddenly, the bravado was missing from her voice.

Packer took a step forward and crouched. Grabbing a handful of Lexie's hair, he yanked her head forward. "Thomas ain't here, is he?"

Whimpering at the agonizing pain from her skull, Lexie cried out louder as Packer shoved her to the ground.

"I've never done a pregnant bitch before."

Lexie's breaths shortened, coming out as short gasps. Packer climbed on top of her. She tried to shove the big man aside, only to have him pin her hands to the dirt with ease. His strength was overwhelming.

"Don't worry. This will be fun." Packer smiled, displaying his brown-stained teeth. "No, wait—I meant fun for *me*. You should worry."

Removing his hand from one of Lexie's wrists, Packer tore her shirt open in one swift jerk. Overexcited brown eyes darted to her red bra.

The rain started to fall hard, hitting Lexie's chilled skin.

At the feel of him hardening against her leg, a new wave of terror and revulsion entered Lexie. Packer's hand went to her breast, and he began to fondle it roughly. Bile rose in her throat.

Just as panic began to take over, Lexie saw a glimmer of metal from the back of Packer's pants.

Gun. It had to be a gun.

Lexie had shot a gun before. Granted, never at a person, but it sure beat being raped.

Body going limp, Lexie closed her eyes. If she fought him, he would restrain her again. She needed to catch him off guard.

"That's it. Just relax."

Packer hadn't grabbed her right wrist again, and the grip on her left loosened. It took everything in Lexie not to gag from pure revulsion to have him on top of her. Touching her.

As Packer reached down to start unbuckling Lexie's jeans, she took a quick breath before making her move.

Reaching up, Lexie made it appear as if she was about to touch him—only to yank the gun from his jeans.

Packer's eyes widened the moment he realized what was happening.

Before he could react, Lexie aimed the gun at his stomach and pulled the trigger.

Packer howled in pain, immediately falling to the ground. Half his body was still on Lexie, forcing her to use all her strength to push him to the side.

"You fucking bitch!" Packer growled as he writhed in the dirt, clutching his wound.

Scrambling to her feet, Lexie took a single step before a hand latched on to her ankle, yanking her back to the ground. Her body hit the dirt hard, the gun falling from her fingers.

Packer pulled her toward him until she lay under him again. Blood leaked from his bullet wound onto her bare skin.

"I'm gonna fucking kill you!"

Terror gripped Lexie when Packer drew back a fist.

Quickly realizing his intent was to punch her in the stomach, not giving her actions a second thought, she swiftly dug her fingers into the bullet wound.

A pain-laced cry escaped Packer's throat as he once again fell to the ground.

Rolling away, Lexie grabbed the gun before lurching to her feet. Then she took off into the woods.

Lexie didn't stop to think about the fact that she'd just shot a man. She didn't pause to look at the blood that coated her hand or the splatters across her torso. She focused on moving. As fast and far as her injured body would allow.

After only a few seconds, Lexie heard Packer's angry voice from behind.

"I'm gonna kill you, bitch!"

There was no time to run any farther. Packer was too close. He would hear her if she kept moving.

Stumbling on a branch, Lexie dove behind the closest tree root and huddled down. Holding the gun in front of her, fingers shaking. She prayed that Packer didn't have the same level of hearing as Asher did. She didn't know if she could shoot to kill.

In the next few minutes, Lexie heard the scuffling of feet, followed by a grunt. Then silence.

Before she could risk a peek to look for Packer, the gun dropped from Lexie's fingers as a sudden, sharp pain hit her in the stomach.

Dropping to her side, Lexie curled into a ball, arms wrapping around her waist.

As more pains hit, Lexie scrunched her eyes shut, curling her body tighter.

Suddenly warm hands touched Lexie's hip, causing her to cry out.

"Lexie, honey, it's me."

Squinting her eyes open, she saw Asher hovering above her, his eyes a mixture of anger and agony. "Where are you hurt, Lex?"

Opening her mouth to speak, another spike of pain hit her stomach, causing her eyes to scrunch shut. "My...my stomach. It hurts, Asher. The baby..." Reaching up, Lexie grabbed on to his hand. "Help me!"

CHAPTER 16

*P*ushing down the anger and fear that simultaneously threatened to suffocate him, Asher pulled his sweater over his head and lay it across Lexie's chilled upper body.

Bending down, he gently lifted her into his arms. Lexie's soft whimper made him want to go back and snap that asshole's neck a second time.

"Everything will be okay, Lex. I'm going to get you help." Asher spoke the words softly into her ear.

Walking through the woods back to his team, Asher wished he could move faster. Fear of jostling Lexie and increasing her pain kept him at a slow, steady pace.

Blood coated her bare skin. Asher wasn't sure what was hers and what wasn't. Black and blue bruising marred her face, making him clench his jaw harder.

Tuning in, he could hear her heartbeat—as well as the faint but fast pitter-patter of the baby's heart.

They were alive. Asher had to focus on that. Not the bruising on the battered woman who trembled in his arms. The beating hearts.

After what felt like too damn long, Asher reached the car.

Mason was waiting. Wyatt and Bodie were likely still in the woods, following the men who remained out there.

A groan of pain emanated from Lexie as she dug her head further into Asher's chest.

"We need to get her to Sage. Now," Asher commanded, already moving to the back seat.

Anger washed over Mason's face at the sight of Lexie. "Are you sure you trust her?"

"No. But we need her. Lexie and the baby need her."

Nodding, Mason climbed into the driver's seat. Wasting no time, he pressed his foot to the accelerator before hitting dial on the car's Bluetooth. Sage picked up on the second ring.

"Sage speaking."

"Sage, it's Mason." He spoke quickly as he turned off the highway. "I'm with Lexie and Asher, and Lexie's injured. She needs medical attention as soon as possible. We're heading to Asher's place."

Sage didn't hesitate. "I'm in town. Give me Asher's address and I'll be there as soon as possible. I have equipment in my car."

Mason rattled off Asher's address before ending the call.

Asher's eyes drew back down to Lexie's pale face. His heart clenched. God, he wished he could take away her pain. She should have been safe. He couldn't forgive himself for not watching closer.

Leaning down, he placed a light kiss on her temple, trying to avoid any bruising.

"Asher..." Lexie's voice was weak. Fragile. He'd never heard her like that before. Lexie was the strongest woman he knew, and she liked everyone to know it. "I'm worried about our baby. I'm hurting."

Lexie's hand held her stomach as though she was trying to protect the growing baby inside.

Asher placed his large hand over hers. He started a slow stroke with his thumb that overlapped onto her stomach. "I haven't told you this, but not long ago, I noticed a light thumping sound whenever you were around. It was too fast to be your heartbeat. I realized it was our baby's heart. And that's what I can hear now, Lex. Our baby's heart is beating."

Tears filled her eyes. She closed them and a tear slid down her cheek.

Catching it with a kiss, Asher didn't take his eyes off her for the remainder of the drive, praying to God that both the woman in his arms and their unborn child would be okay.

The moment the car stopped, Asher was out. Moving up the stairs to his home, he was relieved to see Sage already waiting by the door, a large medical bag in her arms.

Sage didn't bat an eye at the sight of Lexie, bruised and covered in blood. Mason pulled the door open and Asher went over to the couch. Laying Lexie down but remaining by her side.

Sage took a seat on the edge of the couch. "Lexie, it's Sage. Can you tell me what you're feeling?"

Brows crinkling, Lexie kept her eyes closed. "I can feel shooting pains in my stomach. They're lessening now but are still strong." Eyes opening, she looked up at Sage, worry clouding her vision. "That's bad, right?"

Pulling out what looked like gel, Sage lifted Asher's shirt from her stomach then lathered some on her skin. Placing a transducer on Lexie's stomach, Sage was quiet for a moment.

A second later, thumping filled the room, loud enough so that everyone could hear. "The heartbeat is a perfect speed," Sage said quietly. "Did you sustain any blows to your abdominal region?"

Asher tensed, waiting for Lexie to respond.

"No. He was going to punch me in the stomach but I got away."

Releasing a tense breath, Asher relaxed slightly, never more thankful for Lexie's strength.

Leaning over her, Sage touched Lexie's shoulder. "You did really well. You protected your baby and yourself."

After a few more tests, Sage put her equipment back in the bag.

"Lexie, your baby is healthy," she said, placing her hand on Lexie's leg. "You don't need to worry at the moment. It looks like you went through something quite traumatic today. Science still doesn't know the full effects of stress during pregnancy, but there are stress-related hormones that have the ability to cause complications."

"Complications?" Lexie gasped before Sage visibly firmed her grip on her leg.

"You're okay. But it's very important from this point on that you avoid any stress. *All* stress. I would recommend a week or two of bed rest, then low-stress activities. Walks, baths, and still plenty of rest."

Asher stroked Lexie's head before turning back to Sage. "We can do that."

Hell, Asher would lock Lexie in the bedroom if he had to.

Nodding, Sage stood. "Good. Now, in terms of other injuries, there's extensive bruising. Possibly a mild concussion. Asher, it would be good for you to help Lexie bathe, then get her something warm to eat before she rests. I'll leave some pain meds—"

"I'm not taking pain meds," Lexie interrupted.

Asher growled. "Lexie."

"This baby has been through a lot and I'm not taking pain meds."

Damn, even after such a traumatic ordeal, the woman was stubborn.

"I'll leave them here in case," Sage replied softly. "They're safe for the baby."

Bending down, Asher lifted Lexie from the couch. Giving Sage a nod of thanks, he then headed to the bedroom.

Moving into the adjoining bathroom, Asher immediately stopped at the gasp from Lexie's lips.

A moment from running Lexie back to Sage, Asher looked down to see Lexie inspecting her face in the mirror.

She looked like she'd been through hell, and now she was seeing it.

Fighting down the rage, Asher moved to the bath and set Lexie on the edge. "If I could murder that asshole a second time for hurting you, I would in a heartbeat."

Lexie's head shot up as he turned on the bath tap. "You killed him?"

"I did." Asher took a moment to inspect Lexie's face, not sure how she would react. The only emotion he could read was relief.

"What about the other guy? Thomas?"

Asher helped Lexie out of her clothes before lifting her into the tub. "Red went after one of the guys, while Jobs went after the other. Both will be questioned when found."

Moving some hair off her face, Asher inspected the damage. Her cheek had swelled and her pupils were wide, likely from shock. She was so damn strong. "Not now, but when you're ready, I would like you to take me through exactly what happened today."

Swallowing, Lexie nodded. Fear lingered in her eyes.

"I'm not letting you out of my sight again, Lex. Consider me your personal bodyguard slash shadow. You're safe."

Some of the fear eased from Lexie's expression.

Good. She understood.

"She didn't seem surprised when we called." Mason's voice sounded from the living room.

"She didn't blink an eye at the sight of Lexie covered in blood and bruises, either," Asher added.

Lexie had only been standing by the bedroom door for a moment. She got the gist of what Asher and Mason were saying, though. They thought Sage was the leak. That she was the reason Project Arma knew about the pregnancy.

"We know you're there, Lex. You can come in."

Dammit, she'd forgotten about Asher's superhearing. He'd probably heard the moment she'd stepped out of bed.

She tread carefully into the room, and Asher was by her side in a moment. Lifting her body, he sat on the couch with Lexie on his lap.

Ordinarily, Lexie would tell him that he didn't need to do that. She'd fight for her independence. But the feel of Asher's big, strong body surrounding her own took away just a small amount of the lingering fear.

"How long have I been asleep for?" Glancing out the window, she could see it was almost dark outside.

Mason stood with his arms crossed beside the couch. "About an hour."

That's why her body still felt exhausted. And she'd probably spent a large chunk of that time tossing and turning.

"How are you feeling?" Asher asked.

Sore. Scared. *Angry.*

Although the latter only came in spurts when she got small bouts of reprieve from the first two.

"I'm okay. I'll be better after some time passes." She hoped.

"We're here for anything you need," Asher said firmly.

Mason nodded. "All of us."

Lexie knew that and she was grateful. So grateful for all of them.

Resting her head on Asher's chest, she glanced over to Mason. "Sage isn't one of the bad guys."

Mason's expression didn't change. "I'd like to believe that. But it's a bit suspicious that as soon as she comes into town, bad things start happening. Your apartment gets broken into, then you're kidnapped."

Cringing, Lexie had to agree that the timing wasn't great, but she still didn't think Sage was the culprit of all this. "Call it women's intuition, whatever you want, but she's got a good heart. She wouldn't sell out a pregnant woman. I can tell by the way she cares for me as a patient. Speaks to me with respect. She's here to help, not hurt me."

The look on Mason's face told Lexie just how much he believed in her women's intuition—which was not at all.

"Do you feel up to telling us what happened?" Asher asked softly, his hand rubbing her back.

No. But she had a feeling the words would never come easily. So now was as good a time as any.

Mason took a step forward. "I can leave if you want."

Lexie shook her head. Mason would hear the story anyway. There wasn't much point in him leaving.

"It's okay." Taking a breath, Lexie drifted her gaze down to her hands, comforted by Asher's touch. "I was coming out of Marino's Pizzeria. A guy grabbed me and threw me in the van. I tested the back door, expecting it to be locked. It wasn't. I opened it and was able to escape when the van slowed."

Lexie's fingers began to explore Asher's hand. The distraction was soothing.

"I didn't get far. They found me, dragged me back to the van. When they saw the flat tires, we hiked through the woods. One of the men separated from us. He got a call and said they needed him back at base."

She felt Asher look up at Mason at her last words. No doubt they were silently communicating the need to search for this "base."

"Did they give any clues about where they were taking you?"

No. Darn it, she wished she could be more help. Shaking her head, she tried not to feel like a failure. "No. Nothing to help with where we were going. They did say that they'd had some kind of ability-enhancing drugs, but that was it. They were told not to hurt me."

Asher cursed. "Well the fuckers didn't do a good job of that."

They didn't do a good job of anything, Lexie thought to herself.

"They weren't nearly as enhanced as you guys. The guy carrying me got tired and needed a break."

"What happened next, Lex?" Asher asked, voice smooth and comforting.

Lexie had a feeling he knew exactly what had happened next. He'd seen her hiding half-naked. But she got it. He needed to be sure.

"Thomas went back to check that they didn't leave tracks. Packer attacked me. He wanted to rape me." Asher stiffened beneath her. She didn't dare raise her gaze. "While he was on top of me, I was able to grab his gun. I shot him. Then when he came after me again, I attacked the bullet wound."

A shiver coursed up her spine at the memory of what she'd done. She'd never injured another person like that in her life. Even thinking about it made her feel nauseous.

"You did what you had to do to protect yourself and our baby. A lot of people wouldn't have been able to."

This time Lexie did glance up to look at Asher. There was still overwhelming anger in his expression, but there was also something else. Admiration?

"I ran. Then you found me," Lexie quickly finished, wanting to stop reliving the ordeal.

"And I would find you again. In a heartbeat."

Lexie believed him. He was the strongest man she'd ever met. Both physically and mentally. She had no doubt that he would find her in a hurricane if he had to.

"I'm glad you had the strength to fight." Mason's voice drew Lexie's attention back to him. "I'm going to check in on Jobs and Red. I'll keep you updated."

"I want to be there," Asher added quickly. "To question the assholes."

Lexie swallowed. She could just imagine what the "questioning" would entail.

"We also need to finish our other discussion."

This time, Lexie shook her head. "You don't need to speak in code. I know you're talking about Sage. And like I said, it wasn't her."

Mason shrugged. "Then we won't find anything incriminating."

Find? What exactly were they planning to do? Before she could question him further, Mason turned and left.

CHAPTER 17

"Sure you want to do this?" Asher asked, climbing out of the car. The cool night air brushed his face as he quietly closed the door.

Mason stepped out the driver's side, while Bodie exited from the back.

"There's a leak," Mason said firmly. "And we need to find out where."

They'd parked a street away from the inn where Sage was staying. The intention was to climb in through the back window of her room, not drawing any attention to their visit.

At almost nine on a Wednesday night, they knew the likelihood of having onlookers was slim.

Even though Sage's stay in town was only temporary, she had begun seeing some local patients. Mondays and Fridays she worked at the hospital to see those patients.

Tonight, the men had received word that one of her patients was rushed to the ER. Shylah had told Eden, not realizing he and the team would take advantage of her absence to search her room under the cover of night.

"I can't believe we didn't catch either of those other assholes who kidnapped Lexie," Bodie growled.

Asher's body immediately stiffened at the mention of the men who got away. He didn't need reminding.

"They didn't leave so much as a trail," Bodie continued.

"They were good," Mason agreed. "It's damn annoying they got away but we'll get them."

Hell yes they would. If nothing else, they knew the assholes would be back.

Asher also knew that from this moment on, he couldn't lose focus for a moment around Lexie. They were no doubt watching. Waiting for him to screw up so they could take her.

Not gonna happen.

Bodie turned to Asher as they silently drew closer to Sage's room. "How did Lexie feel having a couple of babysitters?"

Asher grimaced at the memory of how he'd left her. "How do you think? I was about ready to go cuff the woman to the bed."

"I'm sure it wouldn't be the first time." Bodie laughed, dodging a hit from Asher.

"When Lex found out Shylah and Hunter were going to stay with her tonight, she suspected what I was doing. She'd make a fine detective." He looked over at Mason. "She's pretty adamant that Sage is innocent in all this."

Not slowing his pace, Mason kept his eyes straight ahead. "Then we won't find anything in her room."

Asher shook his head. Mason had been adamant for days that Sage was hiding something. He called it a hunch but the man was bordering on obsessive.

Nearing the exterior of room seven, Mason tested the window, letting out a curse as it slid open easily. "The woman doesn't lock her window."

Bodie raised his brows. "Seems like that's an indicator of innocence right there."

"Dangerous ignorance, more like it," Mason grunted as he lifted himself through the window.

Asher and Bodie followed closely, pulling the window shut behind them.

Splitting up, the three men each went to different sections of the room. Asher went straight to the bed, Bodie to the lounge area, Mason to the bathroom.

"How's Lexie doing with recovering from the kidnapping?" Bodie asked as they searched.

"She's so damn strong." And that was Asher downplaying it. She was a warrior. "She's been having a hard time dealing with what happened on a psychological level—vivid nightmares, trouble sleeping—but the woman would rather walk over hot coals than admit that to me."

"That's Lexie. Never one to show any weakness."

That *was* her weakness. Her one and only, as far as Asher saw it.

"All her most recent test results have been coming back healthy. Baby just keeps sucking up all of Lexie's nutrients at an alarming rate."

"Well, it is your kid," Bodie joked as he searched Sage's suitcase. "You always have been a greedy fucker. I mean, when we first opened Marble Protection, you didn't give any of us so much as a chance with Lexie."

Straightening, Asher narrowed his gaze. "That's still the case, asshole."

"Lexie was always Striker's," Mason said from where he stood searching the bathroom cabinet. "Never a doubt."

Damn straight she was.

Ten minutes of silence passed with all three men combing through the room. So far, Asher had found nothing. Nothing but normal everyday necessities.

It made Asher feel like an invasive prick for going through her things.

"Found something," Bodie called, causing both Asher and Mason to shift their focus to where Bodie stood beside the couch. Walking over, Asher saw he held a small black bag in one hand and an unzipped couch cushion in the other.

Mason visibly tensed beside Asher. "Open it."

Dropping the cushion, Bodie stuck his hand in the bag. The first item he pulled out was a wad of cash.

Asher cursed under his breath. That was a lot of money. Too much for any average person to need to have on hand in cash.

Bodie turned the wad of cash over in his hand, studying it. "This has got to be ten thousand at least."

Mason kept quiet, attention glued to the bag.

Dropping it to the couch, Bodie stuck his hand back in, this time pulling out a gun.

Mason reached over and took the weapon. Checking it out, he swore under his breath. "It's loaded, and the safety isn't on."

Did the lady have a death wish? No sane person left a fully loaded gun in a bag without the safety on.

"Maybe she has it for protection and doesn't even know how to use it," Bodie suggested.

All three men tensed at that idea. In the wrong hands, guns killed people. Only those trained in how to use the weapon should have one in their possession.

Next, Bodie pulled out what looked like a burner phone.

"Looks unused," Bodie remarked, chucking it down.

The last item was a picture. The three men leaned in to have a closer look at the image. It was of a young girl and boy, both of whom looked to be about ten, sitting on a step with their arms around each other.

Bodie frowned. "Do you think that's—"

"Sage," Mason finished.

Asher leaned a bit closer. "The boy?"

Bodie cocked his head to the side. "Friend? He looks too different to be a brother."

While Sage had fair skin, blue eyes, and light blond hair, the boy boasted more of an olive complexion, with brown eyes and hair.

Mason took the photo and studied it closer. "We've never actually seen a picture of her twin brother so it could be him. Twins don't always look similar."

"That would be easy for Jobs or Evie to look into."

Asher's gaze darted back and forth between the items they'd uncovered. "It's her go bag that she doesn't want anyone to find."

Bodie's brows furrowed. "Why not use the safe?"

"It would take too long to get to." Mason lifted his gaze to Bodie. "Didn't find anything in her suitcase?"

Shaking his head, Bodie began placing the items back in the bag. "Nothing to arouse suspicion."

"I still don't think it's her," Asher said quietly. "She has a secret, but I don't think it's that she's working with Project Arma."

"Agreed." Bodie nodded.

Mason was already walking back to the bathroom. "Let's put this place back together."

Asher noticed his body was tense. He also hadn't commented on his opinion of Sage's innocence.

Spending the next few minutes putting everything back the way it was, the men stilled as footsteps sounded from the other side of the closed door. Light footsteps.

A woman's footsteps.

All three men immediately moved to the back window. Bodie exited first, followed by Asher. Mason just managed to slip out before they heard the sound of the door opening.

With no time to close the window, the three men hurried behind a nearby car.

After a moment, Asher poked his head up to see Sage glancing through the window. There was no way she would be able to see

them, not through the darkness. But they could see everything…
right down to the worry in her eyes.

Guilt hit Asher hard. His gut told him this woman needed
help. If she had a hidden enemy, they had done nothing tonight
but increase her fear.

Sage shut her window, the lock sounding through the night.
Bodie and Asher started slinking away, only to realize Mason
wasn't following.

Asher turned his head to look at Mason. "Coming, Eagle?"

"I'm going to stay. Listen in until she falls asleep. Make sure
she's okay." Mason didn't take his eyes from the window as he
spoke.

Bodie placed a hand on his shoulder. "You sure?"

"Yes."

One unyielding word.

Asher and Bodie left Mason and headed back to the car,
knowing that once their friend had decided something, that was
it. There was no changing his mind.

"TELL me again what my baby daddy is up to tonight," Lexie said
to Eden as he helped Shylah put away the dishes.

Lexie sat at the kitchen island feeling like a fat blob. No one
would let her help.

She knew most people would love to be waited on hand and
foot, but not her. She had been spending all day, every day, sitting
since being kidnapped. Or lying. But always immobile.

There was pent-up energy inside her that she needed to use.

Eden shrugged. "Not sure."

The man clearly did not care in the least that his ambiguous
answers were driving Lexie mad.

Shylah swiped the big man with the pan she was drying. "We
know they're searching Sage's room at the inn."

At Eden's continued silence, Lexie rolled her eyes. "The poor woman is helping us, and you guys are invading her privacy."

This time, Eden stopped to look at Lexie. "Project Arma has proven that they're not an organization to mess with. Someone told them about your pregnancy. We do what we have to do to protect our own."

Their own. That felt nice. Like she was important. Special.

Then reality hit. He was probably referring to the genetically enhanced baby in her belly.

Lexie shook her head. "Project Arma could have already wired this place and Marble Protection. They could be listening right now." She ignored the uneasy knot of tension that the thought left in her stomach.

"We do weekly sweeps of our homes and Marble Protection, so it's not possible. Plus, we have a fantastic sense of smell and can usually tell if someone has been in our home."

Lexie pursed her lips. "You guys are just fantastic at everything, aren't you?"

"Pretty much," Eden responded with a hint of a smile.

Lexie huffed her annoyance. She appreciated that he was trying to protect her from any information that may stress her out, but could really do with the old Eden right about now. The one who didn't smile or joke and just said it how it was even if it upset people.

Pushing away from the kitchen island, Lexie headed to the couch. "I'm going to watch some TV."

And by "watch TV" she meant stare at the screen and aimlessly flip through channels.

Plonking down with the remote, she began pressing buttons all the while not really seeing what was on the screen. A moment later, Shylah came to sit beside her.

"Are you okay?"

No. She felt guilty. Guilty that Sage was suspect number one when she was trying to help her.

Taking a breath, Lexie turned her head to face her friend. "I don't think it was Sage who passed on the information. She's a good person. The first time I met her, she was protective of my rights and privacy. Would an undercover Project Arma operative really care about a pregnant woman like that?"

Shylah nodded. "I agree. I've run into her a couple of times at the hospital. She's lovely. Don't worry. The boys will figure it out in their own time."

"I hope so."

Shylah cocked her head to the side. "Is something else bothering you?"

Jeez, she was transparent.

Lexie pulled at a piece of thread that had escaped the cushion on her lap. "Eden said that none of the places are wired."

"That's true."

A moment of silence passed before Lexie looked up at her friend.

Concern entered Shylah's eyes. "What is it?"

"I have this sick feeling that it might have been my mother who told them."

Saying the words out loud made the sick feeling increase.

Lexie and her mother had never had a great relationship but if the wrong person asked Gwen for information, there wasn't much the woman wouldn't do to get her hands on money to feed her addiction.

Sympathy showed in Shylah's eyes. Lexie hadn't told her or Evie about her alcoholic mother or their dysfunctional relationship. Heck, Asher hadn't even known less than a month ago.

"Have you called her?" Shylah asked.

Lexie was grateful she didn't pry by asking why she suspected her own mother.

"I tried her number, but she didn't pick up."

By "tried her number," Lexie meant she had called about a dozen times. No one answered. Not a single call.

Shylah lifted Lexie's phone from the end table and handed it to her. "Want to try again?"

No. Yes. She had no idea whether she actually wanted to know. Or how she would react if her suspicions were confirmed.

Taking the phone from Shylah's fingers, Lexie quickly scrolled until she arrived at her mother's number and pressed call before she could talk her way out of it.

Popping the phone to her ear, she didn't need to wait long.

Turning to Shylah, she frowned. "The number's been disconnected."

Shylah's brows rose. "Is that normal?"

"She's had the same number her whole life." So no. Not normal in the slightest.

"Maybe Wyatt or Evie can look into it?" Shylah suggested.

"Hmm." Lexie nodded absently. "Maybe I'll give it a week and if I don't hear anything, I'll let them know."

Shylah bit her lip, clearly wanting to say something but hesitating.

"You think I should say something now?"

Shylah gave a small shrug. "You have this bad feeling, plus she didn't answer your call and now the line is disconnected. There's no harm in having one of our resident tech gurus have a quick search."

Dang it. Shylah was right. "I'll talk to Asher when he gets home."

"Good idea. And don't overthink it before then," Shylah pressed.

Yeah right, that was like asking a starving man not to eat a loaf of bread that was sitting right in front of him. Impossible.

"My mother and I don't have the best relationship," Lexie admitted.

That was the understatement of the century.

Shylah gave a small smile. "I know all about that. I try to talk to mine as little as possible. Heck, once a year often feels excessive."

Lexie turned to her friend in surprise. "No way? I pictured you growing up in a house with a white picket fence and perfect family. There was even a puppy in my made-up Kemp family."

Shylah snorted. "My family is far from perfect. Unless you think an overcritical, overbearing mother and an absentee father is perfect."

Lexie leaned back against the sofa, still facing her friend. "My mother's an alcoholic."

"Okay. You win."

Lexie couldn't stop the laugh. Her mother being an alcoholic was in no way funny. But sharing her far-from-perfect family history felt good.

CHAPTER 18

*R*eaching across the table, Asher swiped another piece of pizza.

The pizza was good. Really good. But what Asher enjoyed the most were the soft moans of pleasure coming from Lexie beside him every time she took a bite of her own slice.

Fuck. If they were at home, Asher would have already dragged the woman to the bedroom and made love to her until he heard that moan a hundred times over.

Looking around at his brothers, he knew that wasn't an option right now.

Unfortunately, the pizza would have to quench his hunger until after their family dinner. Shame it didn't dampen his arousal. Not even a bit.

"You guys are going to eat me out of house and home," Bill chuckled as he placed another two pizzas on the round table.

"Don't pretend you don't love it," Kye bellowed from across the table.

"Bill, not only are we funding your next holiday with all this pizza we're buying, but the ladies will be flocking in when they see us from the window," Bodie joked, earning laughs from around the table.

"In your dreams," Lexie said, shaking her head. Although Asher could see a hint of a smile on her face.

Leaning down, Asher touched his lips to her ear. "I know what's in my dreams," he whispered, enjoying the rosy pink that tinged her cheeks.

Swatting him away with her hand, Lexie gave Asher a full smile. Damn, but the woman was breathtaking.

"You keep your mind out of the gutter, Asher."

Kissing her cheek, Asher straightened before he did something he'd regret, like throw her over his shoulder and cart her off to the closest bed.

To be fair, he wouldn't regret it. But something told him Lexie wouldn't appreciate it.

"I'd like to know about those dreams," Bodie interrupted from beside Asher.

Shoving the asshole in the shoulder, Asher shook his head. "Not a chance." Sitting back, he looked around the table and took a moment to appreciate his friends.

Each man was built like a warrior and could fight like one, too. But what you couldn't see from the outside was that they were good men. Hell, they were the best men Asher had ever met.

They did the right thing not because they were told to, but because they had principles. Good values and ethics. It was the foundation of being SEAL, but Asher knew that not every SEAL lived that way.

The best thing about them though...they had each other's backs. More than once one of his brothers had saved his ass, just as he had saved theirs. They could count on each other. Through anything and everything.

Glancing beside him at Lexie's angelic face as she spoke to Evie, he experienced one of those moments where, just for a minute in time, everything felt perfect in his world.

Yes, danger loomed. Immoral people were after them, and they had to watch each other's backs.

But Asher had family. Men who would back him up and lay down their lives for him. And he had Lexie.

He took another bite of his pizza—only to jump at Lexie's sudden squeal. He dropped the slice back to his plate, head swiveling around, searching for the threat.

From his peripheral vision, he noticed all seven of his brothers doing the same.

When Asher saw nothing amiss, his attention drew to Lexie. Pure joy shone on her face. The woman was beaming. Without a word, she took Asher's hand and placed it on her stomach. That was when he felt it.

The softest movement. A light flick on his palm.

Asher's gaze shot back to Lexie's, and he saw her eyes glistening with tears. "Our baby just kicked."

Smiling, Asher nodded. "I felt it."

Some moments, it was surreal that he was going to be a father. A dream. Moments like this solidified the fact that Lexie was growing their baby. A real-life son or daughter.

But it was Lexie's smile that almost undid him. The woman looked beautiful at the best of times. But with a smile that size on her face, she looked fucking gorgeous.

Tilting her chin up, she placed a kiss on his lips before turning back to Evie.

Bodie clapped his hand on Asher's shoulder. "Congrats, man."

Not taking his eyes from Lexie, Asher nodded. "Thanks."

"Lucky son of a bitch."

Asher looked back at his friend. "You want a woman of your own?"

Bodie liked to be the comedian of the group. Laid-back. Easygoing. But right now, there was no humor in his expression.

"Do I want a woman to connect with? Someone who can't get

enough of me? Fuck yeah I do. The question is, how do you find that?"

Asher shrugged. "You don't. It finds you."

He sure hadn't gone looking for Lexie. The woman had just walked into his life. Shown up at Marble Protection, demanded they hire her, and captured Asher's attention.

"You're saying I have to wait for destiny to step in?" Bodie drawled. "I've got to wait and see what the big man has planned? Shit."

Laughing, Asher leaned back in his seat while throwing an arm around Lexie's shoulders. "I wouldn't go so far as to say it's fate or anything. More random good luck."

"Damn, I've got the worst luck." Bodie's gaze shot to the roof. "If anyone's listening, throw me a bone. Someone to grow old with would be nice. Someone to play cards with in the old folks' home. Someone to eat soup with when I have no teeth."

Shaking his head, Asher chuckled. "You're looking too far into the future, Red. Even if you did meet someone at this very moment, two people can't guarantee that they'll grow old together. That they'll change together at exactly the same pace. Love is fluid. It changes as quickly as we do."

Feeling eyes on him, Asher turned to see that Lexie was no longer speaking to Evie. Instead, her eyes were on him. Confusion swirling in their depths.

Before Asher could question it, her phone dinged, causing her to look away.

Was she upset at what he'd said? Asher bit back a curse. He didn't always say what he was supposed to. Christ, he never even knew what that was. Did any man know the right thing to say all the time?

Lexie's shoulders tensed beneath Asher's arm. Looking down, he leaned forward to read the text message, but she quickly locked the screen before he could.

Eyes going back to her face, he studied her for a moment.

Worry. She tried to hide it, but it was as visible on her face as a huge neon sign in a dark room.

"Who was that?" Asher kept his voice casual while stroking her shoulder with his thumb.

Lexie kept her eyes downcast as she pocketed her phone. "No one. Just one of those marketing messages."

Lexie took another bite of pizza. But the exhilarating high of a few minutes ago was gone. So were the delectable moans. Both replaced with something new. Something darker.

Something she wasn't telling him.

LOOKING ANYWHERE BUT AT ASHER, Lexie tried to focus on the joy of the first kick she'd felt moments ago. In reality, she was really trying to forget the two things that followed.

The first being Asher's comment.

Love is fluid. She wanted to ask him what he'd meant by that. The only reasonable meaning she could think of was that love changes. Was that what he meant? That he didn't think his love was forever?

Lexie snuck a glance at the man beside her. He was now laughing with the guys across the table. The conversation seemingly wiped from his memory.

Unfortunately, Lexie couldn't forget it so easily.

Nibbling on her lip, she tried to push the hurt to the back of her mind. But if she was honest with herself, even though she wanted answers, she wasn't sure she was brave enough to ask.

She was scared. Scared about what his answer might be. That he might have meant exactly what she thought he meant. That he didn't believe love was forever.

The heaviness of her phone in her pocket reminded Lexie of the second thing that had happened—a message had come through from her mother.

She had been thinking about Gwen since the kidnapping. Every time she'd attempted to call her mother, there was no answer. Then the line was disconnected. Now, the woman was contacting her from a new number?

Baby it's me. I've got a new number. I'll call soon.

That was the short message she'd just read.

Lexie had wanted to respond immediately. A million questions ran through her head.

But Asher had been hovering over her shoulder. And for some reason she didn't want him to see.

Even though he knew about Gwen's number disconnecting and had immediately organized Evie and Wyatt to search for her, she didn't want to tell him about the message. Because his comment had thrown her.

"Hey, it's Sage." Evie's voice distracted Lexie from her thoughts.

Her gaze shot to the door. Sure enough, Sage had stepped inside the pizzeria and was walking to the counter. The doctor's spine was a little straighter than usual, her steps slightly stilted.

Was it Lexie's imagination or did Sage have fear lurking in her eyes?

Pushing her chair back, Lexie stood. "I'm going to say hi."

Sage and Lexie had become somewhat friends since her weekly visits. The other woman was kind and friendly. She had a sincerity about her that Lexie was drawn to.

When she drew closer to the counter, she noticed the shadows under Sage's eyes.

Crap. Lexie would bet her last dollar the woman was scared for one reason—and that reason involved some former SEALs breaking into her place.

"Sage!"

Her head popped up at the sound of Lexie's voice.

"Lexie! Hi." Shock registered briefly on the other woman's face, but she quickly recovered. "Are you here with Asher?"

"I'm here with everyone from Marble Protection." Lexie indicated with her head toward the table.

Sage glanced over to the group before turning back to Lexie. "How lovely. Do you do this often?"

Shrugging, Lexie answered, "Once a month, maybe? We usually go to someone's home but everyone agreed that pizza with no cleanup was in the cards for tonight."

Just then Bill popped behind the counter. "Can I help you?"

"Yes." She nodded, stepping forward. "I have an order for Sage."

Bill turned to grab her pizza before Sage handed over the money.

"You're welcome to sit with us for a bit if you want," Lexie offered.

She hoped the other woman said yes. The primary reason she was in town was for Lexie. To look after Lexie and her baby's health. But she knew no one. No one but them. That had to be lonely.

Sage's gaze swung back to the table. A moment of longing washed over her face before she cleared it. "No, I shouldn't. I'm working tomorrow. Seeing some of my local patients. I should have an early night. Thank you for offering."

Lexie wanted to push. Try to persuade the other woman to change her mind. But her features were set.

Sage placed a hand on Lexie's arm. "Before I go, how are you feeling?"

She smiled as her hands went to her stomach. "I just felt the first kick."

Sage's lips spread into a wide, genuine smile.

Nope, there was no way this woman was the villain. She was too real. And too kind.

"I'm so happy for you. That must have been such a magical moment, Lexie. And while surrounded by all your friends, too.

How amazing. Get ready, because that's only the beginning." Sage squeezed her arm.

"I cannot wait. This baby can kick away."

Sage took a step toward the door. "Well, I should get going."

"Wait." Lexie quickly closed the space between them again. "I wanted to ask if *you* were okay? You looked a bit stressed when you walked in here."

Sage glanced around before nodding her head. "I'm okay."

Lexie didn't need Asher's lie detector abilities to see through that one. "You can talk to me if you need to, Sage. I know we haven't known each other that long, but with you staying in town for a while and probably not knowing many people, I'm happy to be an ear to listen. A friend."

Plus, she felt ginormous guilt that Sage had traveled to Marble Falls for her, and now the guys had searched her room in an attempt to protect Lexie.

Sage nibbled at her bottom lip for a moment. It was like she was trying to decide whether to share her concerns. "It's nothing. I mean, there was something small that happened the other week. I got back to my room at the inn and found my window open. Since then, I can't shake the feeling of being watched. I don't know. I'm probably being silly."

Lexie's heart went out for the other woman. There was real fear in her expression.

She also felt angry at the men. Angry that they had left the window open. Surely they were better than that?

"I wouldn't think too much on it. I'm sure it was nothing."

She wanted to reassure Sage. Lessen some of the anxiety on the other woman's features.

Shaking her head, she gave a tight smile. "Of course. I'm just overthinking things. I'll see you at our next appointment, Lexie."

Then she was gone. Leaving as quickly as she'd arrived.

Heading back to the table, Lexie glanced around at the men. Maybe she should speak to them? Ask them to tell Sage what they had done so that she knew she has nothing to worry about.

That's when she noticed Mason. His gaze tracked Sage through the window. Intensely.

He'd probably listened to every word they'd said.

Lexie's brows knitted together as she watched Mason watch Sage. It was almost as if he was interested in her.

Sage was pretty. Correction, she was stunning. And intelligent and kind. What normal, red-blooded man wouldn't be into her?

Maybe Mason would be the one to speak to her then. Let her know that she was safe.

Lexie was about to take a seat when she remembered the message that had come through from her mother. Pulling out her phone, she quickly sent off a reply.

Are you okay? I've been trying to call you.

The response from Gwen was instant.

Yes, I'm okay. I left Albert. I'll explain later. I got a new phone to cut off contact with him. Can't talk now. Will call soon.

Reading the message a couple of times, Lexie didn't know how to feel about that information. On one hand, Albert was an asshole. Lexie didn't need to meet him more than once to know that. So the fact that Gwen was no longer with him was a positive.

But Lexie didn't understand why her mother needed a new phone. Surely she could've just blocked his number.

Asher threw his arm around her shoulders again when she took her seat.

While his touch usually made her feel secure and cared for, this time she just felt uncertain. Almost to the point where she wanted to pull out from under him.

Asher turned to study Lexie's face. "All okay?"

No. No on so many levels. The threats from Project Arma weren't okay, her mother's actions were worrying, and Asher's words were confusing.

And mixed together they created a pool of anxiety in her stomach.

But she didn't say that. Instead, turning her head, she smiled at the man she loved and lied through her teeth. "Everything's okay."

CHAPTER 19

"She was quiet the entire drive home?"

"Quiet as a mouse," Asher responded as he climbed into the driver's seat, Luca getting in on the other side. "Quiet in the car, from the car to the house, even when we got into bed. And every time I asked what was wrong, I got the same 'nothing.'"

Which was a flat-out lie. It had to have been the longest Lexie had ever kept quiet in her life. Because he'd said one thing. Damn, he was an idiot.

Once behind the wheel, Asher pulled out of the police station parking lot. He and Luca had run a refresher session on acquiring and detaining people for the city police force.

The job was an easy one, and it allowed the guys to maintain a good relationship with the boys in blue.

"Sounds like you upset her, my friend," Luca laughed.

Asher had come to realize that. He just didn't know how to fix it. "How do I make it better?"

Because so far nothing had worked. Even in bed when he'd put an arm around her, she'd been stiff as a board.

Lexie was the most strong-willed person he'd ever known. It

was a large part of the reason he'd been so drawn to her. That's why the knowledge that he'd hurt her pulled at his chest so damn hard.

Luca shrugged. "She obviously misinterpreted what you meant. Women read too much into things sometimes. Just talk to her. Clarify what you said to Red."

The trouble was, Asher wasn't entirely sure *what* he'd meant. He cared about Lexie. More than cared; he loved the woman. That was why he was struggling to make a lifelong commitment to her.

He just couldn't drop the notion that she deserved better.

When Asher was quiet for a moment too long, Luca turned toward him, cocking his head with a look.

"Don't be a damn fool, Striker. Lexie is perfect for your dumb ass."

"Exactly," he replied. "She's too perfect. What we feel for each other is too perfect. How can something so perfect last until the day we die?"

The concept seemed impossible to Asher.

"Ahh," Luca chimed in, like he'd had an epiphany.

"What?"

Nodding, he clapped his hand on Asher's shoulder. "You're scared to lose her. That's why you haven't told her you love her."

Swallowing, Asher tightened his hands around the wheel. "Of course I'm fucking scared to lose her. If I convince myself I can have her forever, something will go wrong. She'll get sick of me or Project Arma will swoop in and screw everything up. She'll realize she's better off without me at some point."

Lexie deserved easy. A husband who worked a nine-to-five job, a puppy in the backyard, and no danger lurking around every corner.

"Or," Luca rebutted, "you'll be happy."

That seemed like a pipe dream.

"You're not scared to lose Evie?" Asher couldn't help but be skeptical of the idea.

"Every damn day. But if I push her away, then I've already lost her. And I'd have no one to blame but myself."

Taking a breath, Asher shook his head. "Look at the danger I've already put Lexie in. She can't even have a normal pregnancy because of our history."

"Ever thought maybe she doesn't want normal? She just wants you?"

Asher took his eyes off the road for a moment to raise a brow at his friend. "Since when did you become a fucking therapist?"

"Since you started needing one."

Asher chuckled.

At that moment, his phone rang. Noticing it was Evie, Asher pressed answer on the car's Bluetooth.

"Ace. What's up?" Asher called, using the nickname the team gave her.

"Hey, sweetheart," Luca said.

"Luca?" Evie sounded confused for a moment.

"We just finished the police refresher session. We're driving back to Marble Protection now." Luca responded.

"Good. I mean, what I have to tell you isn't so good. Or maybe it is, I'm not sure."

Asher tensed. Evie sounded frazzled, which meant she had information.

"What is it, Ace?" Asher kept his tone even, when internally he was trying to hold himself together.

"Remember how you asked me to search for Lexie's mother and her boyfriend, Albert Boyd?"

Yes, Asher remembered. How could he forget? "Because they left the house they were living in and disappeared into thin air. Not to mention her disconnected phone line. I remember."

"Well, I found Albert," Evie began, then stopped. When she didn't immediately continue, Asher almost lost his composure.

"What did you find, Evie?" Luca asked calmly.

Another moment of silence passed before Evie spoke. "He's here. In Marble Falls. I don't know where, exactly, but I found him through facial recognition at the bus stop and then the supermarket."

Asher's breath caught for a moment before he pressed his foot harder on the accelerator.

"Thanks, sweetheart. We're heading to Marble now." Hanging up, Luca called Bodie. When the phone continued to ring, he then tried Wyatt, but again no answer. Both men were at Marble Protection and both should have answered.

Asher tried not to panic. There were a number of reasons the guys might not be answering their phones.

But he had a bad feeling in his gut.

After Lexie had mentioned that her mother's number was disconnected, Oliver and Kye had paid a visit to her house. But the house had been empty. Empty and trashed.

Asher hadn't told Lexie the last part. It would do nothing but cause her stress. Stress that she didn't need.

Evie had been searching for Albert and Gwen ever since. Asher's instincts told him their absence had something to do with Lexie. He just didn't know what.

Albert may not have the abilities or athleticism that Asher and his team had, but he could still be a threat.

There was only one reason he could think of why Albert would be in Marble Falls.

"Lexie is at Marble with Red and Jobs, Striker. She's protected."

Unfortunately, Asher knew that nothing was ever certain.

Luca clamped his hand on Asher's shoulder again. "Our brothers will protect her with their lives."

~

Lexie was tired. Tired and unsure and hurt. And her tea just wasn't cutting it.

What she really needed was a steaming mug of coffee. An extra-large mug with ten sugars.

Unfortunately, she'd already had the one daily coffee she was allowing herself as soon as she'd woken. Why? Because she had naively assumed it would carry her through the day.

Which was an incorrect assumption.

If there was one thing Lexie didn't understand about pregnancy, it was why women needed to limit their caffeine consumption. What a load of baloney. If there was ever a day Lexie needed coffee in an IV drip, it was today.

She couldn't wipe Asher's words from her mind.

She'd thought they'd been making progress in their relationship. Moving forward. Lexie had *felt* the relationship shift.

But maybe she hadn't. Maybe she'd only seen and felt what she'd wanted to.

That one sentence had made her feel like maybe they were right back where they began.

And that was a terrifying thought.

Because not only did her baby need a father who was committed and stable and present. She needed a partner who was all those things, too.

It just brought back all the memories of their relationship before she'd become pregnant. The lack of commitment. Feeling unwanted. Used.

Lexie thought they were past all that. But now that she'd had time to think about it, she was reminded of the fact that something was still missing. Something huge.

Neither of them had shared that four-letter word with each other. *Love.*

Lexie lifted a pile of papers and stapled them. When she went to place the items down, she noticed there was no staple in the top corner.

Trying again, the same thing happened. Lexie attempted to staple the pages another three times, progressively getting more agitated. In the next moment the stapler was quickly taken from her fingers.

Lifting her head, she noticed Wyatt standing in front of the desk, but no stapler in sight.

"All okay over here, Lex?"

"Everything's fine." At least everything would be fine when the stapler decided to do what it was supposed to. When she saw the look of disbelief on Wyatt's face, she continued, "The stapler isn't working."

"This stapler?" He lifted the piece of stationery before moving behind the desk. Opening a drawer, he began to load it with staples.

Lexie scrubbed a hand over her face, wishing for the coffee again.

"Want to tell me what's wrong?"

Picking up her mug, Lexie grimaced as the warm liquid slid down her throat. "I'm a pregnant lady. I have many problems."

If she got into all of them, she'd probably be there all day. And bawling her eyes out.

Wyatt leaned against the counter. "I'm guessing the main problem has something to do with a tall, brown-eyed man who likes to think he's God's gift to women?"

Lexie chuckled. Yep. He hit the nail on the head with that one.

"You always were the smart one, Wyatt."

Shrugging, he didn't argue the point. "As the smart one, let me give you my two cents. Some guys take more time than others. Rocket, for example, is a dive-in-headfirst, think-of-the-conse-quences-later kind of guy. And that's how he approached his relationship with Evie. Striker, on the other hand, likes to come across as easygoing, when in reality, he'll overthink every minute detail."

Lexie shook her head. "I'm at a point where I need the guy to figure it out. I don't have time for an overthinker."

"He'll get there."

Would he? And even if he did, how long would it take? Lexie had waited. She was done waiting.

Unfortunately, just like Lexie, Wyatt didn't have a magic eight ball with all the answers.

"Thanks, Wyatt."

"Don't give up on him too soon." Wyatt handed her back the stapler before heading down the hall.

Shaking her head, Lexie went back to stapling the papers.

Asher didn't just take his time, he moved at a snail's pace. Every time Lexie thought they were getting somewhere, making progress, he would turn around and take ten steps back.

The sound of the front door opening drew Lexie's gaze up. At the sight of a middle-aged man entering Marble Protection, her eyes widened.

The man was in bad shape. Really bad.

Black and blue bruises covered his face. One eye was so swollen it barely opened. Not only that, the man was limping, heavily favoring one leg over the other.

He looked like he'd been beaten to within an inch of his life.

Finally, when his eyes lifted to meet Lexie's, her breath caught. She took a step back as recognition slammed into her.

Albert. Her mother's partner.

Correction, ex-partner.

Lexie was so surprised at the sight of the man, that she just stood there. Silent. Confused by the fact that he looked like he was barely holding himself up.

Albert didn't say anything. Nor did he stop at the desk. Limping forward, he neared the end of the counter, advancing toward her.

Lexie glanced behind her but the other side of the counter

was connected to the wall. Albert was effectively boxing her in. Trapping her.

Words. She needed to say words so that Wyatt would come back.

"What are you doing here?"

What she really wanted to do was scream for help. But that might cause Albert to lash out. She couldn't afford to risk being injured.

"They're trying to kill me—and it's your fucking fault."

Calm. She needed to stay calm. "Who's trying to kill you?"

Oh lord, she hoped Wyatt hadn't gone out the back.

"I don't fucking know, do I?" Albert shouted, so close that spit hit Lexie in the face. "They followed you and your boyfriend that night. Came back the next day to ask what you wanted. They offered me money. I wasn't about to say no to that."

So it wasn't her mother who had given them information. It was Albert.

"Thought that would be the end of it," he continued. The closer he got, the stronger the smell of alcohol became. "When your mother found out I outed you, she up and left me. Apparently, they'd offered *her* money that day, too, but she refused. Bitch should have taken the money."

Albert limped forward another step. Too close for Lexie's comfort.

She eyed the small gap next to him. Maybe she could squeeze through and outrun him.

Yeah right, her pregnant belly, although not huge, still wouldn't likely fit.

"Then this soldier boy came. Looked awfully like your lover boy. Beat me to within an inch of my life before I pulled a gun on him and shot until he was still on the floor."

Anger flashed in Albert's eyes.

"It's your fucking fault!" he shouted.

Reaching behind him, Albert pulled something out. Lexie's breath hitched at the sight of a gun.

Before he could aim it at her, he was yanked backward.

Wyatt shoved Albert against the wall, dwarfing the man. The gun slipped from his fingers onto the ground.

"Stay the fuck away from her," Wyatt growled.

Bodie slipped behind Wyatt, reaching for Lexie. Placing his hands on her arms, he lowered his head so that they were eye level. "You okay?"

His touch felt warm against her chilled skin. "He didn't touch me," Lexie confirmed.

Relief flashed across Bodie's face. "Good."

"The pregnant bitch has put my life in danger!" Albert yelled. He fought Wyatt's hold but made no ground.

"You better check how you talk about her," Wyatt snarled.

Then the front door opened, and Asher ran in with Luca closely behind. "What the fuck are you doing here?"

Luca took ahold of Asher's arm before he could reach Albert.

He drew his gaze to Lexie and did a once-over of her body. When he saw she was unharmed, he turned back to Albert.

"He asked you a question," Wyatt said, pulling Albert forward and slamming him back against the wall.

"The fucker tried to kill me!"

"Who?"

"How the fuck do I know? Someone who was probably sent by the people in white suits." Albert looked brave for a man facing men who could squash him in a second flat.

"How about I make you a deal." Wyatt's voice was now eerily calm, still holding Albert against the wall in a punishing grip. "You come with me, see if you can identify these people who paid you a visit, and we won't hand you over to the police. Or worse, end you right now."

Would they really kill him? Lexie doubted it. But at the same time, she didn't entirely recognize this deadly side of Wyatt.

Albert sneered. "You wouldn't kill me."

"Let's find out, shall we?"

Wyatt kept ahold of Albert's arm and pulled him into the office. Luca and Bodie following closely behind.

Asher turned to Lexie, concern on his face. "Are you okay?"

She felt far from okay. Her bubble of safety had yet again been disrupted.

"I'm fine."

CHAPTER 20

*L*exie was not fine. Her eyes were too wide and her body too tense.

Taking a step closer, Asher touched her shoulder. "You're safe, Lex. None of us would let anyone hurt you."

Silent for another moment, she finally raised her eyes to his. "Does that include you?"

Asher's brows pulled together in confusion. He wasn't entirely sure what she was getting at. "If you're asking whether I would hurt you, the answer is no, Lex. You know I would never hurt you. And I would never let anyone else hurt you, either. Especially an asshole like Albert."

Something in her eyes changed at Asher's words. "I trust you to keep me safe physically. I had faith that Wyatt and Bodie would come out before Albert actually hurt me. Was I scared? Yes. But I know how protected I am at Marble Protection. What I care about is us. You and me."

Asher still didn't quite understand where she was going with this. "You and me are good."

"Good? Really? Compared to what?"

Asher scrubbed a hand over his face. "Is this about last night?"

He was struggling to catch up with the events. One minute, he was racing to protect Lexie from Albert, the next, he was arguing with her about their relationship.

"Tell me the truth, Asher. Would I be living with you and going out to dinners with you if I wasn't pregnant? Would you have told me the truth about your background and what you can do?"

Ah, hell. Suddenly, Asher wanted to be anywhere but where he was.

It would be easy for him to lie. To tell Lexie what he knew she wanted to hear and save her from what would likely hurt her.

But that wasn't how Asher operated. If it wasn't true, he wouldn't say it.

"No."

As soon as the word left his lips, he regretted it.

He wished he was a different person. The kind who was able to lie to make life easier. If he was, Lexie wouldn't be standing in front of him, looking all kinds of hurt.

She shook her head, a mixture of emotions passing over her face. First there was hurt. Then anger. Then something that almost resembled hopelessness.

Were those tears shining in her eyes? Lexie never cried. A car once ran over her foot right outside of Marble Protection and she hadn't so much as shed a tear.

"I don't know why I'm upset about that. You've always been honest and upfront with me. I shouldn't have expected anything different. It must be in my genetics."

Asher didn't really know what she meant by that, but he didn't have a good feeling about where she was going. "What do you mean?"

"Just look at my mother. She loved my father so much and just assumed that one day, he would love her back. But he never did. He left. And here I am, making the exact same mistake, pregnant and all."

"I'm not going to leave you."

"Really?" Lexie cocked her head to the side. "Weren't you just giving Bodie your worldly advice last night, saying how *love is fluid*? Come on, Asher, can you really stand there and tell me that you see yourself with me forever?"

Running his hands through his hair, he took a step back. "Lexie, can we not do this now?"

Her bottom lip trembled at his avoidance of the question, but in the next moment, she tensed her jaw and crossed her arms over her chest.

"I've got to go help the guys," Asher said quietly, feeling all kinds of pathetic for not being the man she needed.

Still, Lexie said nothing. A voice in his head told him not to leave. Yelled it. But even if he did stay, he didn't know what to say, dammit. His honesty would just hurt her more. Because the truth was, he didn't know what the future held. No one did.

Leaning down, Asher placed a kiss on her head. Then turning, he headed to the office, every step heavier than the last.

LEXIE WATCHED as Asher walked to the office.

And a small part of her broke. He'd left because forcing answers from a violent drunk was easier than being honest with her.

It was quite possible, the man was never going to be what she needed. What her baby needed. The sooner she accepted that, the easier it would be for everyone.

Blinking back tears, Lexie refused to give in to them.

She wasn't upset about Albert. Albert was an old man who drank too much and had a loose tongue. What upset her was the six-foot-four tower of muscle who time and again let her down on an emotional level.

Deciding it was close enough to closing time for her to leave,

Lexie drew out her phone and sent a quick text to Evie. Trying not to overthink it, she typed exactly what she needed from her friend.

Not ten minutes later, Evie entered Marble Protection. Walking straight to Lexie, she wrapped her arms around her. "Are you okay?"

Nodding against Evie's shoulder, Lexie remained in the embrace for at least a minute longer than was acceptable before reluctantly pulling away.

"My mom's ex came in, but the guys stopped him before he could do anything. Turns out he's the one who shared the information about me being pregnant to the people behind Project Arma. But that's not why I need to leave."

"Asher?" Evie knew. Of course she did.

"Can we go out to the car in case he's listening?"

Evie quickly pulled her phone out and typed something before shoving it back into her pocket. Then, taking Lexie's hand, she led them both outside. Once they arrived at the car, Evie got into the back with Lexie.

"I just messaged Luca to meet us here. Now tell me."

Spreading her fingers across her stomach, Lexie rubbed her belly while she spoke. "It's been building up, this argument with Asher. We've never been completely secure. The pregnancy brought us closer together, and I've probably been in a bit of a bubble since then. Anyway, last night, Asher made a comment to Bodie, saying that two people can't guarantee they'll change at the same rate. He said that love is fluid. At first I didn't know what to think. Then it reminded me that he hasn't actually made any promises to me about forever. He hasn't even said he loves me."

Saying that out loud hurt more than Lexie had thought it would.

Concern flickered across Evie's features. "Not once?"

"Not a single time." Cherishing her bump, Lexie wished bubs

would kick. She felt like she needed a bit of sunshine. "To be fair I haven't said it to him, either. But I'm scared."

God, that was hard to admit, but it was true.

She paused for a moment before she continued, "I'm scared about Asher leaving. About not being enough for my baby."

Not being *good* enough.

"Lexie, look at me." She pulled her gaze up to Evie's. "I'm going to remind you of something that you seem to have forgotten, just like you reminded me when I needed it. You are amazing. This kid growing inside your stomach is the luckiest baby on the planet to have you as its mother, and it doesn't even know it yet. You are fierce and loyal and strong. Don't you dare forget that. You can't control Asher or what he does. You can only control your own actions and how *you're* going to parent. Asher or no Asher, you are going to kill it, Lexie. No question about it."

Without hesitation, Lexie leaned over and pulled Evie in for a hug. A huge, body-against-body, never-want-to-let-go hug.

Boy had she needed to hear those words. Out loud, from someone else, made it real.

She held Evie tight, just as Evie held her. It wasn't until the driver's door opened that both women eventually separated.

Luca paused as he got behind the wheel. "Evie?" He looked at both women through the rearview mirror.

"Lexie's staying with us for a few nights," Evie said, her voice firm.

Luca frowned. "I don't know—"

"Luca, Lexie needs a place to stay. She also needs someone around who can protect her. I'm her best friend, we have a spare room, and you can protect her. So, she stays with us." Luca opened his mouth but stopped when Evie added, "Also, we need you to keep Asher out of the house until Lexie is ready to speak to him."

Lexie hid her smile. That was the most assertive she had ever seen her friend. The woman hadn't so much as taken a breath. And she'd done it to protect Lexie.

Reaching out, she laced her fingers through Evie's.

Luca sat there for another moment before grabbing his phone and shooting off a quick message. Then he started driving.

Lexie was pretty certain she knew exactly who he'd just messaged.

So was Evie. "What did you just text to Asher?" Evie asked, tone light and innocent.

Raising a brow, Luca glanced at the women through the mirror before his eyes shot back to the road. "I told him he fucked up. That Lexie is staying with us for a bit and to stay away for a while. Give her some space."

Lexie released a long breath. She was touched that Luca would come to her aid so quickly. He might think she was just being a hormonal pregnant lady, but even if that was the case, he still didn't hesitate to have her back.

Evie smiled as she leaned back against the seat, clearly pleased by Luca's quick acceptance of the situation.

For the remainder of the drive, Lexie tried to keep a calm mind. Clearing out all thoughts of Asher.

But no matter how hard she tried, her mind kept drifting back to him. To his lopsided grin that made her heart gallop. His hazel eyes that crinkled in the corners whenever he smiled. He was gorgeous, funny, empathetic. The moment Lexie had laid eyes on him, she had felt like they were meant to be together.

But that didn't seem to be the case.

The idea of living a life without Asher made her heart hurt.

Just when she began feeling sorry for herself, though, a kick fluttered within Lexie. Placing her free hand on her stomach, Lexie closed her eyes.

You won't be unloved, bubs. I'm going to love you so much that it won't matter if he stays or goes.

CHAPTER 21

"*J* swear, Rocket, if you don't get out of my way right the hell now, you won't like what happens next."

Asher was trying to keep as calm as possible, but he was close to hitting his friend square in the face. Either that or bowling the guy over.

Crossing his arms over his chest, Luca continued to block the entrance of his home. "I told you this would happen if you didn't smarten up."

The last thing Asher needed was an "I told you so." He knew how much of an idiot he was.

Gritting his teeth, he stared down Luca. "This is none of your business. Let me see my woman."

Asher hadn't noticed the text from Luca until after he was done questioning Albert. By then, Lexie was already in Luca's home. Phone off, unreachable. He had sped over here, only to be greeted by a barricade in the form of Luca.

Luca's gaze remained steely. "It's evening, she doesn't want to see you right now. Give her tonight, Striker, and see if she feels differently tomorrow."

"You know I can't do that."

Asher had fucked up big-time, and he needed to make it right. He wasn't leaving without at least *attempting* to see her.

At the sound of a car engine behind him, Asher turned his head to see Eden pulling up with Shylah.

Facing Luca again, Asher raised a brow. "You called for backup?"

Shrugging his big shoulders, Luca didn't appear remorseful in the least. "I knew you'd come and not take no for an answer. It's what I would do for Evie."

Eden came to stand beside Asher, with Shylah trailing closely behind. "All okay here?"

Asher rolled his eyes. "We're fine, go home."

Shylah pushed her way in front of Eden and looked around hesitantly. "Um, I'm going to go see the girls."

When Luca stepped aside to allow Shylah into the house Asher had a strong urge to use the moment to barrel his way in.

"Don't even think about it," Eden said.

"You wouldn't make it," Luca added.

Clearly, Asher had made that thought too obvious.

Swallowing a curse, Asher knew he was a good fighter, but Luca and Eden were equally good. One on one would be an even fight physically, although Asher would probably have the upper hand from sheer will. Two on one, Asher didn't stand a chance.

"I don't want to leave here without seeing her."

Luca cocked his head to the side. "Why?"

"Because it tears my fucking chest apart that she's upset because of me. That I can't comfort my woman."

"Because you love her," Eden added.

Of course he damn well loved her. He loved her so much that every fiber of his being told him not to tie her to him for all of eternity.

"Let me ask you something, Striker." Luca leaned his shoulder against the door frame. "Is there someone else you can picture her with? Someone else you want her to run to in hard times? Celebrate with in good times?"

"No." She was his. End of story.

"Then grow some damn balls and tell the woman that you're hers. Forever." Luca barked the last word.

Eden clapped his hand on Asher's back. "Rocket may not be right a lot of the time, but right now he's spot on."

Asher blew out a long breath. "You're right. Both you assholes are right."

"Finally, he says something true," Luca shouted, throwing his arms in the air.

Eden chuckled while Asher racked his brain to work out how to fix this. He needed to fix it and quickly. He didn't want Lexie upset for a minute longer than necessary.

A faint cry echoed through the house, causing all three men to still.

Lexie.

Shoving Luca aside, Asher sprinted through the house. He knew Luca's home like the back of his hand. The cry had come from the upstairs guest bathroom.

Not stopping once he reached the bathroom, Asher turned the knob, breaking the lock easily.

As soon as he stepped inside, Asher's body went cold.

Lexie lay on the cold tiles, on her side, struggling to push herself up.

Scanning the small room, he noticed nothing amiss. No threat in sight.

Dropping by her side, Asher helped ease her onto her back. "Easy."

Lexie's eyes flew up to his face at the sound of his voice. "Asher?"

Her attention immediately shifted to the door, giving a hurt look to, Asher assumed, Luca.

"It's not his fault. I forced my way in."

Taking a moment, Asher listened to both her and the baby's heartbeats. Both were normal. Next, he studied her face, unable to ignore the stress lines around her eyes.

Lifting his hand, he stroked the side of her face.

"Both your and our baby's heart rates are steady. Are you okay? What happened?"

Lexie attempted to push herself into a sitting position but her arms shook so violently, it was impossible. Asher's worry increased. Placing a hand on each arm, he helped her sit up.

"I'm okay, Asher. I just got light-headed for a moment." Lexie's voice was flatter than normal. Her usual fiery tone absent.

"Call Sage," Asher called to the guys in the doorway.

Lexie closed her eyes. "Asher—"

"Should we get you to the bed?" he asked.

"Asher! I'd like you to go."

Asher immediately wanted to refuse. There was no way he wanted to leave her like this. She needed him. Both her and their baby.

They needed support. And *he* wanted to be the one to provide that.

As if swapping roles, she now placed her hand on his arm. "I think I passed out because I'm stressed. Remember how Sage said that I needed to avoid all stress?" Lexie paused for a moment before she continued. "You and me...this is stressing me out."

Guilt hit Asher hard. He was causing her stress. Asher was the reason Lexie had fallen, while pregnant, onto the cold, hard floor of the bathroom.

Biting back his frustration, Asher helped Lexie to her feet. *He'd* caused this. The wreckage. The pain. All of it.

"I'll get you to bed, then I'll leave," Asher finally conceded as he lifted Lexie into his arms and took her to the spare room.

Placing her on the bed, he sat on the edge. Taking a closer look at her, he noticed the dark circles that shadowed her eyes had returned. So too had the too-pale skin. Just like before. Those weeks when she'd first been pregnant. The sickness. The worry.

Asher had to do better. For the health of Lexie and the baby.

"Are you sure you're okay?" He was stalling, not wanting to leave her.

"I'm okay, Asher." Lexie's voice was strong.

That was Lexie, though. Always strong, no matter the problem.

"I'll be back tomorrow."

"I'll message when I'm ready to see you."

Asher held her gaze a moment longer. "I'm an idiot. But I'm working on it." When her eyes softened a fraction, Asher's hope grew that she would forgive him. "I'll see you soon."

And maybe I can weasel my way back into your life and prove how much you mean to me.

He didn't say those words out loud, though.

Asher turned and left the room. He didn't stop to say goodbye to anyone; he went straight to his car. Climbing in, Asher sat there.

He had something he needed to do but he'd be back. Not tomorrow. Tonight. Because wherever Lexie was, was where Asher needed to be.

"It's stress," Sage said, confirming Lexie's thoughts.

She had known it was stress. Of course it was. Just when her life had seemed to be back on track, her mother's boyfriend had tried to attack her and Asher had revealed he didn't actually see himself with her long term, like she'd thought.

It was as though she was a magnet for problems.

"I thought so." Her voice was quiet as she responded. The

desolation she felt likely evident through her tone. "I really appreciate you coming whenever we call."

"Of course. Any time at all, Lexie." Sage leaned closer. "I know I've said this a dozen times already, but you are the main reason I am here. You are my priority."

She was glad she was someone's priority.

"Is there anything I can do?" Sage asked, concern filling her voice.

That question could mean only one thing. Not only did Lexie feel like shit, but she looked it, too.

"Thank you for offering, but no, I'm okay. I'm just not feeling myself at the moment."

"That's quite common for women during pregnancy," Sage explained. "There are so many changes happening to your body. I mean, you're growing another entire human. And for you, the human you're growing has a different genetic makeup to most others."

Giving a small smile, Lexie appreciated the other woman's attempt at humor.

A knock came at the door before Evie's muffled voice sounded, "Can we come in?"

By "we," Lexie knew Evie meant her and Shylah. The two of them had probably been waiting on the other side of the door the entire time Lexie and Sage had been in the room.

Sage laughed while Lexie shook her head.

"Get in here, guys."

The door crept open and Evie stuck her head in. Then a smile curved her lips before she made her way to the bed with Shylah in tow. The women took the other side of the double.

Shylah was the first to speak. "Are you okay?"

"I'm okay. The diagnosis is in and I'm stressed, which isn't good for me or the baby."

The concern didn't clear from Evie's or Shylah's expressions.

"What can we do?" Evie asked.

"I can take over all meals for you. Eden always tells me if I wasn't a nurse, I would make a great chef," Shylah suggested.

"I can take your shifts at Marble Protection. I can work on the team's IT needs while I'm there, anyway," Evie added.

Appreciation hit Lexie hard. Holy moly, how lucky was she to have these women in her life. Even though their friendships were still fairly new, it was like Lexie had known them for years.

"I'm okay. But I wouldn't turn down any of your peach cobbler if you made it, Shylah."

"Done." Shylah smiled, looking slightly relieved. Probably because she had a job to do.

If only the love of Lexie's life, the father of her baby, could love her as hard and fast as her friends.

Lexie's expression must have given her away, because the concern deepened on the faces of the women around her.

"Are you worried about Albert?" Shylah asked. "Eden said he left town after they spoke to him."

"Plus, I'm going to be keeping an eye out in case he returns," Evie finished.

Lexie *wished* that old man was her only concern.

"I'm not worried about Albert. He's probably halfway across the country by now. That's if the people behind Project Arma haven't caught him already." Lexie felt no sympathy for the guy. He'd gotten himself into this mess. "It's Asher's words from the other night that keep replaying in my head. A part of me wonders if I should end this before I get any deeper."

"This" being any sort of romantic relationship with Asher. Crap, just saying those words out loud almost tore her heart in two.

"I mean, we can coparent while separated."

Everything Lexie said left a sour taste in her mouth and a lump in her throat. The idea made sense to her on a practical level. She didn't want to end up so broken it compromised her parenting.

The only problem was, she was so deeply in love with the guy that it probably didn't make a difference whether they broke up now or later. The damage to her heart was done.

The three women around Lexie sat silently. Each had a look of contemplation on their face.

"Just say it," Lexie said firmly.

"Lexie"—it was Evie who eventually spoke—"it isn't like you to give up. Where's the old Lexie? The woman who told *me* not to give up? To get my damn strength back?"

Lexie didn't know where she was, either. The thing was, she was tired of fighting for something that may never eventuate.

"The other night when we were at Marino's Pizzeria, I thought Asher and I were in a good place. So when I heard what he said to Bodie, it was kind of like, what else do I need to do? How many more times can I be knocked down before I stop getting back up? I'm tired of fighting for us and always ending up in the same place." Looking down, she rubbed her stomach. "It's not just me anymore. I want to be a good mother."

"You're going to be the best mother," Shylah said firmly, the other women nodding in agreement.

"That means that I need to focus one hundred percent on *him*. Not Asher."

Evie's eyes widened. "Him?"

"Oh my God, did you find out the gender and not tell us?" Shylah shrieked.

Shaking her head, Lexie kept her eyes on her bump. "It's just a feeling. I don't know for sure."

But every time she pictured her baby, it was with the same big brown eyes as Asher's. With the same smile and the same boyish good looks.

"Whatever you have, your baby will be beautiful and loved," Sage responded gently as she placed her hand over Lexie's.

Shylah planted accusing eyes on Sage. "You know, don't you?"

The doctor gave a small shrug. She definitely knew.

"Not fair." Shylah pouted.

Lexie let out a laugh that she didn't really feel. "That's okay. I'm just glad you're here to look after me, Sage." Turning her head to look at the time, she saw that it was getting late. Late for a pregnant mama, not for the average person. "I feel pretty wrecked. I might go to sleep now."

In truth, she was feeling more depressed by the minute and was struggling to pull herself out of the funk. Damn pregnancy hormones. Usually Lexie would be fighting her way out of any depressing emotions. But tonight, it felt impossible. Everything felt impossible.

"Of course. We'll see you in the morning, sweetie." Evie leaned over and kissed Lexie on the cheek.

Shylah did the same.

"Remember, call if you need anything," Sage said as she followed the other women out of the room and pulled the door closed behind them.

Once it was just Lexie, she quickly stripped off her clothes before climbing back into bed. Her empty bed.

Growing up, Lexie had promised herself that she would do everything in her power to ensure her life was different than her mother's. Lexie was supposed to either find a man who loved the absolute heck out of her, marry the guy, and make cute babies together, or not have any kids.

Yet here she was, pregnant and alone.

She couldn't imagine herself going back to live with Asher. Sharing a bed with the man she so desperately loved, then seeing him every day at work felt too painful. It would break her.

But then, distance seemed just as gut-wrenching.

Tucking her head into the pillow, Lexie was surprised when the first tear fell. She never cried. Crying made her feel weak, and she hated that.

Quickly rubbing the tear into the pillow, Lexie scrunched her eyes shut. She did *not* want to cry over him.

But soon, more tears fell. They fell so hard and fast that she gave in to the heartache and pain, crying into the pillow. Never in her life had Lexie felt more alone and unloved.

CHAPTER 22

$\mathcal{A}$sher arrived back at Luca's house and threw his car into park.

The relief he felt after what he'd achieved tonight was huge. It was a giant weight off his chest. Not so much the act itself, more what it meant. An indication of the decision he'd made about his future. Their future.

If Lexie forgave him, of course.

Asher should have done it sooner. Hell, he should have gotten over his personal issues and made a commitment to the woman the moment she'd stepped foot inside Marble Protection.

Asher smiled at the memory. His stars had aligned that day, because it had been him standing at the desk when the sassy redhead had walked in. Lexie had literally demanded he hire her.

Not that it would have changed anything if it had been one of the others standing at the desk. Asher would have met her eventually and threatened any asshole who got too close.

He'd asked her straight out why he should hire her. He remembered her response like she said it yesterday—"Why the heck not?"

Asher had fallen for the woman right there and then. It had just taken him too long to realize it.

If he had any luck on his side, Lexie would take his sorry ass back. Otherwise, he didn't know what he'd do.

Reclining his seat, Asher tried to make himself comfortable. He wasn't going anywhere. He was staying as close to Lexie as physically possible. Firstly, because she was in danger and it was his job to protect her. Secondly, because there was nowhere in the world he'd rather be than close to her.

Besides, he'd definitely slept in a lot of worse places than the front seat of a Nissan. One time he'd had to sleep in the trunk of a car while in ninety-degree heat.

About to close his eyes, he heard a shuffling noise from outside. It wasn't the normal rustling of leaves in the wind. This sound was branches snapping beneath footsteps.

Asher listened closer.

There it was again.

Flicking his gaze toward the house, he scanned the area. Even though it was pitch-black, he saw every minute detail. But he didn't spot anyone. Which meant the asshole was either good at staying hidden or had hightailed it out of there.

Sliding out of his car, Asher made as little noise as possible as he moved forward. The sound had been faint and muffled but it had come from the right side of the house.

As Asher passed the front, the door opened and Luca exited. He would have heard it, too, no doubt.

Asher didn't stop. Simply signaled with his hand that the sound had come from around the house.

Both men moved at a slow, quiet pace, creeping to the location. No one would hear anything that Asher or Luca didn't want them to hear.

When they arrived, there was no other person in sight, but there were track marks. Asher crouched to touch the shoe indents in the dirt.

Fresh. And male. Definitely male. By the depth of the marks, Asher would say the man who created them was about two hundred and fifty pounds. If the length was anything to go by, he was tall.

Asher ran his gaze up Luca's house—and sucked in a sharp breath.

He was standing directly below Lexie's window.

Lexie was on the second floor, but anyone with training would be able to scale the wall.

Son of a bitch. Someone had been here, and they were here for Lexie.

Eyes darting back to the prints, he noticed they led into the forest behind Luca's house. The asshole must have seen Asher coming and left.

He took a step toward the woods, intending to pursue the stranger, when he heard it…

The softest of whimpers, followed by a gentle sniff.

Stare shooting back up to Lexie's room, Asher went still. She was crying.

His heart hurt at the sound of Lexie in pain.

"Go to her," Luca whispered. "I'll call some of the guys to come follow the tracks."

Before Asher could respond, Luca was on his phone.

It took him less than a minute to move through the house, up to Lexie's room. When he opened her door, Asher's entire body tightened.

Lexie lay under the sheets, looking small. Her body shook with silent sobs.

This was his fault. He'd done this to her. Made her feel this way. And he would fix it.

Closing the door behind him, Asher quickly stripped off his shoes, shirt, and jeans before sliding between the sheets.

~

ONCE THE TEARS STARTED, Lexie couldn't stop them. It was like she'd opened a floodgate and all the pain and heartache was bleeding out of her.

She cried for her childhood. The one that had lacked any form of security and support. She cried because she had never felt important enough for anyone to love. Not the people she'd needed it from most.

She hated feeling weak. Lexie tried to be the best, strongest version of herself every day of her life. Bigger than her circumstances. She tried to count her blessings. She was pregnant with a healthy baby; how much luckier could she get? But this pregnancy was kicking her ass.

The biggest reason she cried was fear *for* her baby. Fear that she couldn't give him the perfect nuclear family that she'd always envisioned. The one with the mother and father who cuddled on the couch watching Hallmark movies while the kids ate popcorn.

She couldn't give her baby the family that she had craved growing up.

Holding her hand to her stomach, Lexie willed the tears to stop flowing. Not a day would pass when her baby would feel unworthy. Unloved.

Then, Lexie stilled as the mattress suddenly dipped behind her. She hadn't heard the door open or a single footstep.

Wondering if it was Evie, Lexie moved her hand to the arm that snaked around her waist. The hairy, muscular arm.

Not Evie.

Her body was pulled against a much larger, hotter body.

"Please don't cry, Lex. You're breaking my heart." Asher's voice was quiet but pained.

Even though she'd gone silent, the tears still flowed. "I can't stop," Lexie whispered.

A voice in her head said that she should push Asher away.

But she felt weak. And Asher was warm and comfortable. His strength made *her* feel stronger. He anchored her. So instead of pulling away, Lexie pushed her body closer to his. Wanting more. Craving it.

"I'm sorry." Asher's lips pressed against her ear.

Sniffling, she let his gentle strokes of her wrist calm some of the turmoil in her chest. "What are you sorry for?"

"Everything. I'm sorry I've been an idiot. That I couldn't admit my true feelings for you. I'm sorry that I couldn't be the man that you've needed me to be. The man you deserve. I'm sorry that I've never told you how fucking important you are to me every single day. I never told you that I can't look at you without losing my damn mind because you're so perfect."

Finally, Lexie's tears began to slow. "What are they?"

Asher was quiet for a moment. "What are what, Lex?"

"Your true feelings."

"I love you. I love you so goddamn much it hurts. Not being around you hurts."

Lexie's breath caught. Asher loved her.

She had been waiting for him to say those words to her for so long that, now that she was actually hearing them, they didn't feel real. A part of her had thought she would never hear them.

Rolling over in his arms, she could just make out his features in the moonlight. Asher's hand splayed the whole of her hip as she faced him.

"Are you just saying these things to make me go back with you? Because I'm pregnant with our baby? What you said at dinner the other night—"

"I meant." Lexie stiffened, but Asher quickly continued. "But I didn't mean what you *think* I meant. You and me are going to be constantly changing through life. There's no way we'll be the exact same people ten years from now. That's why love is fluid, because it changes with us. Moves with us."

Lexie watched Asher's eyes through the dim light. "And you've only just worked all this out?"

She wanted to believe him. There was nothing in the world

she wanted more. But if she believed that it could all work out, that Asher could love her as fiercely as she loved him, and then it turned out to be untrue, Lexie didn't know if she could recover from that.

Asher reached out and rubbed his thumb over the path where her tears had fallen.

"I'm flawed, Lexie. I knew I loved you before I understood what that meant and required. All I understood was that I needed you. Needed to be close to you. Hear your voice. Touch your skin. That was love. It always has been." Asher lowered his head so that their foreheads touched. "I know I'm late. So damn late that I don't deserve you. You should tell me to leave and not come back. But I'm going to be a selfish bastard and ask you to take me back anyway."

Lexie raised her hand to his cheek, thumb stroking his strong jawline. "I don't know how *not* to love you, Asher."

His mouth crashed onto Lexie's. His kiss was both perfect and marred. Perfect, because his lips healed her, marred because she didn't want to come up for air.

Lexie leaned closer, her bump hitting Asher's stomach.

"I don't deserve you," he whispered between kisses.

Hooking her leg over his hip, Lexie felt like she couldn't get close enough.

Asher rolled her onto her back before climbing on top of her. His lips never left her own.

Slowly, he began to trail his mouth down her neck. Lexie watched his dark head in the moonlight, transfixed.

Pulling down the cup of her bra, Asher lowered his head to her breast, taking her nipple into his mouth. He sucked the peak, flicking his tongue over it.

The heat inside Lexie grew at an alarming pace. Her body quivering with need. She still wasn't close enough to him, though. She needed Asher. All of him.

When his mouth left her breast, Lexie couldn't stop the

protest that released from her chest. With his mouth still on her body, Asher worked his way down, leaving a trail of kisses as he went.

When he reached her panties, he quickly removed them before separating her thighs.

Asher's mouth touched her core.

Lexie jolted at the searing pleasure that washed over her.

He began to lick her clit in firm thrusts, leaving Lexie feeling feverish. Soon, he began alternating back and forth between swiping his tongue and sucking her bundle of nerves.

Asher was merciless.

Lexie cried out, her back arching and breaths becoming labored. He reached a hand up to her breast and squeezed the sensitive nipple, pushing her higher.

Thrashing wildly on the sheets, Lexie jerked against his mouth, then erupted in an intense orgasm.

Closing her eyes, she felt weightless.

Not a moment later, Asher had crawled over her body and positioned himself at her entrance.

Lexie's eyes opened to find him above her. Their eyes caught as he sank into her, stretching her in the most divine way. Her walls were still throbbing.

Finally, Lexie got the level of closeness that she needed. That her body craved.

Asher paused, and Lexie felt something new between them. A new connection. A bond that made her heart swell as her body heated.

Then Asher's mouth lowered to hers before lifting again. "You're fucking gorgeous, Lex. I'm never letting you go."

At the first thrust of his hips, she groaned as a new round of need grew inside her. Then Asher started to move harder, faster, pulling out and thrusting in.

He was intense and fierce above her. Her warrior.

Fingers scraped against his rock-hard chest, every thrust inciting more need.

"Asher…"

Head flying to the side, Lexie whimpered below him. She felt every surge deep to her core.

Soon, their lovemaking became erratic. Both needing to be closer than was physically possible.

A moment later, her body spasmed, and Lexie shattered beneath him. At almost the same moment, Asher's body shuddered before he let out a deep, guttural growl.

Lexie held on to his shoulders as she came down from her high. Her body still throbbed, him still swollen within her.

"I love you, Asher." She gasped the words. Feeling at peace that she was now free to say them.

"I love you, Lex. Today, tomorrow, and every day after that. Forever."

Forever. Lexie liked the sound of that.

CHAPTER 23

*A*s the morning light drifted into the room, Lexie peeled her eyes open. They felt swollen and puffy from all the crying she'd done.

The crying that took place before one of the best moments of her life. The moment Asher admitted he loved her.

Heck, she felt like a new woman. A woman whose love was reciprocated.

Rolling onto her back, Lexie reached for Asher, only to realize she was alone in bed. There was no heavy arm slung across her waist. No steamy warmth from his big, hot body.

Pushing up to her elbows, Lexie searched the room. *Where would he have gotten to?*

She didn't have to wonder long. A wet Asher walked through the door wearing nothing but a towel low on his waist.

Lexie's mouth went dry as she scanned his muscular body. Firm muscles rippled across his chest, his arms reminding her of giant tree trunks.

The man was a walking sex god. Lucky he already loved her, because she was pretty sure she'd just drooled a little.

"You keep looking at me like that and we won't be leaving this room today." Asher's voice was husky. Sexy.

Hmm, that didn't sound like such a bad idea to her.

"I can't see a problem with that," she responded, sure she came across as a wanton pregnant lady.

Asher stalked closer with a predatory look in his eyes. "The thing is, Rocket and Evie will know exactly what we're doing. Plus, Rocket will hear us."

Small price to pay for an hour of lovemaking with Asher, Lexie thought with a smile.

"Also, I have something to show you. Back at my place."

Asher sat on the edge of the bed, an arm wrapping around Lexie's legs. In a very *nonsexual* way.

Ah, crap. Looked like Lexie wouldn't be getting any special Asher time this morning.

He leaned his head down so that his lips hovered over hers. "Still love me?"

"Yes," Lexie grumbled. Although she'd prefer to be loving him naked under the sheets.

Asher's mouth finally touched hers, causing her heart to speed up. His lips were soft. The *only* part of him that was soft.

Too soon, he drew his head away, making Lexie want to latch on to the man and drag him back to her.

Asher chuckled as he stood. "You're trouble."

"Excuse me, buddy, you're the one who walked in here looking too sexy for his own good." Climbing out of bed, she threw on a dressing gown. "Guess I'll go have a lonely shower."

Before Lexie could reach the door, she was spun around into Asher's arms, his mouth slamming onto hers. This time, his lips didn't simply touch her. They consumed her.

His tongue invaded Lexie's mouth, her limbs immediately heating before turning limp. Asher's mouth was insistent. Sure.

Holy heck. There was a good chance she might light up in flames right there and then.

Lexie clung to his solid shoulders, needing an anchor to keep her upright. Just as her heart started to gallop—and other parts of Lexie's body began to come to life—Asher broke the kiss.

No!

Well, it was official. The man was trying to kill her.

"Don't take too long," Asher whispered.

The man wasn't even breathing heavily. While Lexie sounded like she'd just run a marathon.

Lexie gave a humph, not liking his knowing smile, before turning and leaving the room.

Don't take too long? What would happen if she *did* take too long? Would he come in after her? Because if that was the case, she might just break a world record in there.

Once in the bathroom, Lexie glanced at herself in the mirror. Her cheeks were rosy and her eyes wide.

Damn Asher, Lexie thought as she jumped in the shower stall.

As she felt the warm water hit her shoulders, memories of the previous night caused a smile to stretch over her lips.

He loved her. He had actually said the words that he loved her. And she'd said them back.

Jeepers it felt amazing. Better than amazing, it was the best feeling in the world. She felt lighter today. That heavy feeling in her chest was gone. The worry, the fear, had vanished.

And their lovemaking after had felt different. More meaningful.

Lexie was still smiling a few minutes later when she stepped out of the shower. Drying off, she returned to the bedroom to find no Asher. But there was a set of her clothes lying on the bed. The supersoldier must have run home to get them for her.

Once dressed, she glanced at herself in the mirror, her hands grazing over her bump. She was getting bigger every day, and the movement inside her stomach was getting stronger.

Lexie loved it. Her baby was growing. Getting ready to meet its parents.

Smiling to herself, Lexie headed downstairs.

"Listen, buddy, all I'm saying is, if you're not gonna organize the strawberries, then why go to the effort of making pancakes?"

Asher's voice filtered through the house. So did the smell of pancake batter and bacon. Holy cow, that smelled good.

Rounding the corner into the kitchen, Lexie saw Luca flipping a pancake.

"Don't anger the man with the pancakes and bacon, Asher," Lexie scolded as she moved to stand next to him.

Luca seemed to be adding the last pancake to the stack while Evie poured some orange juice. Lexie wasn't entirely sure what Asher was doing, but she *was* almost entirely sure it wasn't helpful.

Evie began to usher her friends to the table. "Sit!"

"Guys, you didn't have to make pancakes." But she sure as heck was glad they had.

"A pregnant woman deserves to be pampered." Evie said with a smile as she and Luca carried the last items over. Everyone took a seat around the table.

Asher began loading his plate. "What about the dad? We deserve some pampering."

Luca laughed. "Yeah, I'm sure watching Lexie be pregnant must really take it out of you."

"You'd be surprised," Asher responded, covering his food in copious amounts of maple syrup.

Evie and Lexie laughed before her friend asked her a question about baby clothes. Lexie turned to her, excited to tell her about the hundred and one things she'd ordered from Amazon.

At the same time, Luca and Asher split off into their own conversation. It wasn't until Lexie overheard a mention of prints from last night that she turned back to the boys.

"What prints?"

Both men fell silent. Luca's gaze went down to his food, while Asher didn't seem to know where to look.

A sinking feeling came over her. "What is it?"

"It's nothing. We saw some tracks outside last night. Someone was walking around the house."

Lexie's eyes widened at Asher's words. That was definitely not nothing.

"A stranger was walking around this house last night?"

Asher nodded.

"Where were the prints?" Lexie asked, glad she'd almost finished her food, because her appetite had vanished.

Putting his fork down, Asher scrubbed his hand over his face before answering. "By the kitchen."

By the kitchen? Holy heck...above the kitchen was the room Lexie had slept in.

A chill crept over her skin as her hand began rubbing her baby bump. "That's pretty brave of them, isn't it? To stalk me with both of you here." A wave of anger washed over her.

"Lexie, look at me."

She turned her head to look into Asher's eyes. He looked just as angry as Lexie felt.

"Nothing and no one is going to hurt you or the baby. Got it?"

"Oh, I got it, Asher. If anyone even tries, I'll be kicking their ass all the way to Antarctica."

A smirk pulled across his face. "There's my Lexie."

If anyone wanted this baby, they wouldn't just have Asher and his buddies to go through. They'd have her.

"Why can't you just tell me what it is you want to show me?" Lexie grumbled.

Asher wanted to chuckle at Lexie's impatience. He restrained himself, though, for fear of angering the pregnant lady.

That was possibly the fiftieth time in only ten minutes that she had begged him to tell her. Same old Lexie. She couldn't blame her impatience on the pregnancy.

"Do you really want me to tell you? Wouldn't you prefer to see it with your own eyes?"

"Yes, I do want you to tell me, and no, I don't need a surprise."

Keeping his eyes on the road, Asher shook his head. "Too bad, Lex. You can wait another five minutes. Also, maybe we should work on your patience before the baby arrives."

Crossing her arms over her chest, Lexie sulked for a moment. "I don't know why you would tell me you have something to show me then refuse to tell me what it is. It's like you want to torture me."

The woman was cute when she sulked. Scratch that, she was cute every minute of every day. "Yeah, wanting to surprise my girlfriend with something nice is akin to torture."

Lexie's head whipped around, her lips pulling into a huge smile. "Did you just call me your girlfriend?"

Asher admired her smile for a moment before pulling his attention back to the road. Christ, she was gorgeous. He hadn't seen that smile enough lately. He sure would be working harder to see it more.

"Girlfriend. Partner. Whatever you want to call it."

Lexie cocked her head to the side. "I thought you hated labels?"

"I do. But you don't. And it's my job to keep you happy. The point is, I'm yours and you're mine. Call it whatever you want."

Lexie's hand slid over to grasp his knee, Asher's hand immediately covering it. "I *am* yours."

"Good."

Asher held her hand for the remainder of the drive.

Arriving at his place, Asher pulled into his parking spot before they made their way to his entrance. Once they'd reached the front door, he stopped.

Lexie's gaze flicked from Asher to the door then back again. "Aren't you going to open it?"

"Nope."

"Then how are we—"

Lexie stopped talking when Asher held out a key. He was immediately rewarded with another of those megawatt smiles.

"*You're* going to open it," Asher confirmed. "With your key."

Lexie's gaze flashed up to Asher's. "You're giving me a key to your home?"

"No. I'm giving you a key to *our* home. Our family's home. If you want to live here, that is."

Shock rendered Lexie frozen for a moment before she swiped the key from his fingers, then jumped into his arms.

"Thank you." Pulling away, she slid the key into the lock before stepping inside, smiling from ear to ear.

Finally, he was doing something right with Lexie. It was about damn time.

Asher closed the door behind them. "There's something else I need to show you."

Lexie's brows lifted but she remained silent.

Taking her hand in his, Asher pulled her toward the spare room. His former junk room. Reaching it, Asher stood behind Lexie.

"Open it."

Confusion marred her expression before she pushed through the door. She'd only taken one step into the room when she abruptly stopped.

Her body went completely still. Then Asher heard her heart speed up and begin to race.

"When did you do this?" she whispered.

"I started collecting the week I found out you were pregnant," Asher said gently as he stepped behind Lexie and wrapped his arms around her middle. His hands pressed against her bump. "I wanted to surprise you. I was stupid, though, and waited too long. Last night I wanted to give you something more than words to prove my commitment to you. So, I came back here and put it all together."

Lexie looked over her shoulder, her eyes tearful. "You started collecting things for our baby's nursery the week you found out I was pregnant?"

The moment it sunk in that he was expecting a son or daughter, he'd begun planning.

Sure, the news had come as a shock. But it had been the best news he'd had in his life. He was going to have a baby with the woman he loved. It didn't get much better than that.

"I did. I'm going to be a partner and father that my family can depend on, Lexie. I'm going to be a man that *you* can depend on. I won't let you down again. I promise."

Lexie continued to stare at Asher, tears still in her eyes. "You made me cry again. This is the best surprise anyone's ever given me."

"You're the best surprise anyone's ever given *me*."

Lexie's eyes heated before she leaned her body back against his, her gaze scanning the room. "The crib is beautiful."

"I'm glad you like it. That was the last addition. I finished it last night."

Her eyes immediately swung back to Asher's. "You built the crib?"

Asher shrugged his big shoulders. It hadn't been hard. He'd put time into it here and there. "Some of the guys helped me. It's been a project I've been working on. I didn't want to show you until it was done."

Lexie turned in his arms and buried her head in his chest. Firming his arms around her, Asher held on tight.

"I love you," she whispered, her voice muffled against his chest.

"You have no idea."

CHAPTER 24

"*A*sher, I don't see why we couldn't have stopped by Mrs. Potter's Bakehouse," Lexie said as she climbed out of the car. "No one ever shows up empty-handed to a family get-together. I feel like a mooch."

Watching Asher round the car, she couldn't figure the guy out. He'd been acting fishy all morning.

"Lex, you're thirty-two weeks pregnant. Enjoy the last couple months of everyone doing everything for you."

Lexie didn't need reminding of how far along she was. She felt every one of those thirty-two weeks.

Rubbing her hand over her belly, the only way Lexie could describe how she felt was massive. More than massive, she felt like she was pregnant with triplets. If one more person asked her if she had only one baby in there, she would not be responsible for her actions.

The baby was measuring way ahead of schedule. She didn't know how she was going to last another eight weeks. Possibly more.

"Stop overthinking everything," Asher whispered by her ear.

Easy for him to say. He didn't have a giant baby he needed to birth from his body in a couple months.

Wrapping an arm around her waist, Asher pulled Lexie toward Mason's backyard.

Glancing up, she was distracted from her thoughts by the sight of Mason's house. Mason's big-ass house. She'd never been to his home before. It was in town but sat on at least one and a half acres of land.

"This place is massive."

The house, the land, all of it was huge.

Asher chuckled. "Eagle likes to be in the thick of it but still have his space. He also has dogs and wants them to have space, too."

Well, they sure have that, Lexie thought to herself. Why did one man need all of this?

Stepping into the backyard, Lexie's feet stopped.

She scanned the area, confused for a moment. All her friends were scattered around the lawn, where they stood smiling at her.

Then Lexie spotted the giant banner that was strung above a food table. The words *Happy Baby-Q* were in bold print.

"Happy Baby-Q!" Everyone sang the words somewhat simultaneously, repeating what she'd just read.

Lexie turned her head to Asher. "Did you know?"

Shrugging his giant shoulders, Asher smiled. "I may have helped with some of the prep yesterday."

Lexie swatted him on the shoulder but quickly reached up to give him a kiss. Good lord, she loved him. All of them. Everyone. Lexie was surrounded by the best people.

"Hey, I made the guacamole, do I get a kiss?" Bodie shouted.

"Try it and die, asshole," Asher called over Lexie's head.

Laughing, Lexie went around to give everyone a hug.

"Baby-Q?" Lexie asked as she reached Evie.

Cringing, Evie's eyes darted to the sign then back to Lexie.

"We wanted to throw you a proper baby shower, but the boys of course insisted that at least one of them had to come."

"One?" Shylah interrupted, holding a cup of juice out for Lexie. "I believe their words were 'at least three of us are present or no party.' We fought it, Lexie,"

Evie nodded. "Sitting in the car wasn't a safe enough option."

Smiling as she took the cup, Lexie could just imagine how that went. "I appreciate it."

Ever since Asher and Luca had discovered the tracks outside Luca's house, Lexie literally hadn't been by herself for a moment. Not that anything had come from the track marks. In fact, nothing even remotely suspicious had happened since.

Although, that may have been because she had barely been separated from the six-foot-four former SEAL of hers. Asher was attached to her day and night, and on the rare occasions he couldn't be there, one of the guys was always present to take his place.

Lexie would have thought she'd feel suffocated. But she didn't. She felt protected. Safe.

"So, we compromised," Evie finished. "A baby shower slash barbecue."

Lexie was touched that her friends had gone to so much effort for her. No doubt, Evie and Shylah were the ringleaders.

"Please tell me we get to watch the men play baby shower games," Lexie begged, way too excited at the possibility.

Evie shrugged, similar excitement lighting her eyes. "There may be one or two games in the works."

Oh sweet Jesus, if Lexie got to watch Asher eat baby food or pop a baby in the form of a balloon under his shirt, her day would be made. Heck, her year would be made.

"Before you get too excited, I told them nothing embarrassing," Asher said into Lexie's ear as his arms wrapped around her middle. Damn, it was like the man was a mind reader on top of everything else he could do.

"Well, that's no fun." Lexie sulked as she tipped her head up to look at her man.

Her man. That sounded good. She also liked the feel of his arms around her while out in public. Something that a few months ago had rarely, if ever, occurred.

Asher's lips lowered to Lexie's, causing a jump of excitement inside her.

Okay, scratch the games idea. Lexie was fine spending her afternoon kissing Asher.

"You know, sex is a natural baby-induction method." Kye's voice pulled Lexie out of her Asher trance.

"And you would know this how?" Lexie asked, lifting a brow.

What she really wanted to do was rant at the man for stopping the pantie-dropping kiss she'd just been enjoying.

"Sage told me," Kye said with a smirk, eyes shooting across the lawn.

Following Kye's line of sight, Lexie saw Sage standing with Wyatt and Bodie, looking beautiful as per usual in a white dress.

"Sage is here," Lexie said, more to herself than anyone else. The sight of the doctor made Lexie smile. She was glad they'd invited her. Sage was definitely a friend now. Lexie secretly hoped that after the baby was born the other lady would remain in Marble Falls.

Not only was Sage a brilliant doctor and incredibly intelligent, she was also a beautiful person.

Shylah nodded. "Mason invited her."

Lexie hoped this wasn't another way for the guys to watch the doctor. If it was, someone needed to have a not-so-subtle word with them. She thought they'd already concluded that Sage was innocent in all the recent drama.

"How would that have come up?" Evie asked Kye.

Lexie was confused for a moment about what Evie was referring to, only to remember Kye's comment about sex and induction.

"I asked her how to get the baby out early. Sage suggested a few things. I only remember sex." Kye winked at Lexie. "I mean, I'm not an expert on the matter, but you are looking pretty big for someone who still has two months to go."

Lexie wanted to throttle him. Lucky for her, Asher thumped him in the arm.

"Ow," Kye howled. "What was that for?"

Evie placed a hand on her waist. "Kye, you never comment on a pregnant lady's size."

Trust her to put it in the nicest way possible.

Shylah frowned. "You don't comment on any woman's size. Ever."

Kye scratched his head. "Even if the woman looks like she's going to topple over, she's so big?"

This time, Asher didn't just whack the man, he went after him. Kye seemed to be aware that it was coming, because he shot off before Asher could touch him.

Lexie shook her head. "I'm gonna go feed my giant baby while Asher teaches that jerk some respect." Lexie laughed as she headed toward the food table.

On her way to the food table, Lexie spotted some of Mrs. Potter's cakes. She quickened her steps immediately. Grabbing the largest plate she could find, she began to load it up.

Thank the lord her baby had come around and didn't make her want to throw her guts up at the sight of baked sugary cakes anymore.

Deciding she couldn't wait any longer, Lexie lifted a cinnamon roll to her lips and took the biggest bite she could. Holy heck, it was good. Better than good. It was orgasmic.

"People weren't joking when they said Mrs. Potter's cakes are the best."

Lexie turned her head to see Sage standing next to her. Swallowing her mouthful of roll, she wasn't the least bit ashamed with how big her bite had been. It was that good.

"Ah, another convert." Lexie knew all too well how addictive the cakes were. Not that she'd ever let that stop her. "I don't know how Mrs. Potter does it. I think she must have secret ingredients that have yet to be discovered by the rest of the world."

Lexie took another bite of roll, only to realize she'd eaten over half of the cake in two mouthfuls.

"That would explain it." Sage picked up her own roll and took a much more reasonably sized bite. "Although, I'd better not eat the whole thing. I hear Marino's pizza will be here soon."

Marino's pizza? Someone better pray for her because Lexie might need to be rolled out by the end of today.

"Well, no one can tell me I'm not feeding this baby." Lexie laughed as she finished off the roll in her hand.

Sage put a hand on Lexie's arm. "Honestly, I am in awe of how you have handled everything. First the twists and turns with the pregnancy. Then the danger you've faced. Lexie, I say this with complete honesty, you are a powerhouse and will make a wonderful mother."

She paused at the other woman's words. Sage had spoken with so much conviction that Lexie felt the words deep down. Asher had said it to her a hundred times over, but he loved her. He had to say it. Sage was Lexie's doctor, and they had only known each other a few months.

"Thank you. That really means a lot to me."

Probably more than the other woman would know.

"Game time!"

Shylah's loud voice echoed across the yard. Lexie's excitement increased tenfold when she saw the other woman holding up diapers and baby food.

Heck yes! It was time to see Asher eat some baby food. Lexie would be savoring every minute of this.

An hour later, she had not only watched Asher's face screw up in distaste as he ate ten different flavors of baby puree, he'd also attempted to change a diaper while blindfolded, chug apple juice from a baby bottle, and waddle across the lawn with a water balloon between his thighs.

It was like ten Christmases rolled into one. Based on the looks on Evie's and Shylah's faces as they'd watched their men, Lexie assumed they agreed.

The sound of a car engine caused Lexie to turn her head. She quickly realized the boys were already looking that way. The fact that they weren't concerned meant that whoever had arrived wasn't a threat.

In fact, rather than appear on edge, they had smiles on their faces. Giant, something-great-is-about-to-happen smiles. That could mean only one thing.

"Pizza!"

Lexie's stomach growled at the sound of Oliver's voice. Since Sage had mentioned it, the cheesy slices of heaven had been firmly rooted in Lexie's mind.

Not a minute later, she saw Bill enter the backyard and place pizza boxes on the table. Wyatt and Oliver headed to the front, coming back with stacks of pizzas in their hands.

It was like they'd ordered enough pizzas for a village. Which worked for Lexie.

As the boys dug in, Lexie went over to thank Bill.

"The pizzas smell amazing. Thanks for always feeding us, Bill."

"I'm here to help."

Lexie frowned. Was it just her imagination, or were there worry lines lurking around Bill's face?

Placing a hand on his arm, she tried to catch his eye. "Is everything okay, Bill?"

Bill nodded as he scrubbed his hand over his face. "Of course. The restaurant's just been busy. I've been a bit run off my feet. I think it's taking its toll."

Taking a step closer, Lexie felt for the other man. He was the hardest worker Lexie knew. "It's okay to ask for help, Bill. All the guys from Marble Protection would help at a moment's notice. All you need to do is ask."

An emotion that Lexie couldn't quite identify flashed across Bill's face before he quickly cleared it. "Thanks, Lexie. I'll see you around."

Then he was gone. Heading toward his truck before she could say any more.

"Come have some pizza, Lex. The baby needs to eat," Asher murmured in her ear from behind.

Lexie dragged her eyes from the driveway. "The baby?" She reeled back. "*I* need to eat, Asher. This mama's hungry!"

Asher chuckled. "Come on. How about we feed you both."

ervous tension hit Lexie as she watched Sage read the number on the measuring tape.

Lexie was big. Bigger than big. She was huge—and she had a feeling she knew exactly what the other woman was about to say to her.

Lexie had researched large babies. She'd researched the absolute heck out of it. According to Dr. Google, most people in the medical profession wanted the baby out as soon as medically safe when this large.

"Thanks for coming to Marble Protection today," she said as Sage wrote some more notes in Lexie's file. The doctor's silence was killing her. "Asher hasn't been here a lot so he wanted to come in today and support the guys. He also knows he'll need some time off when the baby comes. And where he goes, I go."

Maybe Lexie could distract the other woman so she wouldn't suggesting something like a scheduled cesarean.

"That's not a problem, Lexie. Anywhere, anytime."

Lexie began nervously tapping her fingers on the desk. Hopefully that anytime was far into the future. Like due-date or later.

Sage put down the file and leaned her hip against the desk.

Oh crap, this was it. The dreaded "let's get the baby out ASAP" chat.

"You've dropped."

Lexie frowned. That was not what she was expecting the other woman to say.

"What do you mean, *I've dropped*?"

Was that doctor talk for some sort of pregnancy stage?

Sage gave a patient smile. "Your baby has dropped. Have you noticed that your bump is a lot lower?"

Lexie had noticed that her bump was bigger. It got bigger every day.

"Not really. What does that mean, exactly?" Although Lexie had a feeling she knew exactly what that meant. Lower baby could only mean...

"It means the baby's coming. Soon."

Eyes widening, Lexie was so shocked she might have toppled off her chair had she not been hanging on so tight. "But I'm only thirty-five weeks pregnant."

And she still had a million things she needed to do. Her due date wasn't for another month. More than a month. She was supposed to have time.

"When you say soon, how long do you mean, exactly?"

Lexie held out hope that the doctor would give her at least a couple of weeks.

"Anywhere between a day to a week. These things aren't an exact science."

Holy crap. That *was* soon.

Breathe in, breathe out.

Focusing on her breaths, she tried to stop herself from having a full-blown anxiety attack.

She would be giving birth in a week or less. Birth. She knew this point would come, but it was always at some stage in the future. And there had always been something else going on to distract her.

From everything Lexie had read, birth was hard. Of course, there were the stories where women had made it sound easy. Magical even. But who knew what her experience would be? Birth was unpredictable.

And then after the birth came the baby. A real, live, breathing baby who would be *her* responsibility.

"Lexie." Sage lowered to her knees and took Lexie's hands in her own. "Here's my suggestion. Tonight, spend the evening with Asher and tell him in your own time what I've told you. Tomorrow, pop into the hospital and we'll do a scan. Baby is healthy. Remember that. This baby has been ahead of schedule the entire pregnancy, so this isn't a huge surprise. If baby comes within the week, that's okay because the main thing a baby needs is love from Mom and Dad. Relax and breathe."

Nodding her head, Lexie felt like she was having an out-of-body experience. "So, a week or less?"

"A week or less."

So many things popped into her head that she needed to buy and do. Lexie had wanted to sleep in until midday, then cook a million meals to pop into the freezer. She had wanted to visit the local shops and buy bits and pieces to decorate the nursery.

"We haven't even chosen a name."

Sage shrugged. "I hear that names often come to parents when they hold their baby in their arms."

Would that happen? Would she look at her baby boy or girl and just know what to call them?

"Is it okay if I sit here for a few minutes? Process everything."

Sage stood but then lowered herself into the seat beside Lexie. "Of course. I'll sit right here with you if you'd like."

Lexie didn't say anything. Instead, she reached over and entwined her fingers with Sage's.

∼

ASHER BIT back a curse when he looked at the time. He'd gotten so caught up in the meeting, he'd missed Lexie's appointment with Sage.

Leaving the office, he went in search of her. But he couldn't wipe the scowl from his face after what he'd just learned.

Evie had finally found a lead on what the "distraction" might have been the day John Roberts had died. The car chase had happened so long ago, Asher had all but forgotten about it.

For months, Evie had been searching for anything out of the ordinary in Marble Falls. She'd found nothing.

So about a month ago, she'd changed tactics and started watching traffic cam footage around Marble Falls. That led to her discovering video surveillance of three military-looking men in various locations around town.

Noticing how out of place and unfamiliar the men appeared, Evie went deeper, hacking private security footage from shops all over town. The same men had been spotted around town sporadically, never in the same place as one another.

The sightings started the day Asher had chased John. Before that, nothing.

When Evie had shown them some footage, Asher had immediately identified one of the men as one who had kidnapped and attacked Lexie. The man Asher had killed.

Asher was betting the other two men were the men who got away.

The team had concluded that all signs pointed to it being John's mission to distract the team while the men moved into Marble Falls. The question remained, though—where the hell were the two remaining men hiding?

When Evie had looked deeper and used facial recognition software, she found the men were ex-military. Dishonorably discharged. Exactly the type of men Project Arma began recruiting after going underground. Basically, taking whoever they could get their hands on.

What was more disturbing—and what really upset Asher—was the likelihood of someone in Marble Falls helping them.

Someone he knew could be entangled in all this...and it made him angry. More than angry, it made him *furious*.

Clenching his fists, Asher attempted to clear his features. No way did he want Lexie finding out the men had been in town all this time. He'd been doing anything and everything to keep stress out of her life, and that was exactly how he intended to keep it.

She could kick his ass for keeping secrets when she was no longer pregnant. Until then, she stayed in the dark.

Spotting Lexie behind the front desk, the first thing Asher noticed was the worry lines around her eyes. Damn, had Evie already told her?

Asher smiled as he pulled Lexie into his arms.

"Ready to go home, baby mama?"

Lexie smiled but the strain on her face remained. "I am past ready. And I'm hungry."

"Hungry? Then I'm not doing my job right looking after you, am I?"

"Lucky for you, this isn't the Dark Ages and women can feed and take care of themselves now."

Shaking his head, Asher pulled Lexie closer. "Incorrect. I take care of you regardless of the period we live in."

Lowering his head, he pressed his lips against hers. She tasted of strawberries. Coaxing her mouth open, he deepened the kiss, loving the soft purr that escaped Lexie's lips.

"Get a room, guys."

Asher growled at the sound of Luca's voice. He reluctantly pulled his mouth away from Lexie's. Keeping her body firmly against his, he turned his head to see Luca, Evie, Mason, and Wyatt. He saw a twinkle in Luca's eye.

"Leaving so soon?" And by that, he meant get the hell out of there so he could get some privacy.

"We are. And the others left through the back, so do what you want but lock up after yourselves," Mason said, urging the others forward.

"Yeah, do what you want but do us all a favor and wipe down the counter before you leave," Luca laughed.

Evie swung her head around. "Luca!"

Asher took a threatening step toward him, but lucky for his friend, Mason ushered them out the building quickly.

Lowering his gaze back to Lexie, he noticed she was frowning again.

"Everything okay?" he pushed some escaped hair behind her ear.

Raising her brows, Lexie nodded quickly. "I'm just hungry."

That was a lie.

Concern shot through Asher's chest. Lexie frequently avoided discussing anything she thought might upset him. But he knew if he pushed, she'd retreat.

He watched her for a moment longer before deciding not to press it. For now.

"What do you feel like? Burgers from the diner, Chinese, pizza...?"

Relief washed over Lexie's features. "Thank God you suggested fast food. I really don't feel like cooking or cleaning up tonight. But please, no pizza. I'm a bit sick of it. Burgers maybe?"

"Done."

Asher watched Lexie as she collected her things. Walking out, she came to a stop before they reached the door. "Actually, can we stop at Marino's? I left my sweater there the other night."

"Your wish is my command."

Asher was rewarded with another lyrical chuckle from her.

There was no way he would ever get sick of that sound.

Locking up, Asher took her hand in his and they headed across the road. When he glanced up at the pizzeria for the first time, he realized all the lights were off.

"It looks like Bill's shut up for the night," Lexie said as she pressed her face to the glass in an attempt to see inside.

Asher didn't need to get any closer. He could see inside perfectly. Seats were on tables and there wasn't a soul in sight. And he spotted her sweater immediately on the coat rack at the back of the room.

"He often shuts on Tuesday nights. But I can see your sweater. I'm sure he won't mind if we grab it." Asher took a step toward Marble Protection, Lexie's hand still in his.

"You want to go in? But the door's locked."

"We have a key at Marble Protection. It will be fine. A quick in and out."

Quickly returning to Marble, Asher grabbed the key, then crossed the road again to the pizzeria.

Bill had given them the key when he'd lost his one time. Said he wanted people he trusted to have a spare.

Unlocking the restaurant door, Asher pushed inside, Lexie following closely behind.

Halfway to the coat rack, he stopped moving. An unusual sound filled the air. A buzzing sound. Coming from upstairs.

"Asher?" Lexie tightened her fingers around his. "Do you hear that?"

His gaze darted to her. It wasn't just him. Lexie heard it, too.

Asher hesitated for a moment, torn between going up or not. He wanted to check what was up there, but he didn't want to pull Lexie into danger. Particularly when he didn't know what that danger could entail.

Lexie studied the stairs. "Maybe we should go up there and check. Just have a quick look through the place then go," Lexie whispered.

There was no need to whisper because there was no one else in the building. Asher would have heard their heartbeat and breathing immediately.

If there had been another person, he would have gotten Lexie out of the building before she could blink.

Lexie took a step forward, tugging at his hand when he didn't budge.

"Asher, I'm sure it's fine. We'll be in and out."

In and out. But if he saw even the slightest chance of danger, they were out of there quick smart.

Moving in front of Lexie, he led the way to the stairs. "Bill never mentioned this space," he said, more to himself than to her.

"He told me he started renting it to someone a few months ago."

Pausing halfway up the stairs, Asher turned to look at Lexie. "Why didn't you tell me?"

She shrugged. "I didn't think it was important information. He told me the night we came here for pizza, just after you found out I was pregnant."

Asher's heartbeat notched up a fraction. Questions started filtering through his mind. Who was Bill renting to? Were they new in town?

Facing forward again, Asher and Lexie walked up the last few steps only to come to a stop in front of a closed door. Trying the handle, Asher wasn't surprised to find it locked. That wasn't a problem.

Turning it hard, Asher broke the lock easily.

The buzzing had become progressively louder as they'd neared the room. With the door cracked open, Asher was almost certain he knew exactly what it was, but he prayed he was wrong.

Pushing inside, he switched on the light and stopped. "Motherfuckers."

He felt Lexie push in beside him and heard her quick intake of breath. "What is this?"

Asher knew exactly what it was, and it made him feel raw with anger. This was Project Arma. There wasn't a doubt in his mind.

Walking over to the window, he glanced out. The view was a direct line of sight into Marble Protection.

Right to the front desk where Lexie worked every single day.

Clenching his fists, Asher spun around. Just as he'd suspected, the buzzing came from the multiple laptops and computers stationed around the room. Scanning the space, he noticed a variety of weapons scattered around, as well. Guns, knives.

Picking up a spray bottle, he inspected the exterior. He was certain the bottle contained the very chemical that had been sprayed into his eyes by John Roberts.

Fuck. He wanted Lexie out of there now. The risk that whoever was living there would return was too great.

A gasp from Lexie had him by her side in a second. She stood in front of a computer. On the screen were images. Hundreds of them. Some of the team. Some of Evie and Shylah, but the vast majority of Lexie.

His muscles bunched.

Whipping out his phone, Asher quickly snapped pictures of everything.

"We need to go." He was already pulling Lexie behind him before the words were out of his mouth.

Every second she stood in the room made Asher's anxiety increase tenfold.

"Shouldn't we call the others?" Lexie asked as she moved behind him.

"We'll call them in the car."

He was betting that the renters were the very same men Evie had spotted around Marble Falls. The same men who had kidnapped Lexie and gotten away.

Asher checked the road before stepping outside. Moving across the street, he tried to cover Lexie's body as much as he could. He had a bad fucking feeling...and it was just getting worse by the minute.

CHAPTER 26

*L*exie stood behind Asher as he banged on Wyatt's door. She could just about see the anger coming off him in waves. His fists were so tightly clenched that the veins in his arms were popping out. The guy looked ready to kill.

As soon as the door opened, Asher didn't hesitate. "We found something."

Walking inside the apartment, Lexie glanced around at the modern interior. It may have been small, but it was like she'd stepped into the future. Gadgets and machines were scattered around the space. She spotted two laptops and a desktop, as well as a ton of other things that she wouldn't even begin to be able to identify. And that was just one room.

Asher ushered her to the couch but remained standing. As Lexie went to sit, she felt a small twinge in her lower abdomen. Stopping for a moment, she placed her hand over her stomach.

"What's wrong?"

Lexie's eyes flew up to meet Asher's worried ones. The man looked about as stressed as she'd ever seen him.

Deciding to keep the twinge to herself, Lexie nodded as she sat. "Nothing. I'm okay."

She would tell Asher what Sage had said later tonight. In private. Hopefully by then, plans had been made and he was less tense.

Asher's eyes remained glued to her a moment longer before swinging over to Wyatt. "Do you have food? Lexie hasn't eaten."

She opened her mouth to tell Wyatt not to worry, but he jumped in before she could.

"Sure. I grabbed some sausage rolls from Mrs. Potter on the way home. I might also have some chicken."

At the mention of sausage rolls and chicken, Lexie's mouth snapped shut. She was hungry, and if Wyatt had the goods, why not accept his hospitality?

Ten minutes later, Wyatt returned with two giant plates of food. As he placed them on the coffee table, Lexie's stomach growled loudly. Any other person may have been embarrassed. She was too fixated on the food in front of her.

Moving to the edge of her seat, she was about to stand when Asher shook his head.

"I got you."

Food and service. She could get used to this.

Asher handed Lexie a loaded plate and she dug in like she hadn't eaten in days. You would think that finding out criminals had been watching you from their secret hideout would kill your appetite.

Nope. Not the case at all. Not for Lexie, at least.

"Okay, so, tell me what you found," Wyatt said, dropping into a seat.

Asher sat next to Lexie, his hand going to her knee. "We went to Marino's Pizzeria after we locked up Marble, but Bill had shut the shop."

Wyatt's expression didn't change. "That's not unusual. He often closes shop at the beginning of the week."

"My thoughts exactly. But Lex left her sweater in there so we used the spare key we have to go in and grab it." Asher's grip firmed on her knee before he continued. "There was a buzzing coming from upstairs. We went up to check it out and found a whole lot of shit suggesting that whoever is living there has been watching us. Watching Lexie." Asher paused for a moment. "Those military guys that Evie discovered around town...I'm pretty sure they've been renting Bill's spare room upstairs."

Wyatt cursed as he ran a hand through his hair.

Lexie paused midbite at Asher's words.

"Evie discovered military guys here in Marble Falls?"

Asher hesitated, almost like he wasn't going to tell her. Lexie was about to demand he tell her when he saved her the trouble. "Three. One of them was the man who attacked you. The man I killed."

Lexie swallowed before gaining the courage to ask her next question. "Do you have pictures of them?"

"Lexie—"

"I've seen him," she hurried, cutting Asher off. "I've seen the man who's renting the apartment from Bill. Or one of them at least. I can confirm whether the man renting the apartment is the man Evie has seen around town."

Asher appeared far from happy, but still, he turned to Wyatt and nodded.

Wyatt reached over to lift a laptop that was sitting on the side table. Opening it, he pressed a few keys before swinging the laptop around.

"His name is Dominic."

Lexie's breath caught. It was him. The man she'd run into at the fundraiser, then the pizzeria. The man with the dead, black eyes who'd made Lexie's skin crawl.

And one of the men who'd kidnapped her.

Holy heck. Why hadn't she recognized those eyes when she'd been taken?

"It's him."

She was angry. Angry at herself for not making the connection. Angry, upset, frustrated…everything.

As if sensing her turmoil, Wyatt's expression turned sympathetic. "Fear does strange things to the brain. It can block you from identifying certain information. Making connections and remembering details."

But they were *important* details. Details that could have helped. Saved everyone time and stress.

"If I'd connected that one of my kidnappers was renting Bill's apartment, we could have been at this point ages ago."

Asher placed his hand on her cheek, turning her face toward him. "We all missed things. Your focus has been on our baby, like it should have been. Don't feel guilty about that for a second."

His words comforted her somewhat. But the guilt was still there. Lurking beneath the surface.

Leaning down, he pressed a kiss to her head before turning back to Wyatt. "I got us out of there as quickly as possible. We need to come up with a plan and send a team in to search the place."

Wyatt spun the laptop back to face him. "I'll message the guys. I'm guessing you came to me because you want me to look into—"

"Bill," Asher interrupted.

Lexie almost choked on the bit of chicken she'd just placed in her mouth. "You think Bill's in on this? No way. Bill is a good guy. Why would he want to hurt us?"

Lexie saw regret wash over Asher's face before he spoke. "I don't like to think he would be out to get us, either, but not everyone is who they say they are. And even if Bill is a good guy like we thought, sometimes there are extenuating circumstances that make good people do bad things."

Bad things like intentionally harboring criminals in his restaurant.

"You think someone threatened him?" Lexie murmured in alarm.

Ah jeez, Lexie didn't like to think he may have known. Or that someone had forced him to keep the secret.

Before Asher could answer, Lexie felt it again. The lightest twinge. Pressure low in her abdomen. She was better at not reacting this time but worry filled her.

"I hope we're wrong," Wyatt continued as his fingers flew across the keys. Jesus, the man was a machine when he had a piece of technology in his hands. "I'll see if I can find any useful information on Bill."

Asher and Lexie sat and waited in silence for what felt like a long time when, in reality, it was likely mere minutes. In that time, Asher had begun drawing circles on Lexie's thigh with his thumb. The movement was comforting, particularly when she felt another twinge.

Lexie knew he was worried about her stress. He was probably cursing himself that he'd discovered the information with her in tow. She had no doubt she never would have heard about it otherwise, or at least not until after their baby was born.

"Shit."

At Wyatt's curse, both Asher and Lexie returned their gazes to him. A sinking feeling grew in the pit of Lexie's stomach.

Oh, Bill, what have you done?

Wyatt looked up, all emotion wiped clean from his face. "I took a look into his finances. Don't ask me how because it was in no way legal. I can see that Bill began getting payments the week we chased John Roberts around town."

"Rental payments?" Asher suggested.

Wyatt nodded. "Amounts look about right."

Well, that wasn't suspicious. He probably didn't realize who he was renting to.

Wyatt looked back to the screen. "A bit over a month ago, the payment changed. It increased."

Asher leaned forward. "How much?"

Wyatt raised his eyes. "More than ten times the original amount."

No. No no no. It just didn't make sense. "Bill is a good person, Wyatt. There's no way he would sell us out."

Lexie just couldn't accept that Bill had done anything malicious without a damn good reason.

If possible, Wyatt's face turned grimmer. "The money doesn't stay in his account for long."

"Where does it go?" Asher asked quietly.

Lexie wasn't sure she wanted to know.

"Mostly El Royale. Also Bovada and Super Slots."

Gambling. Bill was a gambler. Lexie never in a million years would have picked that. But then, no one had picked her mother for an alcoholic growing up, either. People let others see what they wanted.

Asher remained silent beside her. His stillness spoke volumes.

Wyatt hit a few more keys. "He has debts spanning over years, showing this is a long-term problem."

Asher scrubbed his free hand over his face. "So, he discovers his new renters aren't playing on the right side of the law, probably threatens to out them, they offer him money to keep his mouth shut."

When Lexie glanced at Asher, she could see the strain on his face. But there was still something that wasn't adding up to her. "Wouldn't it have been easier for them to kill him?"

Why would the people behind Project Arma pay out a large sum of money when the simple solution would be to get rid of the problem?

Wyatt shook his head. "No. Not if they wanted to remain hidden. Bill going missing would raise too many questions."

Oh yes, that made sense.

Another twinge hit Lexie's stomach. Holy heck, if this was the beginnings of labor, baby was not good with timing.

About a month ago, she had grilled Sage about anything and everything to do with labor and birth. Sage had told her that she could feel mild, uneven contractions hours or even days before giving birth. Some women feel them for weeks.

Yikes. Lexie didn't know if she wanted that to be the case for her or not. She did know that now was not a good time to go into labor.

"How the fuck did we not see it?" Asher growled.

Wyatt scowled. "No clue. We *should* have seen it."

Bringing her mind back to the problem at hand, Lexie flicked her gaze between the men. She knew exactly what Asher was doing. Likely what Wyatt was doing, too. Blaming themselves.

Well, that was bullshit. "Addiction of any type is hard to spot. Sometimes, impossible. I would know, I grew up with an addict and no one around us spotted it. Not a single teacher or parent. So in this case, absolutely all the blame for this whole mess lies on Bill for taking the money and those assholes at Project Arma. Now get your asses on the phone and let your team know what's going on."

Wyatt's scowl lessened at Lexie's words, whereas Asher showed a hint of a smile. Wyatt reached for his phone. Asher remained still for another moment.

"You, too, Asher."

Rather than immediately pulling out his cell, he leaned over and planted his lips on Lexie's.

"Damn, I love you."

"I love you, too. Now get on the phone."

Shaking his head, Asher joined Wyatt in calling the team.

AN HOUR LATER, everyone knew what was going on. A raid had been organized for six the next morning.

Leaving Wyatt's home, Asher felt slightly better. Only slightly.

The team knew what was going on, they had a game plan, and if everything worked out, Marble Falls would be that bit safer. But it didn't change the fact that some assholes from out of town had been watching Lexie every damn day.

Clenching the wheel a bit tighter, Asher glanced over to Lexie. He was in awe of her strength. When he had wanted to lose it, it had been her who had kept him on track. Act now, think later.

Reaching over, he placed a hand on her leg.

He loved the woman. But he hated that tonight she'd been in a dangerous situation at the pizzeria because of him. He'd put her life in danger. He'd brought it right to her doorstep.

"Stop it," Lexie gently scolded.

Asher's mouth pulled up at the corner. "Stop what?"

"Whatever thoughts are running through your head about anything and everything being your fault."

"Are you a mind reader, woman?"

Lexie shrugged. "Don't need to be a mind reader to know when you're tearing yourself down internally. It's written all over your face."

Christ, he should be better than that. He *was* better than that. When the problem didn't involve Lexie. "I don't mask my emotions enough in front of you."

"Enough? You should never mask your emotions in front of me."

Asher looked over and smiled—but the smile dropped when Lexie's face pinched in pain. She'd been doing that all evening. Every time he'd asked her about it, she'd avoided the question.

"You okay, Lex?"

She looked over to Asher, her amber eyes shining in the moonlight. "There's actually something I need to tell you."

He got another of those bad feelings. Was there another hidden threat? Were there more plans he needed to make? Did he need to go after this whole damn town to make sure his woman was safe?

"It's about my appointment with Sage." Lexie rubbed her hand over her stomach. Asher's body tensed in anticipation about what she was going to say. "I had this plan for us to have an intimate dinner and tell you then."

Forcing calm into his limbs, Asher rubbed Lexie's leg. "It's okay. You can tell me now."

Lexie paused. Desperation to know what she was hiding tore at him.

Opening his mouth, Asher was about to attempt to soothe Lexie into opening up to him—but his full attention returned to the road when a car suddenly sped out from a side street.

The high beams were on and the car was close. Too close.

Cursing out loud, Asher swung his rearview mirror away so the light wasn't directly hitting him.

Pressing his foot harder on the accelerator, he could see in the side mirrors that the car behind him also accelerated.

Lexie started to turn her body around, but Asher stopped her by placing an arm across her chest.

"Don't move. Keep your seat belt on and go as low in the seat as is safe," Asher commanded, leaving no room for debate.

He could hear Lexie's heartbeat accelerate but pushed that fact to the back of his mind. Taking a corner much faster than he was comfortable with while Lexie was in the car, Asher hit dial on his phone.

He didn't know who he'd called, just that it was one of the guys.

"Striker," Bodie answered.

"Got a tail. He's speeding up and blinding me with his high beams." Asher bit the words out.

"Location?"

"Coming up to Lakeside Pavilion. I'm gonna take some detours and try to lose them."

"I'll call the guys and circle the area. Stay safe until then."

The line went dead as Asher reached into his IWB holster and withdrew his gun. Ignoring the small gasp from Lexie, he placed the weapon on the middle console in case he needed it.

The vehicle behind again inched closer, forcing Asher to speed up.

"Asher"—Lexie's voice trembled—"maybe we should stop. You're a good shot."

Asher's gaze flicked to Lexie before pulling back to the road. "No."

That was a *hell no*. Not with Lexie in tow. Asher had no idea how many people were in that car or how much of a threat they posed.

"Lexie, brace your hands on the car dash. Make sure your seat belt isn't on your stomach."

Lexie sucked in a shaky breath but did as he said.

Her panic was thick in the air. He needed to get her to safety. He just had to run this guy around long enough for his team to get to them.

In the next moment, a second car suddenly appeared from another side street and hit the back bumper of Asher's car.

Asher fought to control the spinning car by working the wheel.

When his car came to a stop, Asher's gaze flew to Lexie. She was gulping in deep breaths, but she had avoided any collisions with the car interior. She seemed unharmed. Tuning in, he could hear that her heart rate was galloping but the baby's was steady.

"Stay down, Lex. Everything will all be okay."

Asher surveyed the scene and waited. The car that had been trailing theirs was parked behind. He could see the outline of two men in the front.

The car that had hit them had moved in front. One man sat in driver's seat.

Asher waited for them to make their move.

Finally, the man in the driver's seat of the car behind stepped out.

Reaching to the ground, Asher lifted his gun before kicking his door off the car. He kept the car so that it was always in his line of sight. So that Lexie was always in his line of sight.

When the man ran toward him, Asher cut out all emotion. Swinging his body around, he kicked a foot out, hitting the enemy in the gut. Before the guy could recover, Asher threw his arm out, punching the guy in the throat.

Showing no emotion, Asher fought the man in front of him. The assailant met Asher blow for blow. He was strong. But Asher was stronger.

When another shadow crept around the car, Asher knew it was time to end it. In one lethal move, he snapped the man's neck before moving to the next.

Grabbing the other man around the throat, Asher was about to follow suit when sudden footsteps near Lexie pulled his attention.

The momentary distraction cost him, as the man flipped Asher onto the ground. A boot came at his ribs, but Asher was able to grab the leg and flip the other man to the ground.

Jumping to his feet, Asher was moments away from killing the asshole when a whimper from Lexie pulled his attention.

Asher stopped dead—and his eyes shot to her.

A gun was pointed at her head. Bill was holding the weapon.

"Don't make me do it, Asher."

Asher sucked in deep breaths to tame his wild rage at seeing Lexie so close to harm. Stepping back, he let his arms drop.

Bill swiftly turned the gun to point at Asher and fired.

The last thing Asher heard was Lexie's cry before his world went black.

CHAPTER 27

*L*exie gave the rope around her wrists another tug. Nothing. Not even an ounce of leeway gained.

She sagged into her restraints. It was no use. She was stuck, tied to this wooden chair until her kidnappers decided otherwise.

Her eyes lifted to Asher's still form across from her. Anxiety shot through her yet again. God, she wished he would open his eyes.

Lexie estimated that at least a couple of hours had passed since he'd been shot. The only thing helping her keep it together was the fact she could see his chest lifting and falling with his breaths. That, and the fact that blood wasn't pouring from his chest.

Lexie could only assume that the gun Bill had used hadn't been a normal handgun. It had to have been some sort of tranquilizer. A strong one, if she went by how long Asher had been out.

While Lexie was tied with rope, Asher sat opposite her also on a chair, but he'd been chained to a metal pole that ran from the floor to the ceiling. His upper body was hunched over.

After Asher had been shot, Bill had tied a rag around her eyes and driven them somewhere. But not before she'd recognized the still form on the ground as Thomas. The man who had kidnapped her all those months ago.

Lexie had tried to talk to Bill in the car. Heck, she'd just about begged the man for help, compassion, anything! But she'd wasted her breath. He'd given her nothing.

The next thing Lexie knew, they were here, in a room with no windows and no natural light. It looked like a basement.

Lexie winced as a strong pain shot through her abdomen. She was about ninety percent sure she was in labor. And it scared the crap out of her. Over the past couple hours, the surges had become progressively stronger and closer together.

Oh, bubs, please wait.

Although Lexie was doing the best she could to hide the pain, it was getting more and more difficult. But the last thing she wanted was some nutty professors from Project Arma to realize her baby was close to being born. The thought of them snatching him away from her left her in a pool of terror.

Lexie needed time. Time for the guys to find her. Time to get to Sage.

Asher's groan drew her gaze up.

Please, heaven almighty, please be waking up.

Finally, Asher's eyes began to open. Immediately, his gaze darted around the room. As soon as it landed on Lexie, a deadly stillness came over him. He did a once-over of her body before he tugged at his restraints.

"They used rope for me. Chains for you," Lexie murmured with regret.

She had hoped that once Asher had woken, he would be able to break them both out. Watching him tug on the unrelenting chains, she doubted that would be happening.

Lexie ground her teeth as another contraction hit. She was lucky that Asher was distracted at that moment because there was no way to hide the pain. It was like nothing she'd felt before. And it was the strongest one yet.

"Are you okay?" Asher asked, his head lifting.

Lexie considered his question. Other than feeling an unbearable pain to her stomach every few minutes while trying to dull an overwhelming fear of birthing their baby in a kidnapper's basement, she was great.

"They didn't hurt me." Lexie deflected from what was currently going on in her body.

Asher blew out a breath. "Good. That's good."

She wasn't sure if he was telling her or trying to convince himself. Probably a bit of both.

Asher went back to struggling with the chains while Lexie attempted to push past the consistent surges that were ripping through her body.

Sitting was becoming more painful by the minute. Her body needed to stand, move, walk around. Heck, a nice hot shower wouldn't go astray.

But she knew she wouldn't be getting any of those things. So, she needed to deal with her circumstances. Survive until help arrived and hold it together for the sake of her baby.

You can do this, Lexie.

Closing her eyes, she had to make herself believe those words. Otherwise, she'd crack.

Footsteps sounded on stairs above them before the door opened. The man who walked in first was the man who had eyes as black as midnight. Eyes that haunted her nightmares.

Dominic.

Behind the man was Bill, and then an older woman wearing a white lab coat.

Swallowing a lump in her throat, she had a bad feeling. Lab coat meant scientist or doctor, right? Neither of those things sounded particularly appealing to Lexie in her current state.

Where Bill and the woman stopped a few feet from the door,

Dominic kept moving forward. He walked straight up to Asher and punched him in the face.

Lexie cried out as blood dripped from Asher's mouth. He barely reacted. Simply spat a mouthful of blood onto the ground before turning back to the man, fire in his eyes.

"That was for Packer and Thomas," the man snarled.

Fear clawed up Lexie's throat at the sound of his familiar voice.

Asher showed no fear as he sneered at the thug. "Who the fuck are you?"

The man crossed his arm. "Consider me the new *you*, asshole. New and improved."

Asher's eyes narrowed. "What the fuck does that mean?"

Dominic suddenly swung his arm again, backhanding Asher.

Swinging her head to Bill, she pleaded with the man. "Bill, do something."

Although Lexie caught a flicker of what she could only assume was remorse on his face, Bill kept his eyes straight ahead. He didn't make a move to help. The man didn't even open his mouth to stop Dominic.

Another surge hit drawing her attention away from the violence and forcing her to focus on her breathing. She'd come to realize that every contraction was like a wave. She breathed through to the peak of the pain, then her body slowly worked its way back to normal.

At the feel of wetness on her hands, Lexie realized she'd clenched her fists so tightly that her nails had cut into her skin.

"That old man's not gonna help you," Dominic snickered once he was done with Asher. "He's here for one reason. To make sure he gets his money."

Lexie had held out hope for Bill. Even with the evidence Wyatt had pulled up and even after he'd tranquilized Asher, she had still had hope that there was some good in him.

Swallowing her disappointment, Lexie turned her attention to the lady in the white coat as she stepped forward. "If you're done, I'm going to do my job."

With a neutral expression and a stiff spine, she dropped a bag to the ground and pulled out a syringe. It was an empty syringe, but that didn't do much to calm Lexie's nerves. Her entire body tensed as the lady walked toward her.

"Don't you fucking touch her!" Asher snarled as he fought his restraints harder. His muscles were visibly tensing, and the metal pole groaned at his movement.

Dominic reeled back and punched Asher in the gut, causing him to cough up more blood.

"Asher, stop it," Lexie begged. "She's just taking blood. I'm okay."

Everything about their situation was hard enough. Add watching Asher get beaten to within an inch of his life and it was almost too much to bear.

Asher went still as the lady reached Lexie. The anger came off him in waves, and Lexie had no doubt, if he wasn't restrained, the woman would be dead.

Taking the cap off the syringe, the woman plunged the needle into a vein in Lexie's right arm. She wasn't surprised that the lady didn't bother with an attempt to be gentle.

On a normal day, Lexie would be spitting fire at the sting. Today, the pain to her arm was nothing compared to the pain in other parts of her body.

As if she'd conjured one up, another contraction hit at the exact moment the lady pulled out the needle.

"It's not that bad, dear," the lady said without an ounce of compassion, obviously mistaking the reason behind Lexie's cringe.

Closing her eyes for a moment, Lexie willed the pain to pass.

When it was over, she glanced at Asher, noticing his eyes were narrowed. Shit, Lexie had no doubt he was catching on to what was happening. That was if he hadn't already.

She attempted to clear her face of any expression, not wanting Asher to do anything that would get him further injured.

Turning to the lady, she watched her package the sample. "What do you plan to do with my blood?"

"The same thing we intend to do with the baby. Study it."

Terror stole Lexie's words. Her body turned icy as panic flared inside her. They wanted to take her baby. Take it and study it. Like it was a specimen that needed to be analyzed, rather than a living, breathing baby. *Her* baby.

The woman hadn't even flinched when she'd said the words. Did she not have a heart?

"Never gonna happen," Asher said quietly.

Lexie looked across to see his eyes on her. He was speaking to her. Not to the woman. Not the men in the room. Just to her. Confirming he was going to stop them.

Some of the fear eased from her body. Because she believed him. If Asher said he was going to protect their child, then that was exactly what he was going to do.

Dominic snorted. "If that's what you think, it's no wonder they needed to upgrade their soldiers."

"Yeah, you're so fucking tough you needed an old man to pull a gun on me to keep you alive."

Dominic took a threatening step forward but stopped when his phone beeped. Pulling it out of his back pocket, he read the message before turning to the lady in the white coat.

"He's gonna need a bit more time to get here. Wants the ultrasound done and images sent through now."

With the same clinical look, the lady nodded. "We'll have to untie her. She needs to be lying flat."

Dominic's brows pulled together. "Can't you just pull the bitch's top up?"

Asher growled. His muscles were visible bunching and she noticed he was still pulling at the chains. Lexie didn't think there was any way he could break them. But then again, she didn't really know the full extent of what he could do.

"No," the lady said, seemingly unfazed by the big thug.

"Fine."

Dominic took a step forward but stopped when Asher lurched against his chains. "You fucking touch her and I'll rip your damn throat out."

Dominic regarded him with a chuckle. "Yeah? And how exactly are you gonna do that? Those are specially made metal chains. Tried and tested against men like us."

"Ever tried and tested them against a man protecting his woman?"

The lady in the lab coat stepped behind Lexie and began working the knot. "For goodness' sake, *I'll* do it." It took her less than a minute to get the knots undone. "Lie on the ground and lift your shirt."

Lexie eyed the dusty floor but did as she was told. Lucky she didn't have an allergy to dust because this place was covered in it.

Just as Lexie crouched on the ground, a huge contraction hit her stomach. *Oh God, not now.*

Bending forward, she pretended to be moving slowly when really she was gritting her teeth through the pain.

"So, if you plan to keep us, why not tell us where we are?" Asher asked, clearly deflecting their attention.

Doing her best to relax her body through the contraction, Lexie sucked in deep breaths. When the worst of the pain was over, she finished moving to her back.

"You haven't figured it out? You're in the basement of the fucking pizzeria."

Lexie's eyes widened, looking around the room again. She'd had no idea there was a basement at the pizzeria.

A spark of hope filled her. The team knew that Bill was involved. When they found out her and Asher were missing, surely Wyatt or Evie would uncover this space under the shop.

"Why would you bring us here?" Asher asked as the woman beside Lexie pulled out her equipment.

"You left us with no fucking choice. Our attempt to take her didn't work out because of you fuckers, then you never left her side."

Asher shrugged. "Okay. That doesn't explain why the pizzeria."

The man kicked Asher in the shin. Again, he barely reacted.

"The organization is in between locations at the moment. So, we'll just wait here until they get us." Dominic smirked. "This worked out better, anyway. This way, we don't just get the baby, we get you, too."

The lady covered Lexie's stomach with cold gel before pulling out a machine. After pressing a few buttons, lights came on. She then proceeded to press a probe to Lexie's stomach.

Why they needed scans of her stomach at this exact moment, Lexie had no idea. But as long as her baby remained unharmed, she would do as she was told and remain calm.

Her gaze drifted to Bill. He had remained quiet since entering the room. The pizza maker looked bad. Sick with fear. Large dark circles shadowed his eyes. And his gaze kept flicking from Dominic to the lady. She could even see sweat soaking into his shirt.

Lexie wondered if he was finally realizing he was in over his head. Or maybe he was feeling guilty. Guilty that he'd exchanged the lives of his friends to sustain his gambling addiction.

But that was probably wishful thinking on Lexie's behalf. Wanting to believe that the man had a conscience.

"I say we just cut the thing from her now and let her bleed out," Dominic sneered.

Asher's leg flew out and hit him in the balls.

Collapsing forward, Dominic growled before his head lifted and he looked at Asher.

Lexie knew exactly what was about to happen. And it sent a bolt of panic through her.

Dominic lunged.

Lexie sat up quickly and watched helplessly as Dominic began to repeatedly hit Asher in the face.

When the man didn't stop. She tried to move forward but was grabbed from behind by the lady. Her surprisingly strong arms stopped Lexie from going anywhere, her fingers digging into Lexie's flesh.

"Asher—" Lexie called, real fear in her voice.

"Stay the hell back, Lexie!" Asher roared from where he was being pummeled in the chair.

Lexie looked to Bill for help, but still, the man just stood there, motionless. Uncertainty in his eyes.

CHAPTER 28

"*E*nough!"

Asher's body throbbed, but at the sound of the familiar voice, he conjured up the energy to lift his head.

It can't be.

Every muscle in Asher's body tightened at the sight of the man he'd once considered a father figure. He looked exactly as Asher remembered. Which shouldn't be a surprise. It had been only a couple of years.

His dark eyes met Asher's. "Striker. It's been a while."

Asher's pain faded into insignificance.

"Commander Hylar. I was starting to wonder if you'd show your face around here." Asher spat blood to the ground, keeping eye contact with the man who'd pulled them into all of this.

The commander stepped forward. He had a scar that ran across his right eye, and he stood well over six feet tall. Asher knew that being slightly older did nothing to detract from the man's physical capabilities. He was strong and knew how to fight.

"You boys have disappointed me."

Asher fought for calm, but his voice dripped with unconcealed rage as he spoke. "We were nothing but loyal to you, and you sold us out. Gambled with our fucking lives."

The commander cocked his head. "Is that what you think? That someone offered me some money and I just volunteered you for an experiment?"

That's exactly what Asher thought.

From his peripheral vision, Asher saw Lexie wince again. He struggled to keep his eyes off her and on Commander Hylar. She was in pain. Which meant he had to get them out, dammit. Away from these psychopaths.

"Tell me it isn't true," Asher growled.

"It isn't true." The commander's response was instant. And Asher couldn't detect one sign of insincerity. His pupils remained the same, his heart rate steady.

But then again, the commander was trained to lie under pressure.

"I wasn't bought, Asher. I was the buyer."

Shock rendered Asher motionless. He had to toss the words over in his head before he could make sense of them.

"What are you saying? That you're responsible for creating Project Arma?"

He prayed the man denied it.

At the sight of Hylar's smile, pain ricocheted through Asher's chest.

"Creating. Masterminding. Call it what you like. The idea was mine."

No. None of it made sense to him. He'd suspected the man was involved due to greed. But not this. It was a level of betrayal that Asher struggled to wrap his head around.

"It came to me when your team was training," the commander continued. "So damn strong and lethal, but still human. Too many weaknesses. At first, it was my goal to make the team stronger. Faster. But you'd always reach a limit, wouldn't you? Then it hit me—what if I could make you *more*? So I got the ball rolling. All it took was reaching out to the right people, putting in some fake paperwork, and Project Arma was born."

Utter disbelief coursed through Asher. He had never had more desire to kill a man than he did in that moment. Commander Hylar hadn't just pulled them into this mess, he'd manufactured the whole thing.

"You could have killed us," Asher snarled.

Asher had seen the images of previous drug recipients. Dead. Disfigured. Others survived but with significant brain damage.

Visions of his brothers injured or worse had lingered in Asher's mind. All because of this man.

The commander frowned. "We tested for years first. Many died to achieve the perfect drug. They died to make you stronger. Faster. You received a tried and tested version, Striker. Everything you are now, I gave to you."

That was bullshit. Physical strength and speed don't make a man who he is. It's mental strength and knowing right from wrong. Asher may be stronger and faster, but what made him the man he was inside was all his own doing. And his brothers'.

Hylar took a step closer to Asher. "That's why I've been watching you. I know how dangerous you are. For a while I hoped you would join us. That was always the plan. But I can see now that's not the case. And I can't have you messing anything up. Project Arma has become too valuable. That's why we had to create weapons against you. You've already experienced Tovid. What a pleasure that was to see it used against Hunter and Shylah. You experienced it, too, didn't you, Striker?"

Asher remained silent. During a mission to one of the Project Arma locations, Asher had been injected with what was, at the time, an unknown drug. It had sent him into a rage. Eden had been injected, too. It was a biological weapon, there was no question about it.

"We're working on improving it. Making it stronger. You also experienced the chemical spray we made."

"So, you're what? Spending all your time coming up with ways to stop us?" Asher snapped.

"And watching you." The commander half smiled. "Dominic here has been in town for a while, and you didn't even know."

Asher didn't need reminding. The fact that the asshole had been close and watching his woman made him want to kick his own ass. He shouldn't have missed it.

"He was assigned to watch your team. That night you went to Lexie's mother's house, he followed. The next day, he returned to the house. That was when we found out she was pregnant. And that was when the target changed from your team—to her."

A hundred different ways to destroy the man were running through Asher's head.

The commander's focus turned to Lexie. Asher immediately wanted to tear the man's head off just for looking at her.

Strain was now visible on her face, her breathing ragged. He was running out of time.

Giving another silent tug on his restraints, he could feel the headway he was making. He was sure he could break the chains.

"But unlike your brothers, you, my son, have earned your way back into my good graces. Look what you've given me. The next generation!"

The commander spoke as if the baby was his. There wasn't a chance the asshole would be getting his hands on their child.

Hylar turned his attention to the lady in the lab coat. "Boy or girl?"

"Boy."

Asher held his breath at the word. They were having a boy. He let that sink in for a moment, gaze meeting Lexie's. Tears gathered in her eyes.

Hylar clapped his hands together. "Excellent."

Asher's attention moved back to him. The excitement in the man's eyes made Asher sick.

"We can test how strong and durable this child is. Train him."

Commander Hylar's gaze returned to Asher. "You will father the first member of the next generation of my army."

Not a chance.

Asher gave his restraints another silent tug.

He noticed the sweat building on Lexie's forehead. The commander would also notice what was going on soon.

"Because the first generation is so damn strong?" Asher snarled, wanting to distract from Lexie. "I've seen them at work. A bit sloppy. I mean, you sent men to trail me who couldn't hide the tail. Men broke into Lexie's apartment by breaking the damn door handle. They couldn't even remember to lock the door of the van they took her in."

Dominic growled from Asher's right.

"You're right," Hylar conceded. "Dominic here is well-trained, but the men I called in when we found out Lexie was pregnant were less so. I assumed Lexie would be an easy target. I assumed wrong, as I underestimated your care for her. That mistake won't be repeated."

There was no question in Asher's mind—Hylar needed to die. Every word the man said just confirmed that he wouldn't stop hunting them and their loved ones. Not until they were dead or working with him.

Just then, Lexie groaned and scrunched her eyes shut, clearly unable to hide the pain any longer.

Fuck. He needed to break the restraints right the hell now.

"And we're in labor! Great, did you get the blood sample?" the commander asked the lady.

"Affirmative."

The commander nodded his head. "Let's move. Shauna, give Asher the sedative. Dominic carry him out of here."

"You fucking, asshole!" Asher seethed, no longer hiding his attempts to break the chains.

"I hope this teaches you the importance of loyalty, Striker. You could have been my number one."

"I can just knock him out for you, Commander," Dominic sneered.

"No. But kill the old man."

Bill's gasp sounded as Shauna neared Asher with the syringe. He gave another tug.

Sticking the needle into his arm, she'd injected half the liquid before he finally managed to snap the chain.

Asher yanked his arm away from the syringe.

"What the hell?" Dominic or the commander gasped. Asher didn't have time to wonder who.

Swiping the syringe from the woman's fingers, he plunged it into her skin. She gave a small hiss of surprise before falling to the ground. Clearly, her body was less tolerant to the drug than his.

Asher caught sight of the gun as Dominic pulled it out. Before the man could even aim, Asher swiped it from his fingers. He held the weapon for only a second before Dominic kicked Asher's arm, then lunged at him, knocking them both to the ground.

Feeling weaker than normal, Asher knew the half dose of sedative was clouding his mind and stealing his strength. He pushed through the fog, unwilling to leave Lexie unprotected.

He rolled away as Dominic swung a fist, then jumped onto the man's back. Ignoring the blood still dripping down his face from the earlier beating, Asher threw an arm around Dominic's neck and swiftly tightened his grip.

Dominic choked and grabbed at the arm taking away his breath.

Just as Asher thought he had him subdued, Dominic flipped their bodies, then stood over Asher.

The man made a lethal error when he pulled his arm back a fraction, giving Asher an extra half second to react.

That was all the time he needed.

As Dominic's fist came down, Asher grabbed his arm with lightning reflexes, twisting until a pop echoed through the room.

In the background, Asher heard a scuffle but couldn't afford the distraction.

Dominic drew back and howled in pain, his arm now hanging from his shoulder.

Asher caught sight of the knife strapped to the man's thigh. Before Dominic could recover, he swiped the knife and lunged, digging it into Dominic's neck.

Blood splattered on Asher's face as the man choked, spewing red liquid.

Not sparing the dead man a second thought, Asher pulled the knife free and shoved it into his belt, looking around wildly.

The room was empty except for Bill shaking in the corner.

Asher didn't stop to think. He needed to get to Lexie. If the commander got her inside a vehicle, it would make Asher's job ten times harder to get her back.

Taking the steps two at a time, he stopped at the top and listened.

Then he heard it—Lexie's heavy breathing.

Moving through the shop, Asher pushed through the back door into the alley.

He spotted the commander immediately. The asshole was dragging Lexie across the grounds.

Another mistake on your part, Commander.

Asher stepped outside just as the commander spun around, placing a gun to Lexie's head.

Outwardly, he showed no reaction. Internally, he was thinking up a million different ways to end the man for holding a gun on his woman.

"Come any closer and I'll shoot her. We don't need her, just the baby."

Lexie's hands were at her stomach, her face pale.

"You're not taking her *or* our baby."

The commander inched closer to the car. "I am, Striker. One way or another, I am taking this baby."

Asher's hand slowly reached for the knife in his belt. But he needed to be careful. One wrong move could prove deadly for Lexie.

"You trained me yourself, Commander. Taught me how to fight. Kill. Then you made me stronger. Faster." Asher paused and cocked his head to the side. "You made a mistake, though. You misjudged my integrity. My ethics. Now we're on opposite teams. You should have known better than to create a killer, then turn that killer into an enemy."

The commander's eyes widened, a hint of fear showing. An emotion Asher had never seen on the other man before.

In the background, Asher could hear Bill's footsteps inching closer to the back door.

"This all could have been different if you'd have come and joined us, Striker."

Different? There wasn't a single scenario in which things could have been different. Not for Asher, at least.

"No thanks, I'd rather destroy you and your minions than join you." Asher's hand wrapped around the knife. His fingers itched to throw it, but he had to wait for the right moment.

Just then, Lexie groaned, holding her stomach tighter. Her legs gave out, but she didn't hit the ground. The commander's tight hold kept her upright.

"It's okay, Lex. You'll be okay," Asher called out, attempting to soothe her even as the commander took another step toward the car. "Before you go, tell me. What is the end plan in all this? What do you hope to achieve?"

Usually so composed, the commander paused, excitement creeping into his eyes. The asshole *wanted* Asher to know. "My plan? I'm going to build an army like the world has never seen. Unstoppable warriors. Lethal in every sense of the word. Can you imagine how powerful I'll be?"

Not a chance that was happening. Not if Asher and his team had anything to say about it.

Just then, a car pulled up beside the one the commander was trying to get to.

Asher cursed under his breath as Carter and the other six members of his team stepped out.

The former SEALs were part of Project Arma at the same time as Asher and his team. And they were just as lethal.

But that was where the similarities stopped. Where Asher and his team were on the right side, fighting for good, Carter's team wanted the same things as the commander.

They positioned themselves in a straight line on either side of the commander. Hylar's mouth stretched into a smile. "This doesn't have to end with you dying, my son. You can join us." There was genuine hope in the man's voice as he spoke.

"I'd rather die ten times over."

"That can be arranged," Carter muttered with a smirk from his position directly beside the commander.

"My boy, you're outnumbered, and we're taking your woman and child. Surely coming with us is a better choice than losing them."

Asher's eyes cut across the eight men in front of him. One on one, he would likely win. Eight on one, not a chance.

Taking a breath, Asher couldn't believe he was considering it. But there was no way he was letting Lexie out of his sight.

"We have company," Carter snarled.

Asher heard them, too. A small smile tugged at his lips. He knew exactly who it was.

In the next few minutes, things happened quickly.

Asher's team converged on the group. Some jumped from nearby windows, others emerged at the end of the alley. They didn't stop to assess. They attacked. Each man on Asher's team taking a man on Carter's.

None of them took the commander—he was for Asher.

Asher already knew that if Lexie hadn't been smack-bang in the middle of the commotion, gunfire or tear gas would have been used. To protect the baby, hand-to-hand combat was necessary.

The commander's eyes flew wide before his gaze zeroed in on the car beside him.

Not a fucking chance, old man.

Before Hylar could make a move, Asher's fingers tightened around the knife.

Flinging the weapon through the air, he hit the commander dead in the hand that was carrying the gun.

Both the gun and Lexie dropped from his hold as his face contorted in pain.

Without a second thought, Asher took off toward the commander. Before he could reach him, gunfire rang out behind him. Asher froze in his tracks.

His gaze flung to Lexie, scanning every inch of her. No blood. No bullet wound. Next his attention moved to Hylar. Blood gushed from the man's right thigh.

Who the hell shot him?

Asher whipped his head around, his gaze flying to the pizzeria door. Bill stood there, gun firmly in hand, pointed at the commander.

The sound of a car engine pulled Asher's attention back to the alley just in time to see Hylar racing away.

No!

Asher took a step toward the retreating vehicle only to stop at Lexie's pained cry. He was by her side in an instant.

Pushing away the anger he felt about the commander's escape, he focused all his attention on Lexie. She had tucked her body into a ball on the ground.

He attempted to shield her body with his own as he crouched beside her.

"The baby's coming, Asher." Her voice was a mix of pain and fear.

"I'm going to get you to Sage," he whispered, lifting her into his arms.

Asher kept her body close to his. His brothers would watch his back. His priority was Lexie and getting her away from the war that was raging around him.

But Asher knew too well that the real war would not be over for a long time. Not until the commander and every man who worked for him was buried deep in the ground.

CHAPTER 29

*L*exie studied every inch of Fletcher's adorable baby face. Her baby. It had been a week since giving birth, and she still had to pinch herself that she was a mother.

"He is the spitting image of his father," Evie cooed from her spot on the sofa beside Lexie.

"Except for those amber eyes," Shylah added. "They're all you, Lex."

Lexie smiled at her friends' comments. They sat in her and Asher's home. Today, everyone got to come around to meet Fletcher for the first time. The girls sat in the living room while the boys were having celebratory drinks in the kitchen.

Asher and Lexie had spent the first week after Fletcher arrived sequestered, just the three of them. Spending some much-needed time together in their newborn bubble.

It had been amazing.

Who was she kidding? It was better than amazing. It had been the best freaking week of her life. She had a beautiful, healthy baby boy and a wonderful partner in Asher. It didn't get much better than that.

"I was worried before he was born that I wouldn't know what

to do." Lexie's eyes were glued to her perfect bundle as she spoke. "But it's true what they say. You just follow your instincts and let your love for the little human take over."

Her fear had been so real and so tangible her entire pregnancy. Even when she thought she was okay. Even when she told herself repeatedly that she would be a kickass mother, there was still fear. Fear that her past would dictate the type of mother that she would be.

But it doesn't. And it took holding Fletcher in her arms to fully realize that. To realize that her past wouldn't touch her. The only person who would decide the type of parent she would be and the future she would provide to her child was her.

Lexie lifted her hand and gently stroked Fletcher's face. He was perfection. Not touching him seemed physically impossible. She was drawn to this little soul in every way possible.

When her eyes finally lifted, Lexie glanced over at Shylah with uncertainty. She knew her friend continued to struggle with the fact that she couldn't have her own babies.

Shylah's stare was stuck on Fletcher, a smile on her face. "Fletcher is absolutely beautiful. Perfect even. I'm really happy for you both."

At the sincerity in her friend's voice, Lexie smiled again. "Thank you. I'm just glad I made it to the hospital in time. There was a real possibility I was going to give birth right there in the alley, in the middle of the chaos."

Lexie joked about it now, but of course, the reality was both she and Fletcher had been at serious risk that day. If the team hadn't arrived when they had, everything could have panned out very differently.

A shiver coursed down Lexie's spine at the thought. She lifted her gaze to Asher as he stood with the guys. His eyes were already on her. Heated. Predatory.

Of course they were. The man was probably listening to every word she said.

Asher had been beyond amazing throughout the last week. He hadn't just been a great dad. He'd been an amazing partner, too, and had far exceeded her expectations.

He'd been a bit over the top with security but Lexie had a feeling that wouldn't change for a while—if ever. Which was fine with her. The safety of her family came first.

"The guys tend to always make it just in time," Evie said, pulling Lexie's attention back to her friends.

Lexie laughed. "A little earlier would have saved me some stress."

"Do you know what's happened with Bill?" Shylah asked, her expression turning somber.

At the mention of the pizzeria owner, Lexie got a sick feeling in her stomach. She felt angry at the man. Angry and betrayed. She knew he had an addiction and she understood addiction to a certain extent.

Addiction, whether that be to alcohol, gambling, or anything, was a disease. And it didn't discriminate. It made people desperate.

Lexie got that. She understood it. But it didn't change what he'd done.

The only reason Bill had shot Hylar in the end was because the man had wanted him dead. Not to save Lexie. Not to save her baby.

"Asher's been sketchy on the details," Lexie said quietly. She knew he was only trying to protect her, though it frustrated her that she wasn't getting all the information.

"No one's stepped foot inside the pizzeria," Shylah said in a hushed tone.

Evie leaned forward and spoke in an equally quiet voice. "I overheard Luca on the phone to one of the guys yesterday. Bill disappeared after he shot the commander. They're going to search for him. It sounded like it would be a race on who would find him first. The guys, or the people behind Project Arma."

Lexie's gaze drifted back down to her sleeping boy. She didn't feel bad for the older man. He was an adult and had made his own decisions.

"Girls' nights won't be the same," Shylah said, changing the subject.

Lexie shook her head. "When people told me babies sleep a lot, they weren't joking. I foresee many girls' nights in the future. Just be prepared to have a sleeping Fletcher around the place. And Sage definitely needs an invite."

Sage had been a powerhouse throughout the pregnancy. Then at the birth, the doctor had been a damn legend. Her calm voice and gentle nature had basically stopped Lexie from losing her mind. As far as Lexie was concerned, the woman was a friend for life and would be receiving yearly Christmas cards.

Evie nodded. "Yes, I agree. She's lovely."

"We just need to convince the supersoldiers over there," Shylah remarked, indicating to the guys with her head.

Lexie shook her head. "Those guys consider everyone outside of this room a threat."

Evie nudged Lexie's shoulder. "So, get ready to never be left unprotected."

"I have a feeling you guys will be more heavily protected than the darn president," Shylah agreed.

Lexie's arms tightened around Fletcher. "That's okay. If I'm protected, Fletcher's protected. They won't be getting their hands on him."

Not while either of us are around.

Lexie glanced up as Asher moved to the door. He pulled it open moments before the bell rang.

Because Asher took up the whole doorway, Lexie was unable to see who it was. Then the woman spoke, and Lexie recognized the voice immediately.

Rising from the sofa, Lexie kept Fletcher securely in her arms as she moved to stand next to Asher.

Her mother stood on the other side of the door, looking unsure.

Shock rendered Lexie speechless for a moment. Gwen looked different. Better. More put together. The shadows under her eyes were lighter. Not gone, but not as distinct. And her usual rumpled clothing actually looked clean.

"Mom. What are you doing here?"

Gwen was wringing her hands, clearly nervous. "Hi, honey. I wanted to pop in to see you. I was wondering if we could talk?"

Lexie's mother had never "popped in" to talk.

Turning to Asher, Lexie transferred Fletcher to his arms. "I'll be back in in a few minutes."

Asher's gaze scanned the area once more before flicking back to Lexie. "Keep the door open." Then he leaned down to kiss her temple before moving back inside.

Lexie stepped out and sat on the steps leading to the street. She only had to wait a moment for her mother to follow. Another minute of silence passed before Lexie eventually broke it.

"How did you know where to find me?"

Gwen was still fidgeting with her hands as she answered, "I knew you were in Marble Falls. I got to town and asked a few people. A lady at a bakery knew where I could find you."

Ah. Mrs. Potter. World-class baker and holder of all of Marble Falls' information. Including everybody's whereabouts.

When Gwen didn't volunteer any more information, Lexie finally asked the big question. "What are you doing here, Mom?"

Gwen swallowed before looking down at her shoes. "I need you to know that I didn't tell them anything."

"Them?"

"The people who came and asked about you. They offered money but I refused." Gwen raised her worried gaze to Lexie. "I swear, Lexie. I didn't say a word."

"I know it was Albert."

Gwen nodded, her eyes becoming misty. "I'm sorry, baby girl.

I didn't know. I got home one day, and he had all this money. I asked him where he got it and he told me. Lex, if I knew he was going to do that, I never would have told him you were pregnant. I was just excited for you. I left him the next day. I swear."

"I believe you, Mom."

There were a couple days when Lexie had questioned whether her mother would have passed that information on. It was obvious after Albert's visit that wasn't the case.

"I've been trying to clean myself up since I left him." Gwen continued to stare at her hands.

"You look good." Better than she had in a long time. Possibly ever. Or at least as far back as Lexie could remember.

Gwen turned her gaze to Lexie again. There was a big pause where she could tell the woman was working up to saying something important. "I'm sorry I was never the mother you needed or deserved."

Lexie sucked in a long breath. Whatever she'd thought her mother was going to say, it wasn't that.

"I appreciate that, Mom."

Lexie couldn't say she forgave Gwen. She didn't know if she'd ever get to that point. But it was nice to hear her mother acknowledge her mistake.

"When your father left me, it destroyed me. But I should have been stronger. For you. I was never as strong as you, Lex." The tears that had been glistening in Gwen's eyes now dropped down her cheeks. "You're everything I'm not. Strong. Independent. I don't deserve you as a daughter. You will be an amazing mother to that baby. Far better than I was."

Lexie's eyes softened. "Fletcher. His name is Fletcher. And thank you."

Gwen smiled but then looked uncertain again. "I was hoping that maybe if I stayed clean and got a place close by, you might let me visit you every so often. Be a small part of the life you've built. I know I don't deserve it—"

"That would be nice."

Hope flickered in Gwen's eyes. "Great. Okay...well, I'll pop around again soon, honey."

Gwen stood and wiped the moisture from her cheeks. Lexie remained seated.

"I look forward to seeing you more often, Mom," Lexie said, wrapping her arms around her legs.

"Me, too, baby girl."

Lexie watched as her mother turned and left.

She hoped like crazy that what Gwen said was true. That her mother was finally ready to clean herself up and get her life together. If that was the case, then Lexie would do whatever she could to help.

A couple minutes later, Lexie felt Asher's heat beside her as he took a seat on the step.

"Everything okay?"

Her heart expanded at the sight of the wonderful man holding their child. "I know you were listening."

But she didn't mind. What affected her life, affected his.

Asher shrugged his big shoulders. "I may have heard bits and pieces."

Bits and pieces my ass, Lexie thought.

"Everything is more than great. It's perfect." About as perfect as Lexie could have pictured her life.

There was still threats in the world. Uncertainty. But she and her child were protected. And loved. And they would get through any hurdles. Together.

"He's so beautiful." Lexie sighed, her gaze once again drawn to their son.

"Takes after his mama," Asher murmured.

Her eyes met Asher's. The grin was gone. All humor absent.

"Have I told you how amazing you are?" Asher asked quietly.

"Only ten thousand times in the last week. Feel free to keep it coming, though."

He leaned toward her, stopping just before their lips touched. "You're amazing. And I love you."

Lexie was sure he'd said that ten thousand times, too, but she wasn't complaining. "I love you, too, Asher. I love our little family."

Finally, his lips touched hers. Closing her eyes, she let the outside world disappear.

Too soon he pulled away. Lexie pouted her lips, receiving a chuckle from Asher.

At the same time, a small coo sounded from Fletcher. Asher and Lexie glanced down at their baby boy.

"I didn't know I could feel this way. As a father. A partner," Asher said quietly.

"What way?"

"So damn happy. Like I have everything I could possibly need or want right here."

"I knew you could feel that way, it just took a while for you to trust me."

She expected a laugh from Asher. But the man didn't even crack a smile. "I don't know what took me so long."

Then his lips returned to Lexie's, and once again, she was at peace.

$\mathcal{M}$ason unscrewed the cap on his beer, eyes sliding to his team around him.

Hell, they weren't just his team. They were his family. Brothers. If Mason had learned anything in his twenty-nine years, it was that family wasn't only born, it was built. Through blood, sweat, and tears.

He'd been in enough life-or-death situations with these guys to know that they had his back, just as he had theirs.

Looking over to the women who sat in Asher's living area, Mason conceded that he now had sisters to add to the family. Women who were just as tough as the men, if not tougher. Plus, the newest addition—baby Fletcher.

"He's so damn gorgeous," Bodie cheered, clapping Asher on the back. "And Lexie's a warrior."

Asher's gaze heated. "She is."

He held Fletcher in his arms while Lexie sat outside talking to her mother. The three of them made a damn cute family.

"I'll tell you what, I'm damn glad you guys got there in time," Asher said quietly.

Mason's grip tightened on the bottle in his hand. It had been close. Too close for any of their liking.

"That was Evie," Wyatt responded as he crossed his arms over his chest. "When we discovered you'd been taken, I searched for Project Arma warehouse-type locations, while she looked at local buildings."

Luca shook his head. "When she realized the pizzeria had a basement, we thought there wasn't a chance they'd taken you there. It was too close to home. Then she hacked different road cameras and found they'd headed to that very spot."

"I'm glad that woman of yours is a genius, Rocket," Asher confessed...before going still.

The whole team listened to the retreating steps of Lexie's mother.

"Time to see my baby mama." Asher smiled before heading outside.

A small smile of his own stretched Mason's lips. He liked seeing his brother happy. More than happy, Asher was fucking beaming. It was about time the man had grown a pair and committed to his woman.

And now they were safe to be a family.

Mason was angry. Angry that they'd missed things. They'd missed the men moving in across the street and Bill's involvement.

Trust didn't come easily to him, and now it took another hit.

The team had searched for Bill over the week. They'd used every resource at their disposal to find him. But they found nothing. Which likely meant he was dead. Project Arma had found him first.

Mason felt zero sympathy for the man. He put too many lives at risk for his own selfish gains.

"I can't believe that asshole Commander Hylar is a part of all this," Oliver said, shaking his head.

Mason immediately tensed at the mention of their commander. He'd seen the man briefly that day a week ago. It had been the first time Mason had set eyes on him in years.

He hadn't had time to stop and chat. He'd been too busy fighting for his life against the other SEAL team. They were the best of the best. Just as Mason's team was.

As soon as the commander had left, the other team had swiftly disengaged and taken off. Clearly, Carter's team had been under orders not to kill. Not that Mason or any of the guys would have let that happen.

Carter's SEAL team were enemies. Just like everyone else connected to the project. And they would be taken out eventually.

"He admitted to being the fucking *mastermind* behind it all," Kye sneered, as angry as the rest of them.

The commander had made a deadly mistake when he'd admitted that bit to Asher. But Mason was glad the older man had confessed. "He made this easy for us. We know what we have to do now. Locate him. He's our target. Cut off the head of the snake."

Silence followed for a moment.

"There was a time I would have questioned whether I could have killed the man," Eden admitted, eyes fixed on Shylah in the living room. "That time has passed."

That time had passed for all of them. The man had lied and betrayed them. Threatened their family. His death was necessary.

"Evie and I will change the parameters for some of our searches," Wyatt said. "It won't be easy to locate him."

Mason snorted. "Since when is anything easy with Project Arma?" He lifted the beer partway to his lips before he heard *her*.

Sage. Her voice filtered in from outside, making Mason's body tighten.

Christ. He didn't know what his deal was. He'd never reacted to a woman the way he reacted to her.

But Sage couldn't be trusted. She was a woman with secrets,

and Mason's gut told him that those secrets led back to Project Arma.

Then why couldn't he get her blue eyes out of his head? Not to mention her sweet curves that made him itch to run his hands over every inch of her body.

Mason's attention caught on Sage as she walked through the front door, Asher and Lexie trailing behind with Fletcher.

Scanning her body, Mason's focus drifted from her shapely legs right up to her intelligent eyes. She was short, much shorter than Mason's six foot five, but the woman had curves in all the right places.

When her gaze clashed with Mason's, he caught her short gasp before she snapped her eyes away. The doctor was affected by him, too. She'd never said the words out loud, but her body language said everything Mason needed to know.

Directing his attention away from Sage, Mason moved closer to Wyatt. "Did you bring it?"

Disapproval washed over Wyatt's face as he looked at him. "You sure you want to do this?"

Mason had gone back and forth on the answer to that question. He always came back to the same place.

Tapping her phone so that he received every message sent and received, every call, wasn't just to ensure she was playing on the right side of the field. It was also to keep her safe. If there was anything that Mason had learned over the years, it was that secrets were deadly.

"Yes."

Wyatt's expression didn't change. Reaching into his pocket, he pulled out the small device.

Taking it from his friend's fingers, Mason slipped it into his own pocket. Mason knew how to insert the bug. He just needed the opportunity.

Luckily, he didn't have to wait long. About twenty minutes in,

Sage's phone rang. Standing, she moved away from the women and headed outside.

Mason didn't hesitate. Placing his hardly touched beer on the kitchen island, he followed the doctor down the steps and outside.

"Hello?" Sage answered, hesitancy in her voice.

Mason observed her from behind. Her spine was straight and her shoulders stiff. Whoever was on the line remained silent.

"Jason, is that you?" Panic mixed with hope in Sage's voice.

Jason. Her twin brother. Also, the boy in the photo that Sage had stored in her go bag.

After going through her room at the inn and discovering the picture, the team had gotten Wyatt to find images of Jason. After all, keeping a gun, cash, a burner phone, and an old picture stashed in a cushion was not normal, everyday behavior.

What Wyatt had discovered was, not only was the boy in the picture her twin, he was also nowhere to be found.

Unfortunately, not even Wyatt or Evie could locate the guy. There was no evidence of him anywhere as of three years ago. It was like he'd dropped off the face of the planet.

"Jase, if you're there, please talk to me. I miss you. Mum and Dad miss you." Sage paused for a moment. "Come home."

The words were whispered from her lips, desperation thick in her voice.

Then the line cut off. Sage's shoulders slumped.

Mason felt a strong urge to reach out and pull Sage into his arms. Provide comfort and reassurance even though he knew nothing of her situation.

Taking a step closer, Mason stopped when Sage turned.

The doctor jolted at the sight of him, a small gasp escaping her lips. His attention was drawn to her chest as it rose and fell in quick succession. Damn but the woman was alluring.

"Mason. What are you doing out here?"

Whatever I can to be close to you.

"I just came to see if you were okay."

Sage's brows rose while, at the same time, she opened and closed her mouth.

"I'm okay." She raised her hands to her chest almost like she was trying to slow her speeding heart.

"Be careful coming out here alone, darlin'. Being involved with us could make you a target."

And he hated that.

Sage's cheeks flushed. "I can look after myself. But thank you for your concern."

Mason almost smiled at that. The five-foot-five doctor barely reached his shoulder. He couldn't imagine how she intended to protect herself against people like him.

Mason took a step to the side, giving her space to move past. The bare minimum of space. "Doesn't hurt to be careful."

"I'll keep that in mind."

Stepping forward, she moved back toward the stairs. Her body brushed his.

Once she had returned inside, Mason lifted the phone he'd swiped from her back pocket. Withdrawing the tool from his pocket, he worked quickly, removing the screen of the smartphone and inserting the chip inside.

Once the phone was back in one piece, he moved up the stairs.

Sage was now sitting on the couch, laughing with the women. Stunning.

Moving to her side, Mason crouched down and handed Sage her phone.

"You dropped this, sweetheart."

Sage swung her head toward the phone in his hand, her eyes widening. "I didn't realize."

As she took the cell from his hand, her fingers brushed against Mason's. A zap went through every limb of his body.

Jesus, what was it with this woman?

Sage's eyes lifted to Mason's, pupils dilating once again. She felt it, too. There wasn't a doubt in his mind.

A moment of guilt hit him about what he'd just done. But he quickly squashed it. He was doing what needed to be done. What was necessary. Sage hadn't been honest with the team. She was hiding something. So it was up to Mason to make sure her secrets didn't put anyone in danger. Including Sage herself.

"Thank you."

Mason stood and moved back to the guys. But his gaze returned to Sage more than once over the afternoon. He couldn't stop looking.

He would figure out her secret, not just to keep his brothers safe...but to keep the delectable doctor out of harm's way. Whether she wanted him to or not.

Order Mason today!

ALSO BY NYSSA KATHRYN

Project Arma SERIES

Uncovering Project Arma

Luca

Eden

Asher

Mason

Wyatt

Bodie

Oliver

Kye

JOIN my newsletter and be the first to find out about sales and new releases!

https://www.nyssakathryn.com/vip-newsletter

ABOUT THE AUTHOR

Nyssa Kathryn is a romantic suspense author. She lives in South Australia with her daughter and hubby and takes every chance she can to be plotting and writing. Always an avid reader of romance novels, she considers alpha males and happily-ever-afters to be her jam.

Don't forget to follow Nyssa and never miss another release.

Facebook | Instagram | Amazon | Goodreads

CPSIA information can be obtained
at www.ICGtesting.com
Printed in the USA
LVHW111650170322
713568LV00011B/1176

9 780648 946229